I0552473

Caleb's Destiny

Troubles in the West

Carole Brown

Story and Logic Media Group
New Carlisle, Ohio
Printed in the USA
... For the discriminating reader
...because we believe story *needs* logic.

Caleb's Destiny: © 2020 by Carole Brown
Troubles in the West

 **Published by STORY AND LOGIC Media Group,
New Carlisle, Ohio 45344
...For the discriminating reader...Because we
believe story *needs* logic.**

Cover Design by SAL media
Published in New Carlisle, OH
Printed in the USA

All rights reserved. No part of this publication may be reproduced, stored in a retrieval system, or transmitted in any form or by any means—now known or hereafter—such as electronic, mechanical, photocopy, recording or otherwise—without the prior written permission of the publisher. The only exception is brief quotations in printed reviews.

This is a work of fiction. Names, characters, dialogue, places, and incidents are either a product of the author's imagination and are used fictitiously. Character's opinions are not necessarily the same as the authors. Any resemblance to persons living or dead is purely coincidental; they are not to be interpreted as real people or events.

ISBN 13: 978-1-941622-63-6
ISBN 10: 1-94-162263-1

Library of Congress Cataloging-in-Publication Data
Brown, Carole
Caleb's Destiny /Carole Brown
ISBN 978-1-941622-63-6 (pbk)

1. Christian Fiction 2. Historical Romantic Suspense 3 Western

I. Title. Library of Congress Control Number: 2020938236

Praise for award winning author
Carole Brown

Carole Brown's first venture into writing a western is a delight. Caleb's Destiny has cowboys, outlaws, intrigue, romance, and a sigh-worthy ending. It's everything readers will delight in, and have them begging for more stories in her new series.

~Jodie Wolfe
Author of *Taming Julia*
and *To Claim Her Heart*

Carole Brown's Caleb's Destiny is an engaging book, filled with suspense, a strong plot, and with characters so real and likable they capture the reader's attention, drawing them into the story from page one, all the way to the very satisfying ending. A hard book to put down.

--Barbara Warren,
author of six published books.

Brown's latest story-telling chops take her fans back to gold rush days, showing all the deviousness mankind has always wrought.
Three youngsters, gathered by tragedy and separated by time, are fated to reunite and re-right some powerful wrongs. Rich setting and always excellent scenes will enchant the lover of the romantic historical suspense.

--Lisa Lickel,
author of the Fancy Cat Mystery series

You can count on Carole Brown to deliver a fast paced story with characters you'll remember long after you close the book.

--Mary Ellis,
award-winning author

Brown skillfully weaves tantalizing glimpses of a past that entwines the characters with an adventurous present in *Caleb's Destiny*. Believable, lovable characters—and some, readers will love to hate—drew me with them into the danger and mystery. Recommended for readers of historical romance set in the Wild West.

-Sandra Merville Hart
Author of Civil War romances,
A Musket in My Hands,
A Rebel in My House,
and *A Stranger on My Land.*

A new master of suspense is in town to rival the old. With vivid characters that dance off the pages and cheeky dialogue to keep you laughing, Carole Brown will quickly become a favorite, earning her place on your bookshelf of best-loved novels.

-Jamin Christian Baldwin
author of romance
and award-winning devotion writer.

Nobody can write a scene like Carole Brown. When you read her books, you might want to grab something, like the back of a chair lest her writing knocks your socks off.

--Mary N. Bull,
award-winning author

Carole Brown is a prolific writer who captures the hearts of her readers. Whether she's writing fiction, non-fiction or children's books, you can expect a blessing.

--Ann Knowles, author, editor,
and owner of Write Pathway Editorial Services

In Memory:

Of precious little **Destiny Jade,**
a tiny bundle of angelic sweetness,
whom God lent to her mama for a short time,
but will never leave the hearts of those who loved her.

Dedication to:

My husband:
The one who gave me the idea for the book,
who is my go-to person for brainstorming and knowledge
about what works and what doesn't.
The man who listened patiently
as I read chapter after chapter to him.

Stevie Beth, who has never ceased loving her baby.

And Sharon, my editor and, most of all, my friend.

Acknowledgments:

To my editors: Sharon, Michelle, and Jamin.
What would I do without these people who helped make my book better?

Special Thanks to Jamin, my forever talented friend, who created for Caleb the song of his heart for his Destiny:

Meadow grass or forest green, rivers or garden fair, with eyes like gems, and skin of cream, my love is uncompared. A voice as sweet as a whippoorwill, at dusk she sings to me, she is my heart, my rose in spring, she is my destiny. Open your heart, clasp tight my love, you've always belonged to me. I loved you then, I love you now, you are my Destiny.

To: Marshall Trimble who is an Official Arizona State Historian at the Scottsdale Community College who generously answered my questions.

And to: Sherry Monahan and her two cook books which was a great help in learning about eating places and all things western food.

Carole Brown

Troubles in the West

It was too late. He couldn't
turn the clock back nor the
rage that had consumed him.

Caleb's
Destiny

Chapter One

The Boy Caleb

Fifteen Years Earlier
May, 1864

"Come on out here. I want to talk to you." Billy Bob Bottoms belligerent voice split the air as if lightning had suddenly split the sky. "I don't believe you. I think you're holding out on us."

The man inside the cave paused, pickax in hand, listened then straightened and spit out the twig he'd held between his teeth. Trouble. How many more times was he gonna have to talk this fool down from downright rash actions?

Leaving the ax behind, he crawled out the small entrance. As he stood, he studied the man opposite him.

He should have never gone in business with him and wished to high heaven, he'd listened to his wife, Julie. The man was smart, he'd give him that, but he was greedy, and getting' worse. His partner trusted no one, least of all him, borderin' on—what did Julie call it?—paranoia.

But he *was* smart, and *that* was the only reason he'd gone into business with him. Still nothing was panning out—as of yet—and who knew when or if it would. Took some mighty hard work and an even stronger determination to find gold.

His gaze shifted to take in the land before him. Beautiful land. Just the place he'd start the life he wanted for Julie and his son. Broad sweeping, grassy plains. Hills and trees for shelter...

"I won't be made fun of."

The sound of a gun cocking drew his attention back to his partner. Bottoms had a trigger-happy reaction anytime he didn't like something. "This was always a

9

gamble."

"So you say." Bottoms waved his pistol. "I think you've already found it and holding out on the rest of us."

"That's plum ignorance."

"Is it? I don't think so." Bottoms shifted his feet. "How long have we been partners? Two years, hasn't it been?"

He sighed, and the wish that he'd gone into this business by himself flashed across his mind. Again. Too late now.

"I'm thinking I need to get a new partner."

Bottoms' threat didn't bother him. He'd heard it too many times, and always he'd been able to talk him out of it. "What are you goin' to do about the other two? They'll be askin' questions."

Bottoms scoffed. "Them? I'm not worried about either of them."

"Well, if yer gonna shoot me then have at it. I'll either die here or get back to work. Yer choice."

"Not so fast, Mister Bottoms. Ain't gonna be any shootin' today, not unless it's you that's cravin' some bullet lead."

His lackadaisical response at his partner's threats and accusations did a complete 180 degree flipflop. Twelve-year-old Caleb, his son, stood twenty feet away pointing their hunting rifle at his partner.

"Caleb." The warning note in his voice pulled the boy's gaze toward him, but he didn't hold it.

"Pa. I ain't having no one shootin' you. I'll kill him right between those mean eyes of his. I can do it, Pa, you know I can. I'm a good shot. Can shoot a rabbit fifty feet away."

"I know you can. No doubt about that. But, son, shootin' a man is a far different thing than an animal for food. Once you pull that trigger there ain't no turnin' back from that."

"I heard what he said. I ain't plannin' on goin' pa-less."

"It's not that easy to get rid of me."

"I aim to keep it that way."

The kid was as stubborn as the mule his parents used to own.

"I might shoot you too while I'm at it." His partner's

lips twisted into a taunting sneer as he glared at the boy.

From the corner of his eyes, he saw Caleb lift the gun a tad bit higher.

"You kin try it, Mister Bottoms, if you think you're faster'n me. Go ahead. Try it."

"Caleb, give me the gun."

"Sorry, Pa, I—"

Too late he caught the slight movement from his partner, and the sound of a gunshot exploded.

He ran to his son, but the boy hadn't fallen. And neither had his partner although he was dancing around as if he'd been hit.

Caleb handed over the rifle, his face radiating pride. "Jest wanted to scare him, Pa. Maybe he'll learn you don't mess with us."

He turned to glance at Bottoms. The man's gun had disappeared. His face was white and definitely less confident than before.

"I'd say you better high-tail it outta here, and quick. When I have something to report, I'll get in touch with you. Otherwise, next time, I'd say this son of mine won't miss."

Like a fish, the man's mouth opened and shut. The fright was being replaced with anger. He reached for his saddle horn then swung onto his horse. "You've not heard the last of this. I'll be back, and when I do I won't be alone."

"You're gonna need all the help you can get." Caleb called out.

The boy's father laid a hand on his son's shoulder. "I should give you a good whoppin'."

"But you won't." Caleb looked up at him, the cheekiness in his voice loud and clear.

He stared after his partner as he left. He'd be back, and he wouldn't be alone.

Glancing down at his tow-headed son, he smiled. No, the boy wouldn't be gettin' any whoppin's today. The lad had no doubt saved his life.

Chapter Two

The girl, Destiny, age six

Fifteen Years Earlier
June, 1864

"**W**e can't keep her, son."

Six-year-old Destiny whimpered and curled into a tighter ball behind the curtain—the corner in the small cabin Caleb had said was hers when she wanted to be by herself. She strained to keep out the low murmuring. She might as well have been standing next to the man and his son.

The boy's musical voice pled with the man. "But, Pa. She's too little. She has no one. And she won't talk to us. How do we know what—"

"It doesn't matter, Son. Look at your ma. She's in a bad way. If she—passes on, then what? Who'll take care of a girl young'un?"

"It jest ain't right, Pa. Mama wouldn't like it."

"Boy, think of what yer sayin'. It's too dangerous. Best place for her is as far away as we can send her. You know Bottoms has threatened me and you're big enough to understand it might jest happen if we don't keep our guard up. What would happen to her? Who would care for her? We gotta think of more than our wants and wishes. You understand what I'm sayin'?"

The sadness in the man's voice caused the tears clinging to her lashes to slide down her cheeks. Pressing a fist to her mouth, she swallowed back her sobs. She wanted to stomp the floor and scream at the kind man, but look where that had gotten her. She'd killed her parents because of her temper, and hadn't Mama always warned she'd regret it someday if she didn't learn to control it?

"But, Pa, we can't just send her off..."

"It's settled, boy. I don't want to hear no more about it. If'n your ma...passes on, then you and I have got to do the right thing by her. After the spring rains is over, we'll send her east."

"I don't want her to go away."

The man's voice softened. "Son, this girl is not one of them critters you're always bringing home. Why, she's not more than a baby. We'll do our duty by her giving her a chance for a good education. She'll be better off back east."

Destiny pulled the limp feather pillow over her head.

Maybe she could run away on ole Blackie, the horse.

Or hide in the rickety barn out back until the stagecoach had come and gone.

Maybe it would rain and not stop. Flood the stream so they couldn't cross.

Destiny wondered if Mama could hear her thoughts way up there in heaven. She would frown and scold her foolishness. She'd say, Hush that whining and mind your elders.

Well, Mama wasn't here, and Destiny knew one thing. She was not going back east. Her mind was made up.

Mama had always said, "When that child makes up her mind, it's worse than pulling a tooth."

She'd just dig in her heels and refuse to go.

Chapter Three

The boy Hunter, age five

Fifteen Years Earlier
September, 1864

"Pa. Don't die, Pa. Don't die." The scrawny, little boy knelt beside his dad, crying, pleading, sobbing out a plea that wouldn't be answered.

The dead father's partner stared down at the man who lay face down in the dirt, only several hundred yards from his shanty. He'd heard the shot, but it didn't matter, cause by the time he got there, it was too late. He'd already been shot in the back. He was gone. Dead.

He laid a gentle hand on the boy's shoulder. "He's gone, Hunter. You've got to buck up now and be the man your pa would have wanted you to be."

The little fellow lifted his tear-drenched face toward him. "I don't wanna be a man. I want my pa."

The father's partner drew in a deep breath and glanced at his own son, Caleb. There was nothing else to do. Nothing else he wanted to do but care for this child. No question about that.

But no kind of assurance would ease the hurt of this useless death.

The little lad swiped at his cheeks, leaving dirt-streaked splotches on his face. He stood to his feet and looked up at him. "I'm going to kill him."

The partner didn't ask who the boy was talking about. He didn't caution him not to feel that way. No, because he knew the answers to both.

He knew it wouldn't do any good to try to soothe the tragic hurt the little fellow was experiencing. He'd never get over it. He'd never forget.

Anger like a gully washer ran through him.

He knew who'd shot this good man.

And he knew who'd be coming for *him* next.

Chapter Four

Every bone in her body was broken.

Or at least, she was pretty sure they were, because that's the way her body felt.

Destiny Rose McCulloch clenched her fingers together, swayed with the motion of the stagecoach, and ignored the leering stare of the man seated across from her.

She would have liked to give the man a piece of her mind, but that action would defy every etiquette lesson instilled within her at Miss Harriet's School for the Genteel Lady. Besides, Reverend Richard Burke back in Boston would definitely not approve, and she wanted his approval very much. To be honest, she was trying her best to behave in a Christ-like manner. In spite of her tendency to speak her thoughts. In spite of the hot temper that refused to be dampened.

Destiny sighed. In spite of the twinge of temptation to stick out her tongue, she'd restrain herself and keep ignoring the rude gentleman—er—creature.

At least second man—the simpering idiot with his fancy eastern hat—hadn't spoken to her. He'd tipped his hat and smirked at her more often than she liked, but his voice was low, and he kept, for the most part, his face turned away from her. His dirty-ish blond hair hung over his ears too much, but his clothes were clean.

A whiff of tobacco smoke drifted her way. Destiny frowned at the coarse woman smoking the cigar with an air of defiance. She'd been more of a trial than the annoying man. If the woman had been any more blatant in her attempts at attracting attention, she might as well have carried a sign signifying her occupation.

As for the young cowboy sitting beside her, he'd been quiet, keeping to himself. He was a handsome man, his brown hair giving a hint of a curl. She smiled, imaging him trying to tame those curls.

Destiny stared out the window, but the scenery was anything but inspiring. Why had she attempted this trip with the foolish hope she could find a man she but vaguely remembered as a boy named Caleb? The vastness of the land did nothing for her but emphasize the enormity of her task.

"Who you meetin'?"

Destiny turned her head slowly and took in the sight of the annoying man. His sneer had grown to a full-fledged grin. He leaned forward and a greasy lock of hair fell across his cheek as he stretched out a hand as if to touch her.

"I'm Earnest Fleming. And this here is—"

The man beside him touched his arm. It was a light touch, barely there, but the Fleming guy cast him a glance—was it a frightened one?—and didn't finish his sentence.

Had the man meant to warn him not to touch her? Or was that touch for another reason?

Ernest was talking again. "Call me Ernie."

He started to withdraw his hand, but just the thought of him touching her, with his words if not by hand, caused Destiny to jerk sideways and thrust out a hand to stop him. But a different hand—strong and rugged—shot forward and gripped the man's wrist.

"She doesn't want to be bothered by the likes of you." The quiet cowboy, sitting next to her and defending her, couldn't be more than fifteen, but he displayed a gentle toughness about him that said life had given him far more experience than fifteen years should warrant.

"Mind yer own business, cowboy."

"She is my business." He stared straight into the other man's eyes.

Ernie's gaze shifted to Destiny. "Pretty shore we'll be meetin' agin soon."

Destiny held her breath, but a second later Ernie laughed and flopped back against the seat. "Have it yer way. This time."

"I reckon I don't mind givin' out my name. I don't aim to be as—highfalutin—as some." The woman flicked a disgusted glance across Destiny's face then turned to bat her lashes at the man. "I'm called Lucy by my friends, Ernie."

The coach lurched sideways, and Destiny would have

landed in the woman's lap, but the cowboy's hand steadied her.

"Ma'am, are you all right?"

Destiny smiled at the young man. "Yes, thank you."

"My name's Hunter, ma'am. Don't you worry none. I'll look out for you." He shot a look of contempt at the annoying man.

"Thank you," Destiny repeated. "Are you headed to Roaring Springs, too?"

"Yes, ma'am. I live close by there."

"Then we'll see each other quite often."

"Oh, no, ma'am, I work for Mr. Michael, and he plum keeps me hoppin' worse than a one-legged rabbit in a cabbage patch." His brow drew together in a serious frown, and the dimple in one cheek deepened.

Destiny laughed. "I see. Doesn't this Mr. Michael give you any days off?"

"Not likely, with the spring rains and calvin', and all that goes with runnin' a successful ranch."

"What do you do, Hunter?"

His puzzled gaze met hers. "Do? I work for Mr. Michael."

"I mean, what do you do for Mr. Michael?"

The brow relaxed. "Why, I'm his head man. I know more about cattle than any man this side of the Mississippi."

Her lips twitched at his serious boasting. "How on earth did you learn so much? You can't be more than..." Too late she remembered Richard's warning. Don't ask questions. Western people don't take to nosiness.

Hunter grinned. "Ma'am, I cut my eye teeth on horses and ropin' cattle. I ain't never done anything more my entire life."

She liked this boy. Leaning close, she whispered, hoping the gent across from her wouldn't hear. "I think it's time you call me by my name."

"I'd be pleased to do that." Hunter's voice was low and husky.

"I'm Destiny McCulloch."

"Pleased to meet you, Miss Destiny." Two fingers touched his hat brim.

Just then the stagecoach lunged over a series of large

rocks, dropped and pitched dangerously to one side. Amidst the driver's cursing and urging the team to stop, Destiny clutched at Hunter's arm to keep from being smashed by the woman pressing against her. The voices inside the coach raised in a collective expression of dismay and anger.

When she could breathe again, Destiny jerked her skirt from the grasping fingers of the brash-faced woman and drew in a long breath. What now?

What now was a bunch of wild, hair-raising yells as three men on horseback galloped up, bandanas pulled up on their faces, guns in hand, their mounts prancing.

Obviously, the shotgun rider had started to raise his shotgun for one of the men circling the coach called out, his gun aimed at the top. "Don't even think about it if you wanna see the sun set tonight, old man. Lookee here, boys, it's old Daly and his pal, Luke. Thinkin' we met them before."

"Right down nice to see 'em agin, ain't it, Boss?"

Hunter whispered softly to the passengers. "Get down. Now."

Destiny leaned forward, her head on her knees, but she kept her eyes open, her head tilted in Hunter's direction. The young man had drawn his gun, and now he raised it, prepared to shoot

A thunk, and Hunter slouched. Destiny straightened and reached out to support Hunter, unconscious and slumped over. On the side of his head was a swiftly swelling bump.

"Why did you do this?" she hissed at Ernie who was sitting back grinning like he'd done something important. "You are a fool. Don't you know we need all the help we can get for protection?"

"Doncha worry that pretty little head of yers any. I've got this under control. He was set to have guns ablazin' and I wasn't anyway anxious to get myself shot. You oughtta be thankin' me." He reached out a hand to touch her.

"Get off me." Destiny jerked away then sent a glance out the window before turning back to Hunter.

The leader leaned on his saddle horn while the other two trained their weapons at the shotgun rider and driver. "Raise those hands heavenward and get down."

He jerked his head when their feet didn't hit the ground immediately, his long hair flopping in his face. "Move it. No one gets hurt if you do like you're told."

Once Daly and Luke were on the ground, the leader motioned with his head. "Now help your genteel passengers out of the coach."

With the help of the driver, Destiny and the other passengers alighted and lined up beside the coach leaving Hunter stretched out on one of the seats.

"Who's that still in the stage? Told everyone to get out. He wantin' to meet his maker today?"

Ernie spoke up. "Doncha worry none about him. He was gonna shoot you, but I took care of him. He won't be wakin' anytime soon."

The leader eyed Ernie then swung off his horse. "Thanks. The boss will hear about this. Keep your eyes on them, boys. Don't want no heroes today."

With repeated orders to hand over any jewelry and other valuables, the leader went down the line stuffing everything in a leather bag. He stopped when he got to Destiny. "What have we here?"

Destiny aimed her glance at the man with as much disdain as she was capable but held her tongue. Nothing to be gained by egging him on.

The man made as if to stroke her face, and Destiny took a step back and pretended to stumble. She didn't miss the knowledgeable gleam in his eye. He knew what she'd done to avoid his touch.

"Smart as well as pretty." He leaned closer. "How 'bout you joinin' us? We sure could use someone like you as a decoy."

She scorned him with another glance, but kept quiet. She wouldn't dignify his insulting question with an answer even though a scorching retort burned her tongue.

"No?" His eyes laughed at her. "Too bad. You'd have been an interesting addition to our gang."

His gaze dropped to the locket pinned to her dress. "What's this?"

Destiny clapped her hand over the piece. It was the only thing she had of her parents.

The man's eyes were mere slits as he stared at her. Then, almost as if reading the message in her eyes, he gently took her hand and moved it. With a jerk, the locket was ripped from her dress and lying in his. "Sorry. Gotta take it."

He turned away, but Destiny wanted to grab his arm and beg. She did neither. It wouldn't do a bit of good. But she hoped he could feel the searing glance she gave him as he walked on. Felt it and burned with its intensity.

The leader glanced at Ernie. "Wanna join us?"

"Got other business I need to take care of."

The leader nodded and climbed on his horse again, his men following suit. Then ordering the passengers to turn their backs, so they'd be facing away from them, he yelled out a boisterous shout, and the pounding of horse hooves filled Destiny's ears as they fled.

She slowly turned to stare at the dust plumes swirling around. Placing a hand over her nose to keep from breathing the worst in, she wanted to groan. Sadness and anger stirred inside her at the loss of the one item she'd held dear to her heart. If she'd owned countless jewels, the loss of all of them would not have meant as much to her. The money she'd brought west with her, pinned to her undergarments—she would have given it all to that man—if only he'd not taken her locket.

But she knew better. He would have taken both.

Hunter swung open the stagecoach door and staggered out, holding his head. "They're gone?"

"Hunter, are you all right? Shouldn't you be sitting down?" Destiny hurried over to him and took his arm.

"You can't keep me down. I'll be fine and dandy in no time." He smiled down at her before glancing at the others. "Anyone identify those men?"

"Never seen any of them, but we all know who they are. Been stealin' all over the state." Daly slapped his hat on his pants.

Hunter's eyes had narrowed when he turned back to the others. "I don't know for sure who gave me this achin' knot, but when I find out, you better be headin' far away from me."

"I reckon you know you'd been shot dead and probably most of us too, if you'd shot even one of them?"

Ernie eyed Hunter as if he expected the boy to pull a gun on him.

"We'll never know now, will we?"

Hunter's eyes had sharpened, but in them lurked an emotion that scared Destiny. Wherever it had come from, whatever had caused it to exist, it hinted at dangerous depths to the boy, she wished she hadn't seen.

Hunter said nothing, only walked over to where Luke and Daly stood beside the stagecoach and stared at the wheel hanging crookedly on the axle. The driver shoved at his hat. "Dag—"

"Luke."

The shotgun rider nodded toward Destiny and the other woman.

The driver's crusty face lit bright red. "Sorry, ladies. Didn't mean no offense."

Destiny nodded, but the other woman spoke up. "None taken. Can you fix it?"

Hunter leaned over and prodded the broken axle. "There's no mendin' this until it sees the insides of a blacksmith's shop."

The quieter man groaned. "What are we supposed to do, I ask you?"

"I reckon we hitch ourselves over there in that patch of shade and sit it out whiles one of us menfolk straddle a horse and hightail it into town." The driver ran a roughened finger alongside his considerable nose.

Lucy shook her skirts. "Well, then, I'm getting' out of this sun." She tilted her head at Ernie. "Would you mind?"

He grinned and gave her his arm.

A loud halloo sent Destiny spinning around.

A large horse, black as an inkwell, charged toward them, the white splash on his forehead gleaming in the sunlight. He galloped as if he had royal blood, his head high, his feet barely skimming the ground. Astride the splendid beast sat a man. Even atop his mount Destiny could tell he was tall and muscled lean, his hat held high in the air in salutation. But what caught her attention was his hair. Like a crown of gold it shone, an ornament that set him apart from other men.

He galloped up, pulled on the reins, and swung off his

horse in one fluid motion, ground-hitching him immediately. Then moving to the bay that had followed them, he tied him to a sturdy bush nearby. Within the space of thirty seconds, his gaze rested on each individual—measuring their worth, Destiny was sure. When his gaze landed on her, a monstrous shiver began at the base of her spine and crept slowly up it. She stared back, willing herself not to blush.

His hand lifted, settled his hat on his head, the oddest expression in his brown eyes. Then he whipped around and approached the driver and shotgun man. "Luke. Daly. What happened?" He squatted and studied the loosened wheel and broken axle.

Destiny edged closer to listen and noticed the others hurrying over to see what was going on.

Daly shoved his hat to the back of his head. "Don't rightly know, Mr. Michael. Been over this same road a hundred times and never seen big rocks here."

"Hmm. Sure about that?"

Daly grabbed at his hat and swatted his leg with it. "Doncha think I know what I'm doing? I tell you, look at that bend in the road. We came a whipping around it, going lickety-split, and next thing I knows we're limpin' where those rocks damaged our wheel."

Mr. Michael stood, and his gaze took in the landscape, eyes narrowed. "You didn't see anything suspicious? No sign of being followed or watched?"

"Reckon not."

"No use crying over spilt milk then."

"Except for the gang who just robbed us of anything of worth."

"What?"

"Yep. Every last one of us had to give up anything of value. It was either that or gettin' shot. Ain't worth the risk, I say."

"Get a good look at them?"

"Shore enough."

"Then I recommend you get that information out to the marshals as soon as you can."

"Not thinkin' it'll do a bit of good."

The man said nothing, only lifted an eyebrow.

"Reckon we's were just robbed by the worst thieves in

this area."

"I see." The man said nothing else, but if his tightened lips were any indication, he knew who the driver was talking of.

"We were gettin' ready to send someone on to town to get the blacksmith. Was going to let him use one of the team horses, but they're pretty worn out."

"Roaring Spring's blacksmith is a cantankerous sort for the person who's making that twenty-mile ride," Mr. Michael shook his head. "Might be for nothing."

"I can go, Mr. Michael." Hunter walked up. "I'll drag him back by his heels if I have to."

"I'm sure you would but I need you. That's why I came this way to intercept the stage before it got to Roaring Springs. I already took care of sending those telegrams so there was no need of you going on."

The man's crooked smile sent Destiny's heart in a spin.

The blond-haired man spoke again. "I think we'd be better off to head to the ranch."

"Yer place that close, Mr. Michael?" Daly ran a hand through his tangled mess of gray-streaked hair before jamming his hat back onto his head.

"Eight or so miles over that ridge there." Mr. Michael nodded to a high hill a mile or so away. "I figure we can use the team horses, set a good pace, but not so much they wear out too quickly, and it won't be too hard on them. No one can take anything but what's absolutely necessary. The rest of the belongings will have to stay here with the stagecoach till we can come back and repair it."

The older gentleman protested, "But we'll lose three or four days like that."

"Maybe. Maybe not. Or you can bed down over there in those trees for the night while one of you takes a horse, rides into town, and convinces a reluctant blacksmith to return in a wagon to carry his tools. Of course, you don't have blankets, which you won't mind, I'm sure. The ladies will get chilly, but they'll make it." Mr. Michael eyed the men, his eyes suddenly hard. "Hunter will ride the extra horse I brought back to the ranch. He doesn't need to waste more time than necessary away from the ranch where he's needed."

"Leave Hunter and take me with you." Lucy suggested, her eyes alight with mischief.

"And leave this other lady without a companion?" Mr. Michael raked his eyes over Destiny's face. "Daly, Luke, it's your call."

"I reckon it best if I stay here and look after the stagecoach while the rest of you head for Mr. Michael's place." Daly ran a finger down one cheek and looked at each of his passengers in turn. "It'll be faster, and my guess is, his blacksmith will be every bit as good as the one in town. We're already behind time. Need to git a move on."

The blond man rose. "Good. I'll send someone back with the tools before dawn breaks. It'll take a day, maybe two, to repair the coach so you all will have to be patient." His head tilted in the direction of the disabled coach. "Hunter, help Luke get those horses unhitched. We'll leave one horse here for Daly and take the other three."

Ernie grimaced. "I don't see why some of us can't jest take the horses and head to town."

Mr. Michael patted his own mount. "No. The ranch is closer, and though Jasper will do fine the eight miles or so, the stagecoach horses are already tired. We'll take it slow and easy."

"But—"

"Look, mister, I'm already explaining more than I normally do. I've invited a bunch of strangers to my home, taken days of work on my ranch from Hunter, and I'm not about to have the loss of the stagecoach horses if one or more of you decide to take off without going on into town. I'm not figuring on having to pay the stagecoach line for them. And I doubt you're going to."

"You callin' me a thief?"

"Are you one?"

His lips spread in a smile, Destiny supposed, but she hoped it was never aimed at her.

"If you don't like my rules, then stay here and wait, or walk the twenty miles into town. Take it or leave it."

He was done talking and signaled for Hunter to lead the horses forward. "Hunter, you take your bay, and this lady. I want you to ride rear, understand? Ma'am, your name?"

"Lucy Martin." The cigar-smoking lady gave him a lazy grin.

"Miss Martin, Hunter is the best around. You don't need to fear with him."

"Oh, I ain't afraid, but I'd rather ride with—"

Whoever she wanted to pair with, Mr. Michael never gave her a chance to speak it. "You'll ride with Hunter, ma'am. He's the best."

He turned to the other three men. "That leaves three horses. Luke, you and you—" he pointed at Ernie, "—take the two roans. You two are bigger men, and these two don't look as worn out as the third one. After the first five miles, we'll all have to walk for a couple miles."

He gathered the reins in one hand and stepped into the stirrup before swinging onto his horse. The horse pranced in a circle, but when Mr. Michael had him straightened out, he stretched down a hand, and Destiny realized he was offering her a hand up. He wanted her to ride with him. Or, at least, he'd decided it was the best arrangement, for whatever reason.

She studied his face, but he didn't crack a smile although she was sure there was something—Curiosity? Mischief?—in his eyes.

"I've never ridden astride before."

"Are you sure?"

Confusion whirled inside her. How did he suspect she'd ridden like that? It'd been years ago, when she was a child, such a dim memory she wasn't even sure herself it'd happened.

"Give me your hand."

She placed her hand in his, and his immediately swallowed it with his grip. With a tug, she landed behind him. Her hands went to his lean, taut waist.

He turned his head so he could speak over his shoulder. "Are you afraid?"

"No."

"Good. You have no need to be. Jasper and I are a team. We'll get you safely to the ranch."

Destiny didn't answer. She couldn't. She was too busy controlling her breath that refused to stay even.

Chapter Five

The jolt woke her.

Destiny opened her eyes and caught her breath. It wasn't her own soft blanket against her cheek. Nor the hard leather seats of the stagecoach. With a jerk she lifted her head and stared horrified at the back of a man's shirt. In slow motion, she let her gaze travel up that back and rest on the hair that curled against a sinewy neck. She gasped. She'd been sleeping on his back.

Mr. Michael turned his head again. "Have a nice nap? It's almost time to stop for a water break."

Was that a grin on his lips? He thought it was funny that she'd fallen asleep on him like they were—like she was—oh, never mind. How could he? He could have sent his horse into a canter. Or moved. Or something. Why hadn't his horse bucked?

Her hand dropped and she patted the horse's big flank. She couldn't blame Jasper. He'd carried them both as if they were no more than two blankets on his back.

"I really wish you wouldn't have let me fall asleep," she rebuked in her best genteel voice.

"You didn't bother me in the least. I hardly felt your weight."

Destiny wanted to groan. He thought she was worried about him. She had no more time to remonstrate with him. With one hand, he guided his horse into a turn and called back, "We'll stop here for twenty minutes before beginning the last leg."

He dismounted and reached up to help her. His hands slid around her waist and lifted her down as if she were a gigantic piece of cotton. He stared down at her, the perplexity real in his eyes. His lips opened as if he would speak, but with a mutter, he whirled away, and she was left swaying from the loss of the sudden sure hold he'd had on her.

"Miss Destiny."

Destiny refocused on her surroundings. "Yes, Hunter?"

"Come with me, and I'll show you and Miss Lucy the best place to get a drink."

He beckoned, and casting one glance at the retreating figure of Mr. Michael, she fell into line behind Lucy.

The spring fed into a strong, full stream that was swift and rock-filled, the water cold and delicious. Destiny drank until her teeth ached then dangled her fingers and wrists in it. She touched two wet fingers to her forehead and temples and closed her eyes at the relief from the heat.

A sigh escaped her lips as she sat back against a gnarled pine. Lucy stood over by the stream bank, lighting another smoke. Hunter squatted, carving a piece of wood, not five feet away. Somewhere above them a lone bird cawed. A warning? An inelegant song?

The rushing stream gave her a sense of peace, easing the unrest inside her, the urgency to find the person she sought. The boy from long ago. Was he dead? He'd never died in her memory. Surely she would have known. She lifted a pine needle then watched it drift to the ground when she let it go.

"Hunter, I want to ask you a question."

"Yes, ma'am, I mean, Miss Destiny." His knife blade sliced another sliver of wood and it dropped into the increasing pile of shavings.

"I suppose you know about everyone in this part of the country?"

He looked up and his lips split into a broad smile.

Destiny felt her own responding to his infectious grin.

"There's not too many I don't know."

"I thought so."

"Why you askin'?"

How to put this to keep any excessive curiosity at bay? "Would you happen to know a man around here named Caleb?"

"Caleb? No, not that I can recall. I know a Carney and Calhoun, but no Caleb. Out here in these parts, first names aren't used much."

Maybe the boy had moved away with his father. Or

worse, died of some unknown disease. But if that was the case, where had the money come from? Money that had kept coming and coming and coming. Year after year. It paid for her schooling, her clothes and whatever else she needed. When she'd grown older, she'd asked numerous questions, but the boarding school matron had either not known or refused to say. Her shrugs conveyed clearly she didn't care.

Surely someone knew something. A judge? Sheriff? Banker?

One thing she knew, she wasn't quitting yet.

~*~

Michael gripped Jasper's bridle and strode away from Destiny, angry at himself. What did he think he was doing? Just because she reminded him of someone from long ago. Just because he could drown in her dark blue velvet eyes. None of that made any difference. If nothing else he'd probably scared her to death.

He passed the other men and ignored them. Except for Luke and Hunter, he had no interest in these men visiting his ranch. Not that he'd turn them away, but he was almost positive two of them at least were trouble. And he made sure to ignore the women with Hunter.

The bitterness and anger that resided deep inside him stirred and, once again, shook his memories awake. Not good ones. One that filled him with humiliation and anger that still prodded him at unexpected times.

It didn't ease the pain remembering that he'd not been the only one duped by Priscilla DeWitt when she'd waltzed into town one morning. In no less than two weeks, she'd captured the hearts of at least a half dozen young bucks—including himself—and probably a few of the old timers' hearts as well, if they hadn't had the sense to keep it to themselves.

She'd singled him out and taken him on a merry chase before she'd coyly—or maybe it hadn't been so much shyness as cleverness—agreed to marry him. Standing at the altar of their primitive church in town, his heart had turned to stone when the minutes had passed, and at last, Hunter had sidled up to him and whispered the news. Priscilla had skipped town with the banker and the town's money. Obviously, he'd not been well-heeled enough to fit into her plans.

He led Jasper to the water and made sure he drank his fill, then ground hitched him so he could feed a few minutes. Upstream a little ways, he refilled his canteen then drank deeply.

He scowled at the lizard scampering across a rock and wished he could live such a bland existence.

All this didn't mean he was justified in treating Miss McCulloch harshly or frivolously. It wasn't her fault he used a rock for a heart or that he held it against every woman for what one had done.

"Mr. Michael."

"Hunter?"

"I reckon we ought to go, Boss. Only a few hours left of daylight. The ladies are pretty tired and don't need to be out in the hills after dark."

"You're right." He raised his voice and stared at each one. "There's some rough patches up ahead. Stay on the trail. Even though over the mountain is the fastest route to the ranch, the safest route is the trail."

Should he have Miss McCulloch ride with one of the other men? No, as annoyingly attractive as she was, that wouldn't work. He trusted none of them. She'd ride with him. But he'd watch the smiles and warm tones.

~*~

Destiny was more tired than she'd ever been in her life, but she wasn't about to let Mr. Sobersides Michael know it. For some reason, he'd not said a word since they'd remounted.

The thought of a hot bath and soft bed caused her to whimper, and she felt the man in front of her shift.

"Are you all right?"

"I'm fine, thank you." She hoped the scorn she felt at his question didn't show in her voice.

"We're almost there. We'll be on the ranch land in a few minutes."

Destiny frowned. His voice—it sounded tense. Or maybe it was more worried. Over what? Indians? She cast a quick glance at the surrounding hills. Was that a feather sticking up behind that bush?

"Mr. Michael? Is that—that an Indian behind that bush?"

"Where?"

"To the right, about thirty feet off. That big bush—"

"I see it. No, it's not an Indian. Whatever gave you the thought?"

"You sound worried. I thought perhaps Indians were behind your anxiety."

He laughed. "There's been no warring parties around here for several years now. The few Indians still living near here are peaceful. If you're worried about them, don't be."

She hadn't known him long. What? Two hours at the most? But she'd known when she first saw him, he was a man to be trusted. Destiny allowed herself to relax. She tilted her head and studied the pink and purple horizon in the predusk evening.

An hour and a half later, they topped a small hill, and down below lay what she figured was Mr. Michael's ranch. She frowned as a warm, fuzzy feeling swept over her. As far as she knew she'd never been here before. Why then did the feeling that she'd come home fill her heart?

Chapter Six

"**P**retty late for a meeting, Boss." Hank leaned back in the rocker.

Michael had built a small cabin on the far side of his home, close to the bunkhouse, for his top managers on the ranch. It wasn't elaborate, but nice with comforts the bunk house didn't have. And it gave Hank, Hunter and Jackson a bit of time to themselves without having to mingle with the cowboys twenty-four hours a day.

"I know, but this will only take a few minutes, and I wanted somewhere away from the house where I could speak without being overheard by our guests."

"No problem, Boss, what gives?" Hunter set down his cup of coffee.

"Where's Jackson?"

"He'll be late. He's makin' the rounds."

Michael knew what he meant. These three men were his top hands, Jackson the newest, but one of the best he'd ever met in handling his horses. He didn't know much about the man, but it hadn't taken long before realizing the young man was not an ordinary cowboy. He didn't speak much—and Michael soon guessed—Jackson was hiding something. Like that accent he did his best to disguise. Like why he always had new clothes with no holes or patches.

But whatever the man's past—Michael's instincts told him—the boy was trustworthy, and he valued that. Highly.

The front door slammed open, and Jackson stepped in. "Mr. Michael."

Something was wrong.

"Yes, Jackson?"

"When I was making the rounds, I went past your house, which is always the last thing I do, and there was a light on in your library. I saw two figures in there moving around and heard a crash. Figured I'd better hightail it here and let you know."

Michael was out of his chair and out the door before Jackson finished talking, with the other three men running after him.

As they approached the house, Michael motioned for Hank to head to the library side door that led outside and for Jackson to take the back door of the house. Then with Hunter following him, they entered the front door, and moved as quietly as they could toward his library.

The door was barely shut, and Michael grasped the doorknob, listening. The soft murmurs came from rough voices, laden with a few curses. Men then. Men who were visitors in his home. Casting a glance at Hunter, he nodded.

With a quick shove, he thrust open the door even as Hunter stepped up beside him, holding the lantern high in the air with one hand, a gun in his other.

Two men stood by his glass-enclosed cabinet that held some of his most prized possessions. On the floor, at their feet, lay the lock they'd succeeded in breaking open. And, leaning against the cabinet was one of his father's guns taken from above the mantel. An original and in excellent condition.

"Hands in the air. Now."

At Michael's command, the two men raised both hands. The anger on Ernie Fleming's face proved he was as mean as Michael figured earlier. The other man, Cain Wilson, didn't say a word.

"What do you two think you're doing here in the library in the middle of the night in my home?"

He didn't expect a truthful answer and didn't get one.

Ernie's hands inched downward until Hunter waved his gun at him.

"Don't see why we can't have a look 'round. Ain't no harm in that, is there? Jest lookin', see." Ernie shot a smirk his direction.

"Is that why my pa's gun is on the floor?"

When Ernie would have argued, Michael interrupted.

"I reckon I expect visitors not to be snooping around my home in the dead of night and breaking locks on private cabinets," Michael snapped then pointed at Cain. "You. What were you aiming to steal?"

"Like Ernie said, Mr. Michael. We were just looking. The lock was already broken when we entered the room." His answer came with raised hands that moved with every word. "Really. I would never take advantage of your hospitality."

"Is that right?"

"Yes, it is. I wouldn't think of taking what wasn't mine, especially since you've been so generous in giving us refuge while stranded."

"Hunter, check his pockets."

"Right, Mr. Michael." Hunter holstered his pistol and walked toward the man.

"You have no right to hold me—us—like we're criminals," Cain protested.

"From where I stand, you're just that."

Hunter pulled out a gold nugget. "What do we have here? Looks an awful lot like that gold nugget you kept in this case, Mr. Michael."

"It does, doesn't it?"

"I found that—"

"I'm sure. Right from my cabinet."

Whatever the case, Michael was done dealing with visitors who refused to respect him and his property.

He turned to Hunter. "See that they're taken to the edge of our property. Give them two slices of bread and enough water to last them a day. After that, they can find their own food and drink. Make sure they leave, then set guards to ensure they don't return."

Hank entered the room and glanced at the items. "Jackson just found two of our horses a ways from the house, bridled and saddled. Looks like gold and a gun aren't the only things they were planning on taking."

"Then make sure when you set them loose, they go walking. They're not taking my horses. Or my gold."

The first gold nugget his father had found. The one that had given his family the beginning of financial stability. And set his family on the path of trouble.

~*~

The sound of loud voices woke Destiny. Moonlight beamed into the room and gave enough light for Destiny to see the time on the mantel clock. Before she could lift her gaze, somewhere down stairs, a clock chimed the hour. Ten. Eleven. Twelve...

Destiny swung her feet to the floor and stood then looked down. She'd gone to bed still dressed as she'd traveled last night? What? She searched her brain for any minute piece of memory that would help her remember how she'd gotten to this room.

Nothing.

Except for...her little carved kitten lay on her pillow. When had she removed that from her bag?

Oh, well. She shrugged.

Hoping to avoid any squeaky boards, she tiptoed to the door, unlocked and twisted the knob.

Better, but she still couldn't make out who was arguing—or yelling.

She cast a quick look up and down the hallway, then stepped out, leaving her door ajar. Just in case. At the top of the stairs she peered over the banister. Voices like angry bees swarmed upward. She could only catch an occasional word, but not enough to tell what the argument was about. Mr. Michael stood facing two men. Ernie? And another gentleman who turned quickly, drew back an arm as if to punch someone, and Destiny recognized him.

The withdrawn man from the stagecoach, who'd not said a handful of words the whole trip, didn't have a chance to land his punch. Mr. Michael's hand thrust out a split second behind the other man's and caught his wrist. He twisted the man's arm behind his back then handed him over to Hank who fast-trotted him toward the door. Right behind him, Jackson followed with Ernie in his grasp.

"Make sure the men keep them off my land, Hunter."

"You've got it."

The door shut, and Mr. Michael stepped to the bottom of the stairs. Before she could flee back to her room, his gaze lifted and pinned her where she stood. His left eyebrow rose, and she could feel heat reddening her cheeks.

"You woke me." Better take the initiative than allow your opponent to do so. Words straight from Richard's mouth. "How did you know I was here?"

He grinned then. "Heard you. No one keeps from

stepping on that third board. A giveaway every time."

She wanted to harrumph at his knowledge. Instead she edged backward to her room.

He called out in a loud whisper, "Hungry? I make a mean omelet."

She'd been too tired last night to do justice to the late supper his cook had laid out. She remembered that much. Now she realized she was starving, and the thought of a soft omelet, with cheese and slices of tomato, and bacon...

Her mouth watered. "Give me one minute."

She didn't wait for a reply. On tiptoe, she ran toward her room, but as she passed the room before hers, a voice stopped her.

"Well, well. What's Miss Prissy doing running around Mr. Michael's house in the middle of the night? What shenanigans are going on? I wonder what that sour cook will think of this?"

Before Destiny could give her a scathing reply, Miss Lucy withdrew and closed the door.

Destiny sighed and wondered if she should knock on the door and try to explain. No, the woman wouldn't listen to her. They hadn't gotten on well in the stagecoach, and excuses and explanations would not change the woman's opinion of her.

Hurrying into her room, she rustled through the carpetbag she'd brought with her to Mr. Michael's house for a comb and brush. Her hasty brushing did little to smooth the curls that were determined to stay loose. She smoothed down her hair the best she could and headed downstairs. She hoped she'd be able to find the kitchen.

At the bottom of the stairs, she met Hunter who was just leaving. Again.

"Hunter, I thought you'd already gone."

He turned toward her, still holding the door half open. "I did, Miss Destiny, but I needed to ask Mr. Michael something before he retired."

"I see. Could you answer a question for me?"

"Yes, Ma'am, I mean Miss Destiny."

"When I woke a few minutes ago, I realized I was still dressed. How on earth did I get to my room? I can't seem to remember."

His grin was both teasing and friendly. "Why, Miss Destiny, someone carried you there after you fell asleep at the table last night."

"I did? Who was it who carried me..."

Hunter was gone.

Several wrong turns later, she entered the kitchen, located clear at the end of the hallway. Destiny peeked in. Mr. Michael stood at a countertop beating eggs in a large bowl, an apron tied around his waist. He looked so incongruous compared to his kingly vision today that Destiny chuckled.

"What? You've never seen a man cook in his own kitchen? Believe me, I've done it plenty of times in my life. If I hadn't I'd have starved."

"Can I help?"

"Sit. It's almost ready."

"Hmmm. That coffee smells divine."

He nodded toward two mugs on the table. "Help yourself. Maria had it measured and ready for morning. I'll have to remember to prepare more or she'll know we raided her kitchen in the middle of the night."

"She may still guess someone drank her coffee."

"How? I haven't lived in my own home and watched the woman making coffee all these years for nothing. She'll never know." His grin was pure mischievousness.

He sounded so much like a child, Destiny laughed. "We had a cook just like that back home. She had a heart of gold, but she made sure everyone knew the kitchen was her domain. No one violated her rules when visiting her territory."

He didn't need to know the woman was the servant of the boarding school where she'd grown up. They'd had a special bond, she and Dotty, because she'd been the only girl there who'd never had anywhere to go when vacation time came. Of course, she was popular and always invited to her friends' homes, but popularity didn't make up for the lack of a family. No one who loved her and accepted her when she was less than perfect.

She bit her lip and shoved aside the memories.

"Maria's worth her weight in gold. Worth every penny I pay her and Hernandez. And she's the real boss of this place. I might own it, but she's the boss." He dumped the yellow eggs into a skillet and reached for a knife to cut bread.

Homemade bread. She snitched a sliver and stuffed it into her mouth. Hmm. Heaven.

"Hold on there. I know you didn't eat much supper, but this will be ready in seconds." He frowned but his eyes belied his gruff tone.

"I doubt that." She wasn't afraid of him. Mesmerized, maybe. "Were those the same men who were on the stagecoach? Were they stealing from you? This time of the night?"

When he didn't answer, Destiny traced one of the big squares in the red and white checked tablecloth and asked. "What were those men doing here this time of the night?"

There went that brow again. A slight raise. His brown eyes as if he found her amusing. Deepening dent in his chin as if controlling a mouth that wanted to smile.

Endearing.

The sudden panic building in her throat threatened to choke her, and she swallowed it down. What was she thinking? She loved Richard.

He turned away to check his eggs. "They were trying to steal things that are mine."

She couldn't see his face, but the hardness in his voice scared her. She'd never want that tone directed at her. "It's the middle of the night. How do you know they were stealing? Maybe they just wanted to borrow the gun."

"No." His head shook. "Hunter and Hank were with me in my managers' cabin when Jackson saw Ernie and Cain sneaking around in the library. If they'd wanted to borrow a gun, they'd have asked. If they can't behave themselves and wait for the coach to be repaired, then they can leave, but only on foot. They're not getting any of my stock which they also tried to steal."

With deft moves he buttered the bread. With an expert flip of the pan, the gigantic omelet landed on a plate. He slid a knife through it, deposited half on another plate, added two slices of bacon to each, and thick slices of the bread on top. He lifted the coffeepot aloft. "More coffee?"

Destiny scooted her cup closer to him. "Please."

After he settled into a seat across from her, he picked up his fork and looked at her. "Dig in."

She hated it, but her cheeks were heating up again. "Do you mind...?"

"Mind?" His first bite headed toward his mouth. "If you eat?"

Why hadn't she just said a silent, quick prayer? "Uh, I'd like to say a prayer. I've grown used to doing it at sch—uh, home." And Richard had always insisted on it.

He dropped his fork. "Of course. Go ahead."

Closing her eyes, she pressed her hands together. "Heavenly Father, we ask for your beautiful—I mean, bountiful blessings on our snack—breakfast, uh, tonight." Destiny wanted to sink through the floor. She, who was the epitome of gracefulness at school; she who wanted to impress this confident man, was stumbling like a drunken cowboy. Whispering a "Father, forgive me" for butchering what should have been a simple prayer, she hastened to finish it. "Thank you for Mr. Michael's hospitality, and help us to further our friendship."

Ugh. He'd think she wanted something more than friendship. Destiny cringed and refused to glance at him. "Amen."

Had that been a snicker? Surely not. She picked up her fork and shoved a tiny bite of egg in her dry mouth. She chewed and swallowed, but the former delicious-looking omelet refused to go down. She reached for her coffee and felt the food slide down with the coffee.

Ah, reprieved.

"Tell me, Miss McCulloch—it is Miss?"

He was laughing. She could hear it in his voice without even seeing his face. Her appetite vanished just as her temper kicked in. "It is Miss McCulloch to you, Mr. Michael, and I'll thank you not to laugh at me."

"I wouldn't dream of it." And this time his voice was serious. "I didn't finish answering your question."

"You didn't?"

He leaned forward. "In this country, men are hanged for horse thieving, but I avoid that consequence of sin if I can."

"Sin? You take matters into your own hands, judge and jury, and mete the punishment to those who cross—

"

"Don't sound so righteous and uptight. Perhaps where you come from, theft is taken—what shall I say?—in a lighter manner? But out here, a horse is part of a man. You take his horse, and you take his means of work, travel, and even his life at times." He drummed his fork on the table. "I was kind tonight."

"But where will they go on foot?" She shivered.

"Unless they make another stop at the only other place between here and in town—and I doubt they know of it—they'll have several long days of walking."

"What if they die?"

"So be it. It's not my worry. I gave them a bit of food and water. I won't go further than that for thieves."

Was he as hard as he sounded or was he trying to impress her? "Won't they cause you any more trouble?"

"Not with Hunter keeping watch."

"How old is Hunter anyway? He seems like a kid." Never mind that she was probably only a few years older.

"He's older than he looks. Nineteen. Been with me for several years and seems like forever." He lifted his cup but stared at her over the rim, a twinkle in his eyes. "I imagine he's in your age bracket."

"Are you asking me how old I am, Mr. Michael?" She injected the right amount of shock in her voice, but secretly she was pleased he wanted to know. How old was he? Did she dare ask?

"Too young to know what you're getting yourself into coming out here by yourself."

Really? She gave him a coy look. "Do you think? Most people think I'm older than I am, very mature for my age."

His eyebrow inched upward again. If she stayed around him much longer, it might be in danger of a permanent lift.

He didn't believe her. No doubt thought she was too young to be here, interrupting his life and everyone else she met. Destiny wanted to scowl at him, but her training stood her in good stead.

He couldn't be that much older than her, could he? Besides, what did he know? He was probably dying to know her reason for traveling to this place. As if she'd confide in him.

All she wanted was to find that kind boy who'd rescued her from a savage death years ago and thank him. Then she could return to Richard and get on with her life. Sanity. Safety. Security.

Destiny stood and smiled sweetly. "Good night, Mr. Michael."

She didn't care about Mr. Michael or his ranch or anything else to do with him.

And who did she think she was kidding?

Chapter Seven

Michael watched Destiny sashay from the room. She was a good-looking woman, especially when those dark blue eyes of hers flashed every time she thought someone was slighting her. Carried a mighty big chip on that tiny shoulder of hers. She'd better shrug it right off if she expected to make the west her home.

He'd angered her, but he hadn't been able to resist teasing her.

She reminded him of a fiery-spirited child he'd known years ago. Poor child. She'd seen the brutal killing of her parents while crouched in the brush twenty feet away. His parents had reluctantly taken her in—not because they didn't want to—but because his own mother had been ill and only three months later, she had died. His father had insisted they couldn't care for her.

Michael stood and gathered the dishes. He was tempted to leave them and let Maria handle them tomorrow, but it wasn't worth irritating her. What he'd said earlier was gospel. He couldn't ask for a better housekeeper and cook, but as much as she adored him, she wouldn't tolerate coming into a messy kitchen.

Half an hour later, Michael stepped outside. A cloud had slipped over the moon leaving the night, temporarily, dark and still. A forewarning of another storm. They needed the water in preparation for the summer dry months, but he hated the spring gully washers that filled every bit of low land, usually killing several head of cattle and effectively closing off any paths to the outside world.

They'd get through it just like the other years, but it wasn't convenient.

He loved the ranch at night. Busy days gave way to peaceful nights when problems were put on hold. Pa had always said when he'd come in from working, and after he'd washed up, *"Time to put down our day chores and burdens, son. The night is calling us."*

He could remember the nights on the front stoop of their small cabin, his legs hanging over the edge, Pa playing the harmonica as his mother crooned gentle songs suited for the dark. There'd been something big and lonesome tugging inside him pushing the tears to squeeze from his eyes, but he'd held them back. Tears were for women and children, Pa'd said.

He'd found out different when Priscilla deceived him.

"Night's quiet, Boss." The low voice of Hank, one of his best hands, reached his ears.

"You escorted them off the property? Made sure?"

"Sure as shootin' we did. Me and Jackson. Just got back in time for his watch."

"Good work, Hank. Appreciate it."

"Ah, it wasn't nothing. The likes of them two—"

"I know, but it means a lot to me. My men's respect."

"You earn it."

Michael strolled away.

There was a feeling in the air, or maybe it was inside him. Trouble. But from where? The two men he'd had escorted off his property? Destiny McCulloch? He smiled. He doubted if she could cause much problem. To some young bronco's heart, maybe, but not his. He wasn't about to be taken in by a pretty face a second time. Not by a long shot.

Then what? He didn't rightly know, but what he did know, he'd fight till his last breath was gone to protect what he'd built from his inheritance. Not likely he'd let some swindler or crook get the best of him.

The moon peeked from between the clouds, over the distant mountain range, showering the low land pasture with beams of silver. There was movement but he knew it to be a few of his cattle. A thousand cattle on the hills. Pa had often quoted the scripture to him, conveying his dreams and hopes to his only child. He hadn't lived to see it come to pass, but Michael had worked hard to capitalize on those dreams. Pa would've been proud.

Past time to turn in. He had a busy day tomorrow, and rising time would come all too early, especially with having to do without Hunter for another couple days. He hadn't wanted to let him go with his blacksmith back to the stagecoach, but Hunter's argument made sense. Hunter knew better than any other man on the ranch—excepting the blacksmith himself—what needed done, and with his help, the task would be handled much quicker.

A few hours rest was better than none. He cast a last glance at his land and headed toward his quarters.

~*~

Destiny wasn't sure if it was the rooster crowing outside her window or the warm sunbeams caressing her cheeks that woke her. Regardless, she knew instantly where she was and smiled at the thought of the late night snack she'd shared with Mr. Michael last night. She glanced at the little carved kitten sitting beside her bed and smiled. That never failed to give her a warm feeling.

It was early still, and she deliberated for a minute on snatching another hour's slumber. But the thought of missing out on anything exciting spurred her to climb out of the bed.

Twenty minutes later, Destiny headed for the kitchen she'd sat in last night. She stuck her head inside the door. "Hi. Could I grab a cup of coffee, Maria?"

The short, dark-haired woman glanced up, and waved imperiously to shoo her away. "Coffee's in the dining room, Miss. Help yourself."

"Anything I can do to help you?"

The black eyes stared at her as if wondering about her mentality.

Destiny smiled. According to Mr. Michael this sharp-tongued woman was a pussy cat. Well, she'd had plenty of practice taming live cats in Boston. Maria couldn't be that bad. "I just thought with the extra guests, I could lend a hand if you needed me."

The features relaxed. "We'll see, Miss. Maybe later."

She nodded. "Fine. I'll check back."

The serving buffet showed individually covered platters of sausage and steak. Browned potatoes, yellow scrambled eggs, and three different bowls of fruit tempted the hungry. Destiny poured her coffee, sipped, then speared several apple and pear quarters into a bowl. That should do for a second breakfast.

43

Where was everyone? She cut off a bit of apple and nibbled at it.

The sound of a distant door closing and footsteps approaching put her on the alert. She hoped it wasn't that Lucy woman from the stagecoach.

Mr. Michael stepped into the room, his gaze resting on her. "You're up?"

She tilted her head at him. "Of course. Did you expect me to sleep till noon?"

"Well..." he drawled out the word, but the infectious grin softened any possible hints of criticism.

"Sorry to disappoint, but I'm an early riser." She delighted in disproving his obvious opinion of her. "I didn't want to miss out on anything exciting."

"You won't stay inside or on the porch sewing? Or painting?"

"No, I won't. I can't sew much and my artwork is severely lacking in talent. I'm here in the west, you know, and interested in exploring. Seeing everything I can."

"Yeah, but—never mind. Well then, I thought you might like to ride out to the orchards with me, but I do look for rain today."

Ah, now she knew where he obtained this sweet fruit. "I'm not afraid of a little rain. I'd love to go. When are we leaving?"

"You sure? Our rains are downpours."

"I'm sure."

"An hour then?"

"I can be ready in twenty minutes." Destiny stood and picked up her bowl and cup, thrilled at the sudden flicker of approval she read in his eyes.

"Meet me at the barn."

"Where are you two secretly headed to?" Lucy's brash voice preceded her entrance into the room. She waltzed over to the buffet and filled a plate with sausages and potatoes, ignored the fruit and poured herself a cup of coffee. She cast sideways glances at the two of them. "Or is the destination too *personal* to reveal?"

Destiny's irritation at the woman's insinuation soared into play. "We're not doing anything secretly, I'll have you know..."

"We're going to inspect my fruit trees for bugs. Would

you like to work on them with us?" Mr. Michael's calm voice broke into Destiny's words.

"Inspect for bugs on fruit trees? I don't think so. Bugs and I don't get along. Besides, I have some things I need to attend to." She scooped up a bite of her fried potatoes but managed to cast a glance at Destiny before the food entered her mouth. One that said *she* knew what this business was all about.

Whirling away, Destiny left the room. That woman was impossibly rude.

At the kitchen door, she leaned in. "Sure there's nothing I can help with?"

Maria's mouth widened in a smile, taking years off her age. "I have a pile of folded shirts for Mr. Michael over there on that bench. I was going to take them up later, but if you insist, you may drop them off in his room. His is the first door on the right."

"I'll be glad to." Destiny lifted the clothes and half-ran up the stairs, delighted at the prospect of a morning out.

She hesitated at the door, knocked gently, listened then opened the door.

Her gaze shifted around the room, studying each detail. Just what she expected. A man's room. And he was neat, although truth be told, Maria had probably already been up to straighten it. No fancy quilt on his bed. Not many items on his nightstand or chest.

Destiny strolled around the room. At the foot of the monstrous, four-poster bed, was a large chest, elaborately carved. Destiny caught her breath. Beautiful. His mother's probably. She was almost tempted...no, she'd better not. Not today anyhow.

She hesitated. What would it hurt? Just one quick glance inside?

No more time to argue with herself, she bent and lifted the heavy lid of the trunk then stared down at the items inside it. One side held shimmering party dresses and one old, well-worn man's suit. But the other side caught her attention.

It was...It was...She reached down and smoothed a hand over the quilt. It was old and beautiful, and reminded her of her mother's quilt.

But that was nonsense. That's what she got for nosing

in things she shouldn't.

With a quiet thump, she had the chest closed. Shrugging off the feeling of depression, she moved away.

On top of a huge clothes closet, a glass-topped box hoarded several old watches, some looking as if they could be valuable. Positioned in front of the fireplace was a huge wing-backed chair, the walnut brown leather buffed till the beams from outside made it shine like a chocolate quartz stone. Beside it stood a small table, two books lying on top of it, one a journal.

Stealing a glance toward the door, Destiny shifted the clothes in her arms and opened the journal. The front page was inscribed with the words: *To Susanna from your loving parents*. The childish hand writing, in the first half of the journal—which went through several years—told her it was likely written by some relative of his from the past. Mr. Michael's mother perhaps? Toward the middle, the handwriting had become more elaborate—but less frequent with entries—as if the young child had grown up. She stared down at it, wanting to pick it up and carry it back to her room to devour in the evenings.

But Mr. Michael would know she'd taken it. No, she'd better not yield to temptation this time. But...maybe she'd have another chance to read a few pages now and then. Maybe.

She'd just make sure she was available to help Maria if and when she needed it. Especially delivering clean clothes.

Opening the door to the large clothes closet, she placed Mr. Michael's clothes neatly on a top shelf. Giving the clothes a last little pat, she shut the door of the chest and turned to leave.

At the door stood Lucy, her face a mask of mockery as she taunted. "My, aren't you the nosy little snob? Find anything interesting?"

Destiny jerked herself from the place where she felt glued and headed toward the door, shutting it firmly as she spoke as casually as she could. "If putting clothes in their proper rooms to help Maria is what you call interesting, then..."

Swishing her skirt, she hurried toward her own room, the woman's soft taunting laugh dogging her steps.

Had the woman been watching her the whole time and seen her wandering around the room? Worse, had she seen her opening that journal? Or even worse than that, the trunk?

Destiny wanted to groan, but she had no time. If she wanted to meet Mr. Michael at the barn in time, she'd better hurry.

~*~

The horse he'd saddled for her, eyed her when she approached eighteen minutes later. She reached for the bridle and patted the horse. "You look like a sweetheart. You won't throw me, will you?"

"She's the safest, sweetest mare I own. Might get a little lazy, but she's a trooper when needed." Mr. Michael's voice came from behind her.

She cast a quick glance over her shoulder. "What's her name?"

"Shyanne. Let me help you up."

"No, thanks—"

His hands gripped her waist and tucked her onto the saddle as neatly as if he'd placed a canteen there. He swung onto Jasper's back and motioned her to follow.

Catching her breath, she touched Shyanne's sides with her heels, and the mare picked up her pace until she drew alongside of the bigger horse. "It's a gorgeous morning. Is it always like this here?"

"Yeah, except in winters. Mornings cool or warm, afternoons we get the heat, but by the time night falls we're enjoying the cool weather again." He shifted in his saddle to look at her. "You've learned a lot about me. Tell me about yourself. What are you doing out here in the middle of nowhere?"

Learned a lot? She knew hardly a thing about the man, and she wasn't about to tell him her real reason for traveling all the way here. That approval she'd seen earlier would quickly turn to skepticism and scorn. She doubted the man who owned this place suffered fools, and he'd place her in that category quicker than that sweet little rabbit hopping off to the left of them. "I'm from Boston, back east. Wanted to get away for the summer."

"I deduced that. Why Roaring Springs?"

What happened to all the western reticence Richard had warned her about? "Why not? I stuck my finger on a map and when I opened my eyes, I was pointing at Roaring Springs. Seemed like a good place to start look—" Aghast at her slip, Destiny broke off.

"I imagine you keep things moving wherever you are."

He was either ignoring her broken-off comment or too eager to make the critical remark to pay attention to her gaff.

"If you mean interesting, then you'd be right. I wasn't famous for genteel activities."

"Back home?"

"Of course, back home. Where do you think I've been?"

"I only thought perhaps you'd traveled some. You seem to adjust better than most women to a different scene."

"You don't have a low opinion of women, do you, Mr. Michael?" She didn't care if he did hear the sarcasm in her voice. He needed to be told sugar accomplished lots more than vinegar.

"I have a very high opinion of most women."

Just not her?

"My mother was a wonderful person," he continued.

"She's gone?"

"She died when I was a lad, but I still remember how gentle and inspiring she was. She smoothed a lot of the rough places from my pa and taught me to enjoy the finer elements of life."

Like writing in journals?

Jasper tossed his head, and Mr. Michael stretched out an arm to pat him on the neck.

"She schooled you?"

"Yes. Made me write dozens of research papers, and when I complained about not having books to look up items, she explained I needed to find the answers to what I wrote about with what I had available." He grinned. "She was a perfect lady all right, but a tough one who frowned on sloppiness and excuses."

"She sounds like a smart woman."

"She was. Insisted on us reading a chapter every night out of one of our cherished books and one from the

Bible. We sang the summer evenings away, and played games in the winter."

If she hadn't been hanging on to every word, she'd never have caught the tinge of tremble in his voice. Her heart responded in kind as a wave of lonesomeness swept through her at the empty memories in her own life.

Vague images of parents who patted her head, who shook their heads at her tantrums and ignored her in turns, floated in her mind.

The locket, with the faded portrait of her parents and her own young self hidden inside. She'd loved that locket partly because of the pictures and partly because of the tiny key that had opened the locket to reveal the pictures. Like a miniature treasure chest. She'd never gone anywhere without it—even after she'd grown up—until it'd gotten stolen on this trip.

It had been her most treasured item, even though the little key had been lost years and years ago. But just knowing she had the pictures safe inside the locket had given her a warm feeling. And someday she had planned find the right locksmith to make her a replacement key. Someday when the time was right had been her plan.

She'd also treasured her white kitten she'd had to leave behind with the boy Caleb, who'd promised over and over he'd love and care for it. Maybe that's why she treasured so much the little carved kitten that sat in her room no matter where she was.

The handmade quilt that her mother had given her. Somewhere, at some time, her own snuggly, warm quilt had vanished, and for the life of her, she couldn't remember where she'd lost it.

Had she dreamed some of her memories? Imagined them? Created them for lack of anything more tangible to give her life a background?

No. Young as she was, even with all she couldn't remember, these were real memories. A part of her life, and she'd never let go of them. Not much to get weepy over, but it was all she had.

She shook her head. "You probably still have those same books."

"I do. Wouldn't part with them. They carry too many

memories."

"Didn't you ever wish for a brother or sister?"

"No. I can't remember that I did."

His gaze was focused on something in the distance. He reined in Jasper and nodded at the trees full of pink and white blossoms.

"Where did you ever get so many fruit trees?"

"I've ordered them for years to build up an orchard. Apples, peaches, pears, cherries and a few rows of grape vines." He swung off his horse and inspected a tree. "Hmm. Looks like I need to have Hernandez bring some of his potent bug killer out here."

"Hernandez?"

"Maria's husband, my houseman and general help. He's put together a poison that actually gets rid of these little blighters. I don't want them to get a head start when the fruits actually appear." Mr. Michael flicked a bug off one of the branches. "Want to get down and rest a few minutes?"

"I'd love to." She started to dismount, but he was there beside Shyanne and swung her off. He set her feet firmly on the ground but didn't let go of her waist.

"You're an awfully tiny woman to be wandering around this land by yourself."

"Are you criticizing me, Mr. Michael, or flattering?" She smiled up into his serious eyes.

He stared back into hers, the tiniest of smiles edging the corners of his lips. "I don't know, Miss McCulloch—yet."

"Then I reckon you ought to let me go until you do know." She was flirting—and knew it. The image of Richard was dim and a little bit blurry, while this man, big and handsome and dangerously close, was vividly real. Here and now.

"I reckon you're right." His fingers loosened and released her, and he stepped back. He started off, inspecting trees.

"How much land do you own?" Destiny followed him slowly, giving Shyanne time to nibble at the grass.

"Enough. My parents were some of the first to settle in this area, so I had the advantage of claiming whatever I had need of. Not so easy nowadays with more people moving in."

Destiny widened her eyes at his comment. "Have you had fights over the land?"

"A few, but the key is using the land, and I've always made sure to do that. Enough land to feed my cattle, fields of wheat and corn, a good water supply and a big vegetable garden, and pigs and chickens to keep our table plenished. I've utilized natural barriers when they're available, and a few of my own devising when necessary to mark my land. So far, it's worked."

"Cattle. Fruit trees. What else do you own?"

Mr. Michael's gaze flicked to her, a question in it.

For a second, Destiny wondered if she'd overstepped the western boundaries again.

The gunshots blasted in the air, distant but loud enough they echoed down the valley. Mr. Michael swiveled on one foot, and he reached out to clutch a handful of Jasper's black mane.

"What is it?" Destiny moved up beside him, and Shyanne nuzzled the big stallion.

He held up a hand. More gunshot sounds poured down the valley, and Mr. Michael placed a foot in his stirrup but paused long enough to glance at her. "Wait here. As long as you stay hidden in the fruit trees, you'll be safe. If I'm not back within an hour, head home." He swung up and reined Jasper to face the opposite direction.

"No, I want to go with you."

"In fact, don't wait. Head back to the ranch and send the boys after me." He wasted no more time, but dug his boot-clad heels into the horse's sides and was off.

Destiny frowned after him and propped two fists on her sides. "He thinks I'll be in the way."

She narrowed her eyes then smiled. Pulling Shyanne close she propped a foot in the stirrup and hoisted herself into the saddle. With a gentle kick, she urged, "Come on, sweetie pie. Let's show Mr. Michael-know-it-all that we can do some things. You're after Jasper, and I'm after Mr. Michael." She blushed then, realizing how her words sounded, but didn't care. Only Shyanne heard, and she'd never tell a soul.

Shyanne leaped forward and kept up the pace for at

least a quarter of a mile. She slowed then, but Destiny didn't mind. It was time to see if she could learn to follow Mr. Michael's sign.

Chapter Eight

Hunter stopped at the creek where he'd led Miss Destiny and that other woman for a drink. Sweetest water this side of the Mississippi. Mr. Michael's father had shore picked the best spot in this country. If only Mr. Michael had not been dragged into the feud.

But Mr. Michael's father was a part of the problem. A big part. The heart of it.

Trouble was, the man had trusted everyone. Couldn't see when someone was double-crossing him. Always positive, the man had been.

Right until his own death. That was what being too trustful brought you.

His own dad had warned Mr. Michael's dad, but the man was too good for this world.

Hunter swept off his hat and wiped his forehead with his shirt sleeve.

If it hadn't been for Hank, Hunter wouldn't have learned as much as he did about the past. Mr. Michael had just stared down at him and tried to get him to forget the past. He'd loved him too much as an adopted little brother and had tried to do for Hunter what he wanted for himself, but couldn't do. Forget the past.

Fortunately, Hank had filled in the gaps. Along with that gap-filling, he'd explained Mr. Michael's own hurt— and his efforts at protecting Hunter.

All that had built an even greater loyalty and admiration for Mr. Michael. The tables had turned, and now, instead of Mr. Michael protecting him, he intended to protect the man he owed everything to.

Chapter Nine

It wasn't hard to follow Mr. Michael's trail. He'd been in a hurry, not caring about the evidence of his passing. Destiny urged a reluctant Shyanne up the side of a hill and topped it. She leaned forward to pat her neck then straightened and caught her breath at the sight below her. Gorgeous, golden brown—something—waved in the air giving the illusion of floating on dry ground. Her eye caught the cattle mingling, trampling, ruining whatever Mr. Michael had planted here. Three men on horseback urged the stampeding cattle on.

She screamed at the destructiveness below her, hurling threats and insults, but the wind captured her words and carried them away.

A demanding voice spoke to her, a few feet away. "What are you doing?"

She whirled. Mr. Michael stood behind a rock, his face an angry cyclone of rolling emotions. If she'd made him angry, she couldn't tell. "Looking for you. I've come to help."

He motioned for her to join him and disappeared.

She tossed Shyanne's reins around a low bush, close to where Jasper stood, and rounded the rock. He knelt, a gun poised on the top of the rock, his steely gaze on the damage below. She knelt beside him.

"I told you to go for help."

"I'm the only help you need." She'd done it again. He'd think for sure she was after him. "By the time I got back to the ranch these men would be gone."

"They'll be gone as soon as I go after them." His dry tone didn't speak well for her reasoning.

"We could shoot."

He stared at her. "Don't you mean I could shoot?"

"I've shot a gun before." Only a couple times, and Richard had shaken his head and said he'd never place another gun in her hands again. But then, what Mr.

54

Michael didn't know wouldn't hurt him. Would it? And surely, in all that space below she could shoot over someone's head. "Give me a gun."

To give him credit, he looked doubtful. "No. This is the plan. We'll ride down there and when we get close—if we can—I'll shoot over their heads. If I can, I'll round them up. If not, scaring them off will work for now."

"And all those cows?"

"All those cattle are prime beef. We'll worry about them after we're rid of the men."

He swung onto Jasper's back again and took off.

Destiny hurried to follow.

Mr. Michael led them down a roundabout way, bringing them closer to the men—almost even. At the bottom of the hill, he motioned for her to stay close.

The men had slowed to a walk as they drove the cattle into a cul-de-sac.

She could hear the men whooping it up, laughing and cursing. Her anger solidified. Destiny veered away and approached an oversized rock.

Mr. Michael was right behind her. He swung off Jasper's back, set his rifle against the rock. "Stay here while I get closer to the men. *Do not* follow me. Do you think you can do that?"

His stare unsettled her for a minute, but obediently, she nodded.

Then with a last warning glance at her, he walked toward the men.

Really? He thought she couldn't do *anything* to help? She swung off her horse, studied the rifle he'd left behind then smiled. Surely he hadn't *forgotten* it? Then he'd left it behind on purpose. Or not.

No matter, it was time she showed Mr. Michael she wasn't entirely useless. She touched then raised and aimed the rifle in the general direction of the men. Closing her eyes, she prayed, "God, don't let me hit anyone."

Jerking the rifle higher, she squeezed the trigger and opened her eyes.

One of the men, the last one in the bunch, cursed and slapped a hand over his ear. She couldn't hear *what* he said, but she could hear his tone, and she was pretty sure it wasn't a compliment to her shooting.

The sight of Mr. Michael heading her way sobered her. With a quick move, she replaced the rifle, slid to the ground and leaned against the massive rock. She even managed to hum a little before an angry voice interrupted.

"What do you think you're doing?"

She swallowed and looked up. "Nothing."

His silence was more than she could bear. "Trying to stop those men."

Mr. Michael's gaze riveted on the three fleeing figures and his lips spread in a slow smile as he shook his head. "I reckon you accomplished your goal."

"What?"

"Where did you learn to shoot like that?"

Was that admiration in his voice? She'd impressed him. She jumped to her feet and waltzed a couple feet away then remembered she needed to show some reserve. "Did I hit one of them?"

She fervently hoped not.

His eyes narrowed. "Since one of them yelled out that someone had shot his ear, and I didn't get a chance to shoot, I'm pretty sure it was you."

She was sure she'd pointed that gun straight up toward the heaven. Better not let him know she'd had her eyes closed. She pasted a self-satisfied smirk on her lips. "Not too bad an aim, for a girl, wouldn't you say?"

His scrutiny did nothing to bolster her confidence. "Let's go see what damage there is."

He didn't bother helping her mount, only took possession of the rifle again. Hmmm. Didn't trust her?

Sobered, she climbed into the saddle, dug her heels into Shyanne's sides, and trotted after Mr. Michael. An action rapidly becoming a habit.

~*~

She was either a good shot or the luckiest person alive. He was positive she'd nipped one of the men's ears with her shot. Plucky little thing.

He heard her gasp of irritation when he snatched the rifle and rode away, but he wasn't about to chance getting himself plugged—just in case. Her muttering dogged him, but when he twisted to check on her, she was fine. He suspected she wasn't quite as experienced as she let on, but he had to admit, she was a fast learner.

She pulled up beside him. "What now, Boss?"

Was she being sarcastic? He disciplined his lips. "We've got our work cut out for us herding the cattle out of here. See that gap in the hills to the southwest? That's where we need to drive them. You up for it?"

Her slender throat contracted as she swallowed, but she didn't whine. Setting her lips, she nodded. "Tell me what you want me to do."

He indicated the direction with a tilt of his head. "You take this side and walk alongside them once they get moving. I'll walk a mite faster so you can follow my lead. I'll keep an eye on you in case you need help. And a loud 'yee-haw' will help keep them moving."

"Like this, 'yaw'?"

Michael laughed. Those cattle had never seen what he was about to let loose on them. Hopefully, they wouldn't stampede. "Just like that. Ready?"

Her eyes gave her away. Fear flickered inside them, but she gamely gave a nod and gathered her reins.

"Let's go then." Jasper pranced in a circle as if anticipating the chase in store. "Stay on your horse. Under no circumstance get off. Understand?"

Another nod from her.

He whipped Jasper around and let out a yell. Grabbing his hat and waving it, he started after his cattle.

~*~

"Father, help me out here." Hadn't Richard said God always listened to his children? Right about now, she needed all the intervention she could round up. Was that extra-large cow staring at her? Planning on grounding her into powder just for the orneriness of it?

She gulped and flapped her hands. "Get, you."

It lowered its head. Getting ready to charge, no doubt. She pulled off her scarf and waved it. "Move, you stupid beast. I don't have all day."

Wonder of wonders, the thing whirled and trotted after the rest of the herd. Maybe she could get the hang of being a cowboy—girl—after all.

Waving it wildly in the air, she let out a tentative, 'yaw!' and watched as the beasts took off. Mr. Michael's golden hair shone in the distance, and Destiny followed.

~*~

Four hours later, Destiny slid off her horse and collapsed on the ground. Mr. Michael was on his knees. He looked over his shoulder. "Get a drink from my canteen if you want."

"What are you doing?" Destiny staggered to Jasper and removed the container. Uncapping it she lifted and swallowed a mouthful of lukewarm water. "Ugh."

His devastating grin didn't help her dry mouth any.

"I think I tucked a few strips of jerky in my pouch, if you're hungry."

Not hungry enough to eat that stuff. "Thanks, but I'll wait till dinner."

"Dinner?" He settled back on his heels.

Destiny caught a glimpse of the fresh meat he was arranging on a forked stick. "When did you have time to go hunting?"

His lips thinned. "I didn't. This is one of the calves that got trampled in the stampede."

"Calves?" Her stomach lurched. "We're going to eat that—that baby?"

"You've never eaten a steak back east?"

"Of course, I have—"

"Well, then..." He turned and laid another small stick on the fire.

"Yes, but—"

"You didn't think about where it came from?"

She had to make him understand. "We're done, aren't we? Why can't we head back to your home and have supper there? It's—what?—afternoon? Plenty of time to eat a proper supper prepared by Maria."

He paused and seemed to be considering her reasoning before resuming his careful feeding of the minuscule flames. "I'll grant you Maria's cooking beats mine any day, but for a make-do feast, I don't do so bad myself." He tossed a grin over his shoulder. "Why don't you give it a try before you reject it?"

"Ugh."

"Otherwise you're going to get mighty hungry."

"I'm strong. I can miss one meal."

"One?" Mr. Michael stood and dusted off his pants. "We're talking three, maybe four meals."

"What on earth do you mean?"

Mr. Michael waved a hand at the grazing cattle. "That's about half the herd I have on this side of the mountain. I can't go home till I track the rest."

"But I can't stay out here all night." She had nothing with her. No comb. No towels to wash her face. No change of clothing. Nothing.

"There's no alternative. We're too far out now for you to ride back without an escort, and I'm none too sure those men aren't lurking to make more trouble."

"But I'm not prepared."

"I am." He gave her a grin. "I never go anywhere, even here on my ranch, without a few things. You never know what might happen. I go prepared."

"I see, but why—"

"I won't risk losing my cattle. You should have gone back when I told you earlier."

Was he blaming her? "I just wanted to help."

He bent to rotate the meat, juice dripping into the coals.

When he said nothing, Destiny went on. "How will you find the rest? Couldn't they be stolen?"

"I hope not."

His grim voice sent shivers scurrying up her spine.

"Why don't you go back and get some of the men to do this?"

He looked at her. Something in his eyes startled her. "Those cattle are mine. It's my duty, Miss McCulloch, to care for them."

"I see." She swallowed, feeling as if he'd placed those big hands around her waist and settled her firmly where he wanted her. Softly, she added, "Tell me what to do."

Mr. Michael picked up a stick, the steak brown and succulent-looking. His gaze snagged hers and held it. "First, we'll eat."

She nodded, but when he looked away, made a face. He might insist she eat, but she was determined she'd not like it. She settled on a flat rock and accepted the tin plate and old fork he gave her. "What's this?" She stabbed the wilted green gob beside the steak.

"Greens. Eat them. They're good for you."

She eyed him as he picked up the second stick holding a steak and took a bite.

Closing her mind to the images that clamored to be viewed inside her head, she lifted her fork and nibbled at the meat. The tender, juicy meat rolled across her taste buds and teased the crying hunger pains in her stomach, promising more succulent satisfaction if she'd give it a chance.

Her eyes flew open.

Mr. Michael's eyes twinkled at her. Again.

"What on earth did you do to it to make it so-so—"

"Delicious?" He laughed. "A few wild herbs and the age of—"

Destiny lifted her hand. "That's enough. Don't remind me if you expect me to finish this."

"I do expect it."

She raised her fork and bit off a bigger chunk. She met his gaze. "Definitely delicious."

"I thought you'd like it. Try the greens."

"Don't push your luck."

Chapter Ten

What Michael wouldn't give to have Hunter here right now. But he knew when he didn't show up for supper, at least two of his men would be on their way without waiting to devour their own. Might take them an hour or so, following his trail, but they'd be here. Hunter should be back at the ranch by early morning. Hopefully with the stagecoach following him. The women needed to move on, and the sooner the better.

Regardless of the assurances he'd given Destiny, he'd feel better when Hank or one of the others could escort her home.

Those strands of her erstwhile tidy hair feathering her cheeks only added character to her features. She was worn out, but rounding up close to a hundred head of cattle wasn't an easy task, by a long shot. She'd been a game little thing, he'd give her that, and deserved to look worn out.

He couldn't see any other way but for her to spend the night out here, and that bothered him. Badly. Not that he'd hurt a hair on her head, or allow anything or anyone to do so, if he could prevent it, but he sensed danger. He wasn't a fool, didn't easily panic, and seldom ignored his feelings. Pa had taught him to always go with his innermost feeling, and so far, his advice had never been wrong.

He checked on the horses and grabbed their blanket rolls and his saddlebag. Returning to the fire, he tossed one of the bedrolls down in front of her. "Might as well get some rest. We'll be up before dawn."

She looked up at him. "But it's light yet. The sun hasn't even set."

"You're right. But you're also worn out. Some of my men will arrive by early morning, knowing something is wrong when I haven't returned." He settled back on his heels, picked up a stick, stirred the ashes, and held up the scarred coffee pot. When she shook her head, he set it down and continued. "I'll have one of them escort you back to the ranch at daylight in the morning. The rest will help me finish rounding up cattle."

And check for signs of the men who'd done this. He was almost positive he'd seen one of them on a hilltop, but he'd been too far away to know for sure. If only he'd brought his telescope.

"Will Hunter be home tomorrow?" She stood and turned her back to him.

"Tomorrow, late, yes, and he'll have the stagecoach with him. You'll be on your way before I ever get home."

Silence. Then...

"No doubt you'll be glad to get the stagecoach intruders out of your hair, and life gets back to normal for you."

Had her back stiffened?

"We don't get many visitors out here."

Was it his imagination or had the air charged as if lightning crisscrossed the reddening sky? Was something wrong with her? Blazes, he hoped she wasn't getting sick.

"Don't worry, Miss McCulloch, we'll make sure you get into town without any more problems."

She actually shook her skirt as she flounced a couple steps farther away. "I'm *not* worried, Mr. Michael. It's all to your good to make sure we have a safe departure, isn't it?"

For sure, that was frustration in her tone. She was piqued about something he'd said.

He scratched his head. Hadn't he been polite and concerned? "I was thinking more about Luke and Daly being behind in their trips. Then you and Lucy—"

The glance she scorched him with stopped him dead.

"I'm sure."

If he'd been the praying man his dad had been, Michael would have prayed for an early sunset. He watched as she made her bed, pulling the blanket tight around her. She turned her back to him, but he knew the minute she allowed sleep to overtake her. Her stiff body softened, her breath slowed. Minutes later, she turned over and moaned, her lashes dark against her pale cheeks.

He still couldn't figure why she'd come here. She was obviously well-schooled, didn't seem to lack for money, and a lady all the way. So why come here? No doubt she had suitors lined up around the block. For that matter, he didn't know she wasn't spoken for. All he knew for sure was—well, nothing.

That brought him up short. He had no right to wonder about anything concerning her. She wasn't his business. His gaze flicked to the darkening sky, the darker mountaintop, skimmed it for any sign of movement, then back to the sleeping woman.

He shook his head. Might as well get some sleep. The boys from the ranch ought to show up toward morning, and it'd be a long day tomorrow. Michael stretched, tilted his hat over his eyes, and dozed.

An hour later, a storm rolled in. The crack of lightning lit up the sky, the thunder reverberating from mountain ridge to ridge.

Michael jumped to his feet, but it was too late. By the time he was on his feet the deluge had soaked him. He reached Destiny and bent to shake her, but she was already stirring. Gasping, she sat up, blinking, her hair lying damp and straggly against her cheeks.

It was too late to run for shelter, but Michael pulled her up anyway, took her hand and they ran to an overhanging rock. The space was a snug fit, but they crawled into it and pressed their backs against the hard rock.

"Where did that come from?"

Not a word of complaint though her teeth chattered. The hand he still held felt as cold as the ice sheets winter brought. His admiration for her rose.

"One of our sudden storms. Knew it was coming. I should have—"

"I'm all right." She shivered and tugged at the heavy, sodden blanket.

Her hand was still like ice. There was nothing for it. He'd have to get her home before she came down with pneumonia or something worse. As soon as the rain let up.

"I use to love to play in the ra...a...in." Her voice

shook.

"You're too cold." Michael shook his head. If nothing worse, she was in for a serious cold.

"Where's Shy-anne and J...as...per?"

"Stay here. I'll be right back."

Crawling out of the cover of the overhang, he ducked his head and ran for his horse. Jasper shifted on his feet and snorted. His head tossed as if indignant at being forced to stand in the rain. Michael patted the animal's neck then loosed his reins. Taking the horse's head in his hands, he murmured to him. "Jasper, the men will be a long time finding us with this rain. I need you to go home. You hear me? Home, Jasper. Home."

With a whinny and shake of his head, the big beast turned and galloped away, and Michael watched him go. He'd be home in an hour if he kept that pace up, and one of the hands would hear him. They'd know then he needed them, if they weren't already on their way. Either way, they'd run into Jasper and bring him back for him.

The wind whipped the rain down upon him determined to measure out as stern a judgment on humanity as they passed out on each other. This high up, the trees laid back their branches as if bowing in obeisance to the force of nature. Lightning streaked the sky, blue and at times a fiery red. Mean, threatening, dangerous.

One touched the mountain across the valley, sizzled and disappeared. Whew. Way too close.

Michael sucked in a sodden breath.

He darted to Shyanne's side and quickly gathered as many pieces of wood that lay beneath the thick-branched pines as he could, then led Shyanne back to the overhang. He tied her reins to a low-hanging branch—hoping she'd shield them from some of the rain—and slid into the space beside Destiny again.

He wasted no time digging into his saddlebag and pulling out some of the jerky she'd eschewed to eat earlier. Like it or not, a watery broth of this stuff would warm her body and give her some needed strength. He dug out a small kettle from the bag and set it outside the overhang, watching as the rain pelted into it, slowly filling. When it was a third full, he drew it into their rough shelter.

Destiny opened her eyes. "I thought you weren't coming back."

"Wanted to make sure Jasper and Shyanne were all right." He dumped the sticks in a pile and rearranged them. Using a bit of flint until he had a spark, he blew softly, and the fire leaped up, not big but enough to boil the water and loosen the flavor in the jerky.

"What are you doing?" She yawned, shivered. "Brrr. It's cold."

"Making you some broth." He grabbed his blanket and tucked it around her.

"Ugh. With that jerky stuff?"

He turned back to the kettle. "This stuff will get some strength in you before you get sick."

"I'll be fine."

But her shivers belied her statement. He smirked at her, trying to coax a smile from her. "I'm sure you'll be fine."

"I will, I prom..." She didn't bother finishing her statement.

He didn't want her to go to sleep yet. Sipping the broth he'd made from Maria's homemade jerky would give her body some strength, and hopefully, ward off a serious cold, if not something worse. She wasn't used to this weather. He'd known it might rain. Why had he insisted on bringing her on this disastrous trip?

"This..." He indicated the steaming broth, "...is an added precaution. You'll thank me for it tomorrow."

"I doubt that." Her words were mumbled, her eyes closed.

Michael reached over to shake her. "Wake up, Destiny. You can't go to sleep yet."

"I'm not asleep."

Twenty minutes later, he checked the broth and pulled it off the fire. Using his bandana to pick up the kettle, he poured a little of the liquid into the cup he always carried with him. Blowing on it, cooling it to taste, he touched Destiny's shoulder. "Wake up. Let's get some of this down you."

Her eyelids rose, and her gaze, sleep-laden, met his. She smiled. "I'm not asleep."

Caleb's Destiny

The next roll of thunder prevented any answer he would have made. Instead he held the cup to her lips. "Here, take a sip."

No protest escaped her lips.

When the cup was drained, he smiled. "Now you can sleep."

Her eyes shut almost of their own accord, and he settled back, glancing at her now and then, but his gaze kept returning to the diminishing storm outside. How many of these had he seen in his life? A hundred? More? He dreaded them because of the havoc they wreaked, but tonight he kind of felt they might be a blessing. Whatever mischief those men earlier had planned would have been put on hold because of tonight's storm. For that he was grateful.

Destiny moved, shifted her position, her head settling on his shoulder. Michael adjusted her blanket again then put his arm around her to shield her head from the rock behind them.

He missed Hunter. The lad might be young, but he had a head on his shoulders far wiser than many older men he'd known. Besides being knowledgeable and a quick learner, he took a load off Michael's shoulders with his responsibility and trustworthiness. He was the brother he'd never had.

Destiny stirred, and once again, Michael cast a quick glance at her. What on earth was a young lady like her doing clear out here? She had an agenda he was sure, but one she seemed disinclined to share with him. Could be she was dreaming about a romance with a western man. In that case, she'd better be mighty careful. Though most of the men living out here were decent, a few would be glad to take advantage of the innocence that pervaded the air around her.

The horizon had lost its midnight blackness. Now streaks of light were barely lighting up the distant sky. The few stars still in the sky twinkled as if bidding the fierce storm adieu till another time. Through the receding potato-wagon rolls of thunder, Michael heard the clear ringing of horses' hooves on rock.

A mutter, then a quiet voice. "There's Shyanne by that big rock. Where's your master, little girl?"

Michael scrambled out of their hiding place, stretched, then whistled. "That you, Hunter?"

"Me, and I've got Hank and a couple others with me. What happened?"

"Afraid our thieves doubled back to rile up a spot of trouble. Ran close to two hundred head of cattle through our valley of wheat."

Mutters all around, and Hank said, "If they've destroyed our bread for this winter, I'll personally see to it they pay."

"We've got our work cut out for us for the next few days. Destiny and I rounded up a little less than a hundred, but there's more out there scattered."

"Miss Destiny with you?"

"Brought her out with me yesterday morning to check on the orchard."

"Hernandez didn't confide that bit of news to me."

Michael caught Hunter's sharp glance at him.

"I reckon you've got her stowed somewheres."

"Sure do." Michael nodded at the overhang behind him. "Had to get her out of the rain. Made a mite of broth to ward off the chills. She's asleep."

Hunter's brow lifted, and his mutter reached Michael's ears. "You sure about that?"

"Plotting things behind my back, Mr. Michael?" Destiny's usually clear voice, now with a slight coarseness to it, dogged Hunter's comment. "Hunter, when did you get home?"

"Around midnight, ma'am, I mean, Miss Destiny. Had to do some powerful moving, but made it. Coach all ready to go tomorrow."

Was that a frown on her lovely face? What was she displeased with now?

"That quickly? I'm sure I don't care about the coach, except, of course, for poor Luke and Daly's sake. Are they taking off in the morning?"

"Yes, ma'am, that's their plan. Don't you fret none. Maria will see to it they wait till you get home."

The sun was brightening the sky, as the clouds scattered, lighting up Destiny's features. Sure enough, it was irritation rippling across her face. Temperamental woman. A body would think she'd be tickled to get back to the ranch. Well, whatever her problem, in another hour, Hunter could accompany her home. That would get this bunch from the stagecoach out of his hair, and he could get on with his life.

Why, then, did it feel like a knife twisting in his gut at the thought of never seeing Destiny McCulloch again?

~*~

Destiny kept her back as straight as she could until she and Hunter were out of sight. If Mr. Michael had poked a ramrod down her spine, she figured it couldn't have been any more so. Hopefully, he'd see it and realize he'd offended her.

Sent home. Like a child. Or a helpless female. Neither of which she was. Her help had been good enough before the cavalry arrived.

"Hunter?"

"Yes, ma'am?" Hunter half-turned in his saddle, but in the dawning light, his gaze continued to sweep over the landscape.

"Who is Mr. Michael?"

"Ma'am?" He tugged on his reins and waited for her to stop beside him.

"Where did he come from? Has he always lived here? Who were his parents?"

His puzzled brown eyes stared at her. His right hand lifted and scraped back a lock of longish hair straggling in his face. "That's a lot of questions to be answerin', Miss Destiny, and I reckon I don't know all the answers. Why are you wantin' to know about Mr. Michael?"

That question would take some getting around. She didn't know the answer to it any more than he. And his bewilderment added to her embarrassment. "He intrigues me. He's confident, well learned, and has manners. Yet he's aloof, as if he's afraid of anyone getting too close. Why is he like that?"

"If you mean, he's leery of trustin' folks, then you've got that right."

"Why?"

"Why? I reckon some folks are not worth trustin', ma'am."

Probably not. But none of this gave her an insight to the man. If she wasn't so determined to find her Caleb, she'd love to pursue her interest in Mr. Michael. Too bad there wasn't a way to do both.

But maybe there was.

Two hours later, Destiny stumbled up the back porch steps and staggered into the kitchen. Maria looked up. "What's wrong?"

"I don't feel so good, Maria." Her sneeze was real and loud.

Hands went to ample hips. Pursed lips allowed a half-snort to escape. "That Mr. Michael. What was he thinking, taking a young girl like you out? I've a good notion—"

Destiny couldn't hear her muttered threat, but it was vehement enough. Destiny was positive Mr. Michael was in for it when he returned to his home. How she wished she could witness the confrontation.

Maria guided her to her room, tucked her in bed, and assured her she'd be back with some warm broth in a few minutes.

Lapping up the attention—after all, she did feel badly—she allowed Maria to mother her. Her fondness for playacting in school was standing her in good stead now. She gave an extra hacking cough for good measure and endured Maria's pats on the head.

"Maria—" Cough. Sniffle.

"Yes, my poor child?" Maria's liquid Spanish eyes dripped with sympathy.

"Please, don't—don't let Daly hold up the coach on my account. I—I couldn't bear them enduring that for me." And she couldn't endure being sent away till she had the answers she wanted.

"Tut. Tut, child. Don't you worry about Mr. Daly. He is chomping at the bits to get away. I will send his sorry self down the road so quickly he won't know what hit him." One more smoothing of the cover. "You're indeed in no shape to be traveling. You'll stay here where Maria can take care of you, right?"

Destiny nodded and held back her grin until the woman hurried back to her domain in the kitchen. Then locking fingers together behind her head, she grinned. So far, so good. There was absolutely no reason she couldn't search for Caleb from here.

And pursue that interest in Mr. Michael.

A shred of unease stirred inside her but she tamped down the feeling. She didn't need reminding that she was digging in her heels again to get her way. Whether her plan succeeded or morphed into a hissing snake had yet to be seen.

Chapter Eleven

It was a long four days before Michael, Hank and two of his other men had rounded up all of the stock. In all, he'd only lost a couple, not counting the baby calf, which made him happy. Not so good, was the damage to his wheat. Almost a third had been ruined beyond repair. His men had done what they could, but little was going to be salvaged from that third.

He'd sent Hank to talk to the Indians. They'd always been quick to help when needed, so hopefully they'd keep watch and guard the stock and his fields. For their cooperation and help, he made sure they had the food they needed for the winter time.

They were a peaceful lot, and he figured well worth sharing with them, both his land and usually well-stocked food supplies, for their help when he needed it.

So though he wasn't entirely happy over the hours wasted and the loss of wheat in his fields, it could have been worse. That was something.

Michael walked wearily into the house. He was tired and looking forward to a few days of quiet. He wondered, briefly, if Destiny had moved on to another town, gone back east or still lingered in Roaring Springs, for whatever her purpose was. And he wasn't entirely sure how he felt about her being gone. She'd sure been an entertaining young woman. But, all in all, it was better this way. He wasn't about to get tangled up in another affair.

He walked into the kitchen and pulled out a chair. "Think I could get some hot water for a bath, Maria? Feels like I haven't had one for months instead of days."

"Mr. Michael. You're home. And yes, if you'll give us thirty minutes or so, I'll have Hernandez heat the water and get the tub ready for you. Do you need something to eat right now?"

He shook his head. "I'll wait, Maria. The bath is all I

need for now."

"Why don't you go rest a bit in your room? Hernandez will call you when it's ready."

"I think I'll do that." He stood and walked to the door. "The passengers get off all right?"

"Sure. Except—"

"Except what?" Michael swung back toward her, and knew he'd spoken too harshly by her quick glance at him.

"Why, Miss Destiny. When Hunter brought her back, she was already sick. By the next day, she was congested and feverish."

"So she's still here." He wanted to sit down again.

"Of course, she's still here. Did you want me to send her away sick?"

"You know that's not what I mean."

Maria sniffed. "It sounded like it."

"But she's better now?"

"Why wouldn't she be with Maria caring for her?" Maria's dark eyes flashed a bit of irritation at him. "She's a strong, usually healthy girl. She's pulling through. Wanted up yesterday, but I insisted she stay in bed."

"I see." And he did see. Very well. Destiny McCulloch was still here at his ranch.

~*~

Destiny woke, and though her body felt as if she'd been scrubbed on a washboard, the headache was gone, and she felt she could breathe again. Her head was clear.

Clear enough to wonder what Mr. Michael's reaction had been when he'd found out she was still here at the ranch.

No sounds floated through her open window. Which meant the hands were away from the ranch. Maybe they hadn't come home yet?

From somewhere below a door slammed shut and loud murmurs intruded on the silence that had been the mainstay for the last few days.

Destiny sat up and listened.

Footsteps.

She swung her legs over the edge of the bed.

Heavy steps started down the hallway, approaching her room, and Destiny panicked. It wasn't Maria. She was like a ghost treading the hallway.

Flying to the door, she twisted the key in the lock just as someone knocked three times. "Miss Destiny?"

Mr. Michael.

Destiny leaned against the door, her knees weak, and dragged in a breath.

"Y—es?" He'd hear the panic in her voice. She swallowed. "Who is it?"

"Mr. Michael. I need to talk with you."

"I'm not dressed. Please go away."

Silence.

"Maria says you're doing fine. Get dressed, and I'll be back in five minutes."

"My head feels woozy. I can't dress right now. I'll have to stay in bed another day or so."

He chuckled. "You're right on the other side of the door, Destiny. Five minutes, or I'll break down the door."

He was serious. She should crawl back into bed and defy him to pull her out. A little powder to her nose and a vigorous pinching of her cheeks should convince him she was still too sick to put up with him. Yet.

Destiny flew to the closet and pulled out a shirtwaist. Ran to the mirror to run a brush through her hair. And, reluctantly, unlocked the door.

Four and a half minutes later, Mr. Michael knocked again.

"Since you're coming in no matter what I say, come on."

The door opened. He walked in. Opened his mouth. Shut it. Then, "How are you feeling?"

"Fine. Thank you." Destiny spoke before she thought and wished she'd bitten her tongue. Now he'd know she was well.

"Good." He nodded. "If you can be packed in an hour, I'll have Jackson drive you into town." He turned away.

What? He was so anxious to get rid of her, he'd throw her out right off her sick bed? Destiny struggled to rearrange her previous nice opinion of him.

"I'm still weak. I don't think I can make it to town without a relapse."

His hand touched the doorknob, twisted, before he acknowledged her complaint. "I thought you'd be anxious to get on with your journey."

"Of course, I am. But I'm just too weak to make the trip today." Or tomorrow.

Destiny leaned against the back of the chair and fanned herself. When nothing came from him, she peeked through her lashes. He stood frowning, his fingers drumming silently on the door.

"What's going on in here, Mr. Michael?"

Maria stood like an angry mother hen facing a thieving raccoon after one of her chicks.

Mr. Michael's mouth opened, but Destiny cut him off. "Mr. Michael thinks I should pack and be ready to leave in a few minutes."

Maria stalked into the room and placed a hand on her forehead.

"I didn't say that." Mr. Michael looked as guilty as a schoolboy caught snitching another child's lunch.

Was that red creeping up his neck? Destiny choked back a chortle.

"I tried to tell him I was too weak to make the trip, but he's insisting I go."

Maria's flashing eyes didn't bode well for anything Mr. Michael had to say. She flounced toward him, her back to Destiny, her hands splayed on her ample hips. For the next two minutes she scolded and fussed. Shoving a finger under his nose, she reiterated every reason—and more than Destiny had thought of—why he was the cruelest man in the world to suggest such a thing.

Mr. Michael's eyes strayed to Destiny, and she couldn't resist.

With a grin, she winked.

~*~

Bested by a pintsize human ball of fury. Michael grinned to himself as he left the house. If he didn't love the woman so much, he'd send Maria packing. He broke off a short piece of straw and stuck it in his mouth, and then let out a snort of laughter at the memory of Destiny winking at him behind Maria's back.

The little scoundrel had enjoyed baiting him. She was as healthy as a—

Well, maybe he had pushed her. She had looked a little peaked around the eyes, although they hadn't had any trouble twinkling mischief at him.

Things were quiet. There'd been no sign of the men—most likely the same two, along with another scoundrel they'd scrounged up, that his men had escorted off his land—who had destroyed a third of his wheat. He felt better after a thirty minute rest and a hot bath. But neither a rest nor a bath took away his worry over the disappearance of the men.

They'd given up awfully easy. His men thought it had been the two stagecoach passengers he'd had Hank and Jackson escort off his property. Why had they targeted him? Payback, of course. Unless they'd been ordered to do so by his enemy. What other answer but the age-old problem he'd inherited from his father's time?

"Mr. Michael?"

He cocked his head. Maria stood behind him, the picture of penitence, hands folded meekly in front of her stomach, eyes downcast.

He wanted to laugh. She was about as penitent as a wily fox. What was she up to now?

"Yes, Maria?"

"I've been thinking—"

Here it came.

"Since we have a young lady visiting—"

Not by his choice. "Yes. Destiny will be leaving soon, whether you—er—we like it or not."

She frowned at him. "Don't interrupt."

"Go ahead."

"I'm thinking it's been a long time since we had a social affair here."

Worse than he thought. "We've never had a social affair here."

Her frown deepened. "Then it's about time we start. What will the neighbors think?"

"I don't much care what they think, Maria. I've never cared before. Why should I begin now?"

She eyed him as if provoked beyond endurance. "We should begin now because we have a young guest here."

"Not through any of my doings." Shame slapped him in the face, but wasn't it true? He'd not wanted guests, but he'd been kind in giving the stagecoach passengers rooms when he could have left them stranded. He was under no obligation—

"You are saying you regret helping the helpless?" Reproach as thick as the molasses Maria used spilled from her mouth.

How could one small woman cause such havoc in his thoughts? "Of course, that's not what I'm saying—"

"Then you agree we should provide an evening of social entertainment to pick up our guest's spirits, hmm?"

What if he said no? She'd not quit her badgering until he gave in. He lifted his hands in surrender. "Do as you wish, Maria. But you have to take care of everything. I'm much too busy."

"Yes. I would not expect you to shirk your work for this. Leave it all to Maria." Her face beamed.

Michael's heart sank.

~*~

It'd been a long week recovering. Maria had watched over her like a baby, but on the whole, Destiny was glad she had. She hadn't felt that bad since, well, since she was thirteen when she'd had a serious cold that laid her up for a month. Maria, fortunately, had plied her with plenty of wild herb hot drinks, filled with her secret ingredients. Whatever had been in those drinks, they had done the trick.

Maria had allowed her get up after Mr. Michael's return but wouldn't hear of her doing anything strenuous, and that included making this trip into town. So...she had to admit, Maria had been right. Those extra four days of taking it easy, had given her, her strength back. And Maria's permission to make the trip into town today.

Now, Destiny stepped down from the ranch wagon, glad to be along with Hank as he picked up supplies for the ranch. "Thank you, Hank."

Hank touched his hat. "Hope the trip wasn't too rough for you, ma'am."

"You handled that team like they were your babies. I enjoyed every minute of the trip. It was so good to get out." She smiled but turned her attention to the store with its large sign proclaiming it to be Jake's Emporium.

"Hank, I'm going to do some shopping. You go and meet me back here in an hour."

"Ma'am? You shore?"

"I am." She ignored his look of skepticism and let out a sigh of relief. At last. After the confrontation with Mr. Michael last week, she'd decided to do what she should have done after first arriving here. So when she told Maria she needed to make a trip to town, she'd told the truth. She'd promised Richard a telegram as soon as she arrived, and already it was many days later than she'd anticipated. Plus she had several small, personal items to buy, and material for a new dress would be a treat. And, most importantly, she wanted to ask about her Caleb. Surely someone would remember the boy.

"Ma'am, Mr. Michael said—"

"Hank, I don't much care what Mr. Michael ordered you to do. He's your boss, not mine. I'll be fine. Please excuse me. I have a telegram to send."

Squaring her shoulders, she turned her back and marched across the street to the telegraph office. She was loathe to do it because, well, she didn't know what to say to Richard. *I still love you?* She couldn't say that. She had no idea how she felt now. *How are you? Keeping busy?* How mundane. *Please come to see me?* Definitely not. He'd hate it here.

She shrugged. Surely she'd think of something.

When at last the telegraph was sent, she walked straight to the emporium and opened the door.

The smells hit her. Molasses and cinnamon. Fresh corn. The pungent smell of axel grease. Lavender soap. And so faint she could barely detect it—probably coming from the owner's quarters in the back of the building: fried potatoes, onions and soup beans. Her stomach growled. She should have eaten breakfast, but she'd been way too excited.

Behind the counter stood a tall, rail-thin—making him look as if a good, strong wind would have him bending like a flag—bald man, glasses perched on the end of his nose. He turned as the bell jangled and grinned in greeting. "Morning, Miss. New in town, aren't you?"

"Yes. I am."

"It's surely good to see a pretty face in town."

"Thank you, Mr.—"

"Call me Jake. Jake Blackston. Owner of the best emporium here in town." His eyes twinkled at her. "The only one too. Still the best though."

"Destiny McCulloch."

He gave her a sharp glance. "McCulloch. That's a good Irish name. Good to meet you. What can I do for you this morning?"

"I'd like to look at your fabric. You wouldn't happen to have some nicer material, would you? Something that would do for a fancy gathering?"

He beamed at her as if she'd given him a long sought-after present and headed toward the back of the store. "Just got in a batch last week. I think you'll not find anything nicer even in the best shops back east, Miss."

He ran a finger past several bolts of material, then stopped at one and pulled the roll partially out from the rest.

Destiny fingered the lovely rose-colored, brocaded fabric. "It's lovely. You're right. I couldn't have gotten any better back in Boston. I'd like nine yards please."

Almost clapping his hands in delight, Jake hurried to carry the bolt to a table where a measuring rod and scissors lay. Unrolling it, he measured the yards, and picked up scissors. "What's a young thing like you doing out here? You have family?"

"No-o-o." At least none she knew of. "I'm looking for a man."

The scissors paused in scoring a straight line through the material. A faded concerned look studied her face. "Ma'am. You come out here looking for a man? Surely back east there's more men suitable for a lady like you."

Destiny laughed. He was such a sweetie. "No. No. Not for me. I mean, I'm looking for me, but he's not *for* me." That made a lot of sense. He'd think she was crazy. An eastern crazy woman. "I'm sorry. What I mean is, I'm looking for a man because of business."

"Well, that makes plum more sense." He scratched his nose. "Business? You ain't looking to hire a gunman, are you?"

Wonderful. If she wasn't careful, the whole town would be gossiping about her. She wasn't about to explain her reason, but how to keep the curiosity at bay?

"Oh, no, nothing like that. It's personal business."

"I see."

Which meant he didn't at all. Her answer would likely increase the town nosiness.

The owner folded and refolded the material into a neat small bundle. "I'll tell you what. The man you need to talk to is Hubert Bottoms. He's our banker here in town, and the way I hear it, he's real good in business."

"Do you really think he could help me?"

"I don't see why not. If anyone knows about business in this area, it'd be him. Cause of him being a banker, I figure he has to be fairly smart."

"Where's his office?"

"Down the street, couple buildings on the left. You can't miss it. Now can I get anything else for you?"

Destiny pulled a small scrap of paper with her list of wanted items and handed it over. "If you'd be so kind as to get these ready for me, I'll stop back in shortly and pick them up."

He nodded. "I'll do that. Take your time now."

She headed to the door and swung it open, the bell jangling again.

"Miss?"

Destiny turned to face the man.

"Hubert Bottoms is smart. Some think too smart. You be careful now."

She smiled, lifted a hand, and stepped outside. It was a beautiful day. Wagons and carriages stirred up mini dust devils in the dirt road. Horses carrying their riders tossed bits of dirt behind them as they trotted toward their destinations. Feet shuffled. Boots clacked on the boardwalks. Murmurs from neighbors greeting neighbors hovered in the air.

The banker's office was easy to find. The sign with its large, curvy prestigious letters was easily the best looking sign in town and guaranteed to fill the viewer and prospective customer with awe and a bit of nervousness.

She wasn't the least bit intimidated. Not after visiting all her friends' homes on vacations with their hoity-toity parents and servants who were just as bad. She'd managed fine and even come back to school with invitations for more visits. Parents hoping she would be the good influence an unruly daughter needed.

The name was interesting at least. Hubert C. Bottoms, President.

The C leaped out, begging for her attention. Could his middle name be Caleb? Her Caleb?

All the more reason to talk with this man. Yet the last name stirred up nothing in her memory. Surely with such a name it would ring a bell in her memory. Destiny gave herself another minute to recollect something— anything. But nothing. Still, she could hope.

There was no jangling bell at this door, and a thread of disappointment ran through her. She loved those noisy things letting everyone know someone else had entered a business.

The girl seated at the desk looked up when Destiny entered.

"May I help you?"

"I hope so. I'd like to speak with Mr. Bottoms please."

The girl's brow wrinkled. "Oh, I'm sorry. He can't be disturbed this afternoon. He's much too busy."

She doubted that. A small town like this couldn't give the man that much business, could it? She was more than willing to take matters into her own hands, and getting past this inexperienced girl was nothing. Hadn't she handled similar situations with her school mistresses?

"Don't let me keep you from your work then." Destiny swept around the tiny desk, turned the knob and stopped as the door swung open.

Behind the massive desk sat a man, and not the elderly gentleman she'd imagined in her mind. But not the man who'd lived in her memory for so many years either. Which meant nothing. How could she remember someone she'd only known as a child and so long ago?

He spoke without looking up. "I told you I didn't want to be disturbed."

"I'd like a moment to speak with you, please." Destiny lifted her voice to overcome the girl's fumbling apology coming from right behind her.

He stopped his scribbling and glanced up. His face changed from one of irritation to surprise. He was on his feet instantly and motioned to the frantic girl. "I'll take care of it, Willa. Shut the door please." He pulled a striped chair up close to the desk. "Please have a seat."

"Thank you."

"What may I help you with, Miss—?"

"McCulloch. Destiny McCulloch."

"What's a young lady like you doing out here?"

"That's what I'd like to talk with you about."

"Of course, if I can be of help."

"I won't take up much of your time. I'm looking for a man."

His eyes brightened. He was laughing.

Ignoring him would be best. "I have a business matter to discuss with this man, but unfortunately I don't know his last name. He goes by Caleb."

"You know him? Heard of him?"

No reason to explain how she knew him. And she wouldn't. Not until she knew Bottoms enough to know he wouldn't spread her information around town. He might be a banker, but even letting tidbits of information slip could start the gossip.

"Jake Blackston said you know quite a few people in this area and could possibly help me find him."

"I might just be able to do that."

"Would you mind telling me what your middle initial stands for?" She dimpled at him. "Wouldn't be Caleb, would it?"

His lips tipped up. "Is that the man you're looking for? Then, yes, my name is Caleb, but unfortunately, I do have several papers I need to finish before an important meeting this afternoon. I have no more time to talk."

Possibly her Caleb. Why wasn't she more excited? She leaned forward. "When could I see you?"

He glanced down at a notebook on his desk. "Would you like to meet for supper, Miss McCulloch? We do have a nice restaurant—the Blue Peacock—in town. Perhaps seven-thirty?"

She'd have to deal with sending Hank home and the chance Mr. Michael would wash his hands of her if it angered him. Then she'd have to find lodging and a way back home in the morning. There was no way she could ask Hank to stay the night and wait on her. She'd have to hope for the best. She lifted her gaze back to the man studying her. "I'd love to."

"Fine. Where shall I pick you up?"

"I'll meet you at the restaurant this evening."

He showed her out, walking her to the exterior door. As she stepped outside, she pulled on her gloves and stared down the street where Hank lounged against the wagon.

Oh, dear. She did hate to upset the sweet man. Now to find the right words to make him think it was his idea for her to spend the night.

~*~

Hubert Bottoms stood at his window and watched Destiny McCulloch hurry down the street until she was out of sight. Attractive, she was. Smart? That was to be seen yet. But a perfect gentlewoman. Not like most of the women in this town. Just what he wanted as a wife.

And who was she? Why was she searching for a Caleb? Well, if he could snag her as a wife, then he'd be the Caleb she wanted—at least until he married her. No problem from him on that.

He stared down at the papers on his desk. Of course, he had to take care of his main focus. His real purpose on settling down here in Roaring Springs. It'd make him even richer and take care of his Achilles heel. Once that was finished, then he could focus on wooing Miss McCulloch, and when had the dames in his life ever refused his attentions?

~*~

That evening, after spending most of the afternoon wandering around town, asking only a few questions about a boy named Caleb and securing a room at the hotel, Destiny paused before The Blue Peacock, impressed at its luxurious front in spite of herself. She smoothed down the front of her dress, glad she'd brought an extra one to town. Had an unconscious idea she'd need it planted itself in her brain? Whatever, she'd have no trouble fitting in, and truth be told, would probably be better dressed than most.

She smiled and scolded herself at her vanity. Mama had always been prone to quote old wise fables at her, and even though she was still a child, she'd never forgotten a couple of them. Maybe because of how she'd spoken them to her. Or maybe it'd just been because of the occasion. Whichever, this one had stuck in her head like a burr. *Beauty is in the eye of the beholder. Don't be vain.*

Destiny let a chuckle slip from between her lips. She'd seen Mama primp a time or two. She couldn't help her looks any more than Mama could, and to pretend to be naive about them was downright stupid. She'd used them as a weapon several times. When other people assumed she was just a pretty blond woman with no valuable thoughts in her head, their assumption had gleaned her a few important tidbits of information.

Would it work on Mr. Bottoms? Yet to be seen.

Destiny entered the restaurant and paused to take in her surroundings. The maître de approached.

"Has Mr. Bottoms arrived?"

Before the head waiter could answer, the man himself walked into the room.

"Miss McCulloch." He turned to the maître de and asked in a low voice. "Our table is ready?"

"Of course, Mr. Bottoms. Please follow me."

Once seated, Mr. Bottoms sat forward and smiled. "Have you had a productive day?"

"That depends on what a person is expecting, don't you think?"

"I do." He picked up a single sheet, handwritten menu, then set it back down. "I'll have to say, I've looked forward to tonight."

"Does that mean you accomplished little in your business pursuits after I left?"

He laughed. "No. I managed to concentrate enough to get the signatures I wanted on a couple of contracts."

"Well done, then."

Bottoms said nothing, but Destiny could tell he was pleased at her praise.

"I haven't seen you around town before today. Did you arrive lately?"

"Oh, no, I've been here only a little over a week."

"That's odd. Why haven't I seen a woman as attractive as you around?"

Destiny laughed. "Because I haven't been in town. I

came on a stagecoach, and it was damaged and robbed before I could reach Roaring Springs. A man—Mr. Michael showed up and invited all the stagecoach people to his ranch until the stagecoach could be repaired."

"An opportunist, I see."

"Me? Of course not, Mr. Bottoms."

"It's Hubert or Bert to you, please, Miss McCulloch. And no, I wasn't calling *you* an opportunist."

"Then who—oh, Mr. Michael?"

"I'm afraid so. He's—never mind, let's not talk about him." He settled back in his chair and frowned. "But I thought the stagecoach arrived days ago? In fact, there have been several that have come through."

"No doubt, but I caught a bad cold, and Maria—the cook—insisted on me staying until I felt better. It's only been a few days since I felt well enough to get out."

"I see. Well, now that you are in town, we should be able to see quite a lot of each other. That sounds quite pleasant, doesn't it?"

How to answer that one? Fortunately, the waiter came up right then. They ordered and Destiny asked, "Tell me about yourself. Are you an only child?"

"I am. My mother died when I was young, and my father about five years or so ago. In fact, that's why I came back to this area. Had some important business to take care of."

Destiny leaned forward. So far so good. "I see. So all your business was taken care of then?"

He laughed. "Hardly. Once I arrived here, I realized there were some—what should I call it?—opportunities that would be profitable for me to seize upon. That and hiring the people I needed to help me proceed has taken all my time. Now that it seems those are on the ground and running, I can concentrate on the one thing I came west for."

"I see. Well, I won't be too curious and ask what all this is about, especially since I came west for a similar reason." She gave him a modest smile.

"Searching for this Caleb? Are you thinking I'm your Caleb?" Head tilted, he studied her face.

Heat rose in her cheeks. "I won't know that until I know more about you."

"What do you know about this man?"

What to say to keep his suspicions abated? "He's a kind man, I believe. Active. An excellent shot." At least he'd been when a boy, if bringing home the supper meat was any indication.

"Tell me, why are you so anxious to find him?" He sat back to allow the waiter to set down their drinks.

Destiny waited until the server left.

Who would have thought she'd have to evade answers about her unusual search? Wasn't it fair though? If she entered a town and asked a myriad of questions, why shouldn't someone else? Fair was fair.

"I knew Caleb when we were children but haven't seen him for years. I hoped to find him and renew our friendship." That was only part of it, but a good part.

"You realize he might be anyone? An outlaw or respected citizen? He may have moved away. Or he could be me."

Her attention rested on his last statement. Was he playing with her? Keeping her in suspense? "Do you remember me?"

"You and—this person—would have been very young, isn't that right?"

She remembered. Why wouldn't he remember a homeless child he'd found? Her hopes sank.

"The memory of a small girl seems to stir a recollection." He pursed lips and seemed to be straining for a clearer thought. "Life has a way of blurring the past, you know."

Not for her. Never for her. Mama and Papa's faces. The journey west. The five freckles across a boyish face still as sharp in her mind as the last day she'd first seen it. She could never forget her past.

She wouldn't let it go; let it slip away.

"I want to be that Caleb, you know." He took a bite of his steak, but his gaze remained on her face. "Regardless of what our past was, we're here now. I've worked hard to become what I am. You interest me. There aren't many women who can meet the expectations of the wife a man in my position needs."

A proposal? At their second meeting? Did the man think she'd come all the way west to get a husband? Not when a perfectly good gentleman waited for her back east.

"You loved animals?"

"I still adore them." She laughed. How many had she smuggled into her dorm rescuing them from the rains and cold? Fun until inevitably the dorm mistress had found her out and ousted the poor critters. "Why do you ask?"

"I'm trying to put something together here. You seem like someone who would care about the less fortunate."

"This tells me nothing though." Frustration ran like a river through her veins. How could he not remember more? "Can't you give me some hint of the past? I can't understand why you can't—or won't—discuss it. How can you forget your past like that? Your childhood? It's not that easy."

"It is when you've tried to put it out of your mind. When you do everything you can to forget."

His forceful words did more to convince her of his truth than anything else he could have done.

He swallowed. "Why don't we forget this now and enjoy the evening? We'll concentrate on your search later. When we've had time to think about what you're really wanting."

Not what she wanted, but he was done talking to her. Destiny picked up her fork and took a small bite of her steak, but her gaze remained on the passive face of Hubert C. Bottoms, prominent and important president of the bank of Roaring Springs.

Her Caleb? That remained to be seen.

Chapter Twelve

"**S**he what?" Of all the crazy notions, this was the worst Michael had ever heard.

Hank had returned from town, late that evening with the supplies the ranch needed, but no Destiny.

"I tried to talk her out of it, Boss." Hank shifted from one foot to another. "It was like talking to one of them cows out there in yer pastures. She was all that respectful, Boss, but right determined she was. Wouldn't listen to a thing I said 'bout the dangers for a woman."

Michael could just about imagine the scene. Hank, worry in his eyes, practically begging Destiny to do the right thing and come back with him, and Destiny, young and eager and...and...well, willful was the only correct description he could call it. Ignorant of the possible trouble waiting to happen to a lady of her caliber. Ignorant of those who liked taking advantage. Ignorant of the scheming minds in the world.

Thinking of the men who'd done their best to ruin his dad, Michael's temper rose. Fortunately, Pa had been smart in worldly ways even though he'd had little schooling and was way too trusting.

Michael had avoided Roaring Springs on purpose. Any money he'd saved had been stored in a bank at Mesquite Valley. Twice as far away, but chosen because of the distance.

Of course, what Destiny McCulloch did was nothing to him. But wasn't she under his care given she was staying at his ranch? She'd chosen to stay in town, so it was on her if it placed him under responsibility for her well-being. Wasn't it?

He leaned against the sturdy post and groaned inside himself. "We'll have to go after her."

"We, Boss?"

"Me." More time away when Hunter and the rest were doing double duty. They didn't need his absence. "I'll leave before dawn in the morning, Hank, if you'll have one of the men get the wagon and horses ready."

"Shore thing, Boss."

Michael glanced up at Destiny's room. The window was dark, and he sourly studied it. He was not anticipating tomorrow.

~*~

She'd had no trouble getting a room at the hotel late yesterday. Though it was more rustic than what hotels back east were, it was comfortable enough. Destiny stretched and smiled, eyes closed, but mind whirling with anticipation for the day ahead. Mr. Bottoms hadn't given her information concerning any other Caleb but that didn't mean there was none. They'd talked so much about himself and his memory—or not, as was the occasion—they'd never gotten around to others.

Forty-five minutes later, Destiny headed to the hotel's small dining area. Reputed to serve an excellent breakfast, she was eager to not only sample it, but to look for other clues leading to her Caleb.

She paused at the entrance. At mid-morning, the place had emptied out. A lone cowboy sat at a table near the far wall, back to her.

A lone cowboy with golden hair.

Mr. Michael.

What was he doing here?

"Have a seat, Miss McCulloch." The man stood and turned to her.

Destiny stopped cold in her tracks. "How did you know..."

"Surprised to see me?" He cocked his head toward the wall behind him. On it was an ornate-framed mirror that gave him a perfect view of any who entered.

Destiny glanced at the mirror, irked that she'd not realized how he'd seen her then glanced back at him. He didn't look any too happy to see her.

His smile was anything but friendly. Smirky? Tolerant? Exasperated? Who ever heard of an exasperated smile? Not in her previous life back east. Not before she'd met Mr. Michael. Thinking back, she could point a finger to several different instances when she'd noticed that same smile on his face. Usually directed at herself. Hmm. What was it telling her?

He was angry. At her probably. What had she done now to disturb his peace of mind? No need to answer that question. She was pretty sure she could come up with the right response.

She moved to his table and did as he commanded. Sitting, she peeked at him. He didn't look pleased she'd obeyed. Probably wishing she'd refused, giving him more ammunition to be angry at her. He said nothing. Brooding, she figured.

"Why are you in town this morning, Mr. Michael?" She picked up a menu and studied it studiously.

"You don't know?"

Real wonder in his voice.

"Why should I?"

A long drawn out sigh. "Do you have any idea how you've put me—Hank out?"

"You? Is that what you were about to say?" Destiny's temper edged up a notch. She gave him no time to answer. "I'll have you know, I didn't expect Hank to wait on me or return for me. I'm perfectly capable of taking care of myself. I've done it my whole life. A few hours on my own makes me mentally stronger."

"Do you have any idea what kind of town this is?"

"A western town? Really, Mr. Michael, it's not like this is the first town I've been in."

"But is it the first western town?"

Destiny felt her face warming. Now he was getting way too close to her past.

She frowned. "If you remember, I'm from the east. How could I have ever been in a western town?"

"That is the question, isn't it?" Mr. Michael leaned on his forearms, his gaze intent. "Why does no one still know anything about why you're in our wild west?"

"Why does anyone need to know?"

"What are you hiding?"

Destiny swallowed. "I'm not—"

His brow cocked upward. "Sure about that?"

She tried. She really did, but her gaze dropped. How could she let him do this to her? Let him? He was being obnoxiously nosy. And mean. And...

Lifting her gaze again, she caught the look in his eyes.

The interest—or was it need? Intense and seriously mocking. She could drown in his eyes. Could—she shook her head.

"What?"

His abrupt question tore her absorbed musing away. "Nothing. Why are you in town?"

"I came after you."

Really? That was both annoying and flattering. "I've already made arrangements to return tomorrow." At least in her head, and hoped all worked out accordingly.

His left brow cocked up. His smile tilted. "I see. When you've socialized enough?"

"I'm here for business—I mean, I do have material to buy and telegrams to send." Which, of course, was already done, but he didn't need to know that.

"Could have easily been accomplished while Hank was waiting."

Uh, oh. "You didn't let me finish."

"I beg your pardon. Go on."

He was laughing at her.

Her shoulders stiffened. "I'll have you know, I don't need a guardian looking over my shoulder. I've done for myself all my life."

"So you've said, and I'm sure you have."

Destiny jumped to her feet. "Good bye, Mr. Michael. I'll see you back at your ranch, thank you."

"Would you prefer staying in town where you'd have handier access to your tastes?"

Destiny halted her beginning march across the floor, her heart sinking. Stay in town and not explore Mr. Michael's ranch with him? Or see him whenever she could? Because she was sure as anything he'd not be riding in every day calling on her. She'd lose her chance to—what?

She turned slowly, fear driving the building anger. "Is that what you want? To get me out of your hair? You could go back to your mundane existence with no one and nothing to interrupt your way of life, couldn't you? You've let me know often enough what a bother the stagecoach guests have been." She placed one gloved hand on a hip and stared at him, daring him to pronounce her statements right.

"Of course—"

She rolled right over his attempt to either correct her or agree. She didn't care which one right now. "Of course? Of course? Have you forgotten Maria's wonderful plans for the dinner party? Doesn't it matter to you she works and cleans and waits on you hand and foot? Now she has this bee in her bonnet, you want to spoil her fun?"

"I thought it was you who put her up to it."

Wrong words to say. "You did, did you? You're quite wrong, you know. Maria gets lonely, or has that not occurred to you? She needs some entertainment; some time to plan for happy times. She wants to do this very much. And you. Big man of the ranch you are. You want to take it all away. Don't consider what could make her happy for a short time, do you?"

Destiny stomped to the door then whirled back to him. It did stop her for a minute to find he'd followed her across the floor. She reached out to balance herself from whirling right into his arms. Nice thought. Her lips twitched with anticipation until she caught his expression.

She opened her mouth to dress him down more when he laid a large forefinger across her lips.

"That's enough. You win. I get the idea and realize what a boor I've been to treat Maria and you so hideously. I won't mention I give her one weekend a month to get away, if she wants. Or the generous pay I bestow on her for all the hard cleaning and working and waiting on me she does every day." He grinned down at her. "You're like one of those little terrier dogs I've seen back—"

Back? East? He'd been back east and pretended to never leave this place? Her eyes narrowed. Hiding more things about his life. It was like prying open a safe to get information from him.

He fingered his hat. "I'm abjectly sorry to cause you—and Maria—any trouble. Would you consider having dinner this evening with me? Would that give you sufficient time to complete your business?"

He was being sarcastic. Sincere or not, she wasn't about to let his invitation go unaccepted. Still, she didn't need to make it easy for him.

"I'm going to be awfully busy today, and I have a person I'll perhaps need to see this evening, but I'll see what I can work out."

His eyes glinted with interest. "Who?"

"Mr. Bottoms will have information I'm after today sometime. I can't afford to ignore that."

"Mr. Bottoms?" His disgust couldn't be any more evident than if he'd spit it out. "You need to stay away from him."

"He's been polite and attentive to me. I couldn't ask for more of a gentleman."

"A wolf in disguise."

"What do you have against him?"

"Just suffice it to say, I do know."

"That means nothing to me." Not exactly true, but he didn't need to know.

"Now, listen, Miss McCulloch, I'm telling you for your own good." His big hand clamped onto her arm. "Not everyone that baas is a sheep. Not everyone in this town, regardless of what you think, is as good as they appear."

She shook off his hand. "I won't believe you unless you tell me how you know this."

His lips pressed thin. "Then just forget I asked about dinner tonight."

She stared at him, not the least bit affected.

"I can't help what you believe, but he's not to be trusted." He swung away but his words carried back to her. "Be careful, Miss McCulloch, you don't bite off more than you can handle. A person can get hurt that way."

His tone scared her more than his words. For one moment she was tempted to run after him and tell him she was ready to go back to the ranch, but Richard's face halted her bold step to do so. She had no business dreaming of Mr. Michael when she and Richard had an unspoken agreement to each other.

Why then did her heart appear to be sinking clear to her daintily clad feet?

~*~

Willful woman. Michael strode away, but his heart lingered with the girl he'd left, and that thought hardened his determination to wash his hands of her.

Oh, he'd make sure she was all right. Even let Maria continue on with her plans for the garden party. But after that he'd see she was either safely tucked away in a secure hotel room or on the next stage back east. He didn't need nor want the responsibility of a person too stubborn for their own good.

And he knew, didn't he? Bottoms might look and talk nice, but under all that sophistication lurked an evil demon. One with no motive but to get what he wanted at all costs.

Since he was in town, albeit a fruitless trip, he might as well stop in to see Jake for awhile. Then he'd head back to his world. Miss McCulloch could find her own way back, if that was what she wanted. And if not?

He wouldn't think about that. That was a danger area his heart wasn't allowed to venture into.

~*~

Destiny kept busy all day. Devising another well-worded telegram for Richard took an hour.

Capturing his attention back in Boston had been a feather in her fashionable hat. Her friends had rejoiced with her and some not-so-happy faces had cast envious glances her way. Coming west dimmed the satisfactory glow from her star though. Compared to many of the men here—she refused to acknowledge the image of Mr. Michael blatantly demanding attention—Richard's manners, his talk, his interests seemed less appealing.

And there was something attractive and dangerously exciting about Mr. Bottoms—Hubert, or Bert, as he'd insisted she call him. Not like Mr. Michael who made her want to do the opposite of his demands, yet tugged at her heartstrings. What Mr. Michael said earlier this morning made sense, and though she wouldn't let him know she agreed, she realized she was flirting with danger when she encouraged Hubert's attention.

Compared to the men here, Richard was—well, stuffy. Destiny touched a cheek as the heat rose to them. The darling and most sought-after bachelor in Boston had sunk to the level of being described as stuffy. Boring. A little overbearing with his presumptuous way. She'd seen the coy looks girls sent him. The batting eyelids and smirking smiles. Whispers about his desirable traits as a husband floated around town from eager mothers and covetous fathers ambitious for their daughters.

She'd scorned all such girlish actions and refused his invitations twice before succumbing to his attentions. All the talk around Boston insisted there was a proposal in the making. Proud and thrilled to have captured such a well-respected gentleman, she'd flaunted her position.

Now...

Now she wasn't sure. She didn't in any way downgrade his respectability or his desirability. Or that he'd make some girl a very nice catch.

But her? Did she even want to live the rest of her life in Boston?

When had life in Roaring Springs become more vivid, more tantalizing? When had life at Mr. Michael's ranch become necessary for her happiness?

Destiny bit back a smile. She'd see him tonight. She hoped. If he hadn't gotten fed up with her and high-tailed it home.

Time for lunch with Hubert at the Blue Peacock. Destiny sashayed down the board walk. It never hurt to have too many friends. Whether she ever took his interest seriously or not, she'd squeeze every bit of "Caleb" information from him she could. After that, who knew?

~*~

"I have something for you." Hubert stood as she approached the table where he always sat at the Blue Peacock. His favorite, and one the proprietor kept for Hubert's personal use. Or so he'd claimed last night.

Destiny dimpled at the man. "That sounds nice."

"I hope you think it is nice for you."

Destiny sat as the maître de helped her into her chair. "Please show me."

"You don't want to wait until after we eat?"

He was teasing her, and she smiled. She definitely didn't want to wait. "Of course not."

He slid a paper across to her but kept a hand on it. "I thought this might be something you're looking for."

"I won't know, will I, until I read it?"

He removed his hand.

Her eyes skimmed the paper, then re-skimmed it. A

birth certificate proving he'd been born on a small ranch close by Roaring Springs. Hubert Caleb Bottoms, born to Jedadiah and Mabel Bottoms in 1847.

Her Caleb was thirty-two? That would mean—she did a quick calculation—he'd been sixteen when he'd found her.

No, that couldn't be right. She remembered him much younger. Older than her for sure, but not an almost-adult, at least as the west counted young men. Of course, she'd never asked. Wouldn't have. Not after the tragedy she'd witnessed. He wouldn't have forgotten either. How could he?

The pulse in her neck throbbed. She'd never forget the nightmare she'd created by her determination to have her way.

"I also remember how much you love dogs. Your choice of pets since a child, am I correct?"

He was correct, yet why couldn't he remember the one detail to squash all doubts in her mind? Yes, she loved dogs. Had two especially loved ones. But the kitten. The white kitten. Her first pet and the only one her father would allow her to bring along on the journey west because it was small and wouldn't eat much food. The beloved little creature who'd been the cause of her tantrum when her parents were murdered.

Destiny swallowed back the grief rearing its ugly head inside her. She couldn't, wouldn't fall apart in front of this man who seemed to be a part of her history. A man she couldn't reconcile with her memory.

"May I keep this? It is a copy, right?"

He hesitated, but only briefly. Had she glanced away for even a moment, she'd not caught it. That flicker of— was it doubt? A question? Whatever it was, it was gone now, and a smile had replaced it.

"Go ahead. Keep it if it'll make you feel better. Are you satisfied?"

"Getting there."

But was she really?

"The town is beginning to plan our summer festival. It's a big thing around here, most everyone attends. And as the prominent business owner, I give the opening speech. I'd like to invite you. Before someone else decides to horn in."

"Sounds like fun. I'd love to come."

"Well, it's not for several months or so, but wanted to get the invitation in before someone else did."

"You succeeded."

"I suppose I have."

Not the affirmative answer he obviously was hoping for. "You are convinced you're the Caleb I'm looking for?"

"I could be him as much as anyone else around here. I've shown you my birth certificate. I've given you information about your childhood. What more could you want?"

Self-satisfied, was he? Destiny sat forward and stiffened her back. "Is there anyone who's lived here longer than you?"

"Of course." He frowned. "A few other families joined together to establish Roaring Springs, but it was only after we settled here that it began to grow."

"Interesting."

"Gold in the area has helped, although it's sporadic finds. Still there's always the hope that spurs people to look. That, along with some good cattle pasture grounds has increased the growth of our little town. Businesses have boomed."

Hubert was a dead end. So interested in impressing her, he wasn't really giving her the information she needed. It was time to expand her search.

Chapter Thirteen

The old livery stable's grayish brown walls gave it a rundown feeling. Destiny sauntered up to it early that afternoon and paused at the doorway to stare into the darkened inside. The dusty, straw-scent assaulted her nose but wasn't unpleasant. Horse sweat, oats and manure mingled together.

Destiny grimaced. Oats and manure?

A horse nickered. Destiny called out softly. "Anyone here?"

When no one answered, Destiny strolled down the aisle, talking to each horse as she passed. There weren't that many. Five and a couple of mules. She stopped at the stall where a horse stood covered in sweat. Poor thing. Didn't the owner even care enough to wipe the creature down?

She looked for a rag and found one against a back wall. Talking softly and moving slowly, she touched the horse. He turned his head and eyed her, his ears flattened.

"Good boy. You want me to give you a nice rub down?"

He snorted and bobbed his head.

"I thought you might enjoy it." She ran a rag-covered hand over his back. "Feels good, doesn't it?"

Humming, she set to work. Growing up in Boston hadn't exactly given her practice in caring for a horse, but how hard could it be?

"Whadda you think yer doing?"

Destiny jumped, dropping the rag. "You scared me to death. I didn't think anyone was around."

"You didn't, did you?" The man's eyes narrowed. "What you aiming to do? Steal that horse?"

Who did he think he was? It was bad enough to leave the poor thing all wet and heated, and now he had the nerve to accuse her of stealing? "Steal *him*? He's nothing but a broken-down flea bag."

Sorry, sweetheart, for the insult. I don't mean it. It wasn't the horse's fault this person didn't have any manners. She smoothed a hand across his back to assure him she really didn't mean it.

The man snorted, much like the horse had done earlier. "Fleabag? I'll have you know, this critter can out-buck, out-bite, and out-stomp anything else in this town. Yer taking yer life in yer own hands bein' in there with him."

The horse gave a stomp of its hoof, barely missing Destiny's dainty—but now dirt-encrusted—shoe.

She moved her foot quickly and gave the beast a quick searching glance. He hadn't seemed to be so terrible. Was he really waiting to kill her?

She looked back at the man.

His lips twitched.

"He's a baby." Trying to scare her, was he? She gave the broad flank of the horse a pat to prove her point.

"We'll see about that when he stomps you to death. Don't be blamin' me. You've been warned." The man harrumphed. "You still ain't said what yer doing here."

Why should she tell him anything? She didn't like his looks, didn't like his manners or his attitude, and she definitely didn't trust him. Still, if he was the owner of this rundown establishment, she'd never get any information out of him by snubbing him.

Charm it was then.

She flashed a brilliant smile at him. "I'm looking for the owner. You wouldn't be him, by any chance, would you?"

"Depends." He spat into the straw. "Whatcha wanna know fer?"

She leaned forward just a little, not enough to take in the sweaty stale smell surrounding him, but enough to give a hint of secrecy. "I need some information."

"Yeah?"

She nodded. "Can I trust you?"

It was his turn to nod, and she almost smirked. As if she would ever. She squashed the temptation to laugh in his face. Definitely not the right move.

"I need to know about a man called Caleb. Do you know of anyone around here by that name?"

"What's his last handle?"

"Handle?"

"Name."

"Oh. I don't know it. I knew him when he was a boy and lost track of him. I'm looking to renew our friendship if I can find him."

"Is that right?"

"It is."

The man rubbed his bearded chin. "Well, now. I jest might know who yer wantin'."

"You do?"

"Could be him."

"How do I find him?" Destiny stretched out a hand and grasped the man's arm.

He looked down at her grip. "Yer never gonna find it. Reckon I kin take you to him."

For the first time, fear rippled its way through her body. *Could* she trust him? Of course not, but the desire to find the boy in her memory outweighed the fear. She had to take the chance.

"When can you leave?"

The man slithered a look into the street, then back at Destiny. "Course, my expert guidance don't come cheap."

"You want me to pay you?" Who did he think he was?

"'Fraid so. I'm an awfully busy man."

"I can see that." Destiny studied him for a minute then dug in her bag and pulled out a coin. "Here."

He gave the coin a glance and nodded. "I kin go now if yer ready."

Destiny glanced down at her skirt, glad she'd worn a full one today, then swallowed down the fear screaming for attention. "I'm ready when you are."

It didn't help anything when they started down the street, each on their own horse, that he seemed to find something awfully amusing.

~*~

Michael sat on one of his horses he kept at Jake's place, staring at the distant mountain range. The reds and oranges, blues and greens of the landscape played his emotions like a guitar-strumming-cowboy's nimble fingers coaxed tear-jerking melodies from his instrument on a lonely night.

He missed his dad, that was true, but something deeper and stronger was teasing feelings from buried areas of his heart tonight. He felt the growl before he heard it coming from inside his body. The horse flicked his ears backward, and Michael leaned forward to pat his neck.

"Not growling at you, Pepper. Just angry at myself and the world tonight."

He knew why.

Wishing he would have gone ahead and shot the man who'd killed his father didn't do any good now. He would have too, except for his dad's pleading eyes.

Don't do it, son.

The feeble words. The love in his parent's voice had stopped him cold, and the man had fled the scene. If only he'd been ten minutes earlier to save his dad's life before the scoundrel had gotten the drop on his dad. But he hadn't been.

At least he knew his dad would have been proud of what his son had done with his inheritance. He hadn't squandered the gold, and he'd developed the land.

Michael shifted in his saddle. Too bad he couldn't get Destiny's accusing blue eyes from his mind. He wasn't worried about losing Maria's affection. Her motherly regard was as steadfast as the sun rising in the mornings. But he really did wish he wasn't quite so disturbed at losing the fiery young blonde's respect. She'd sashayed into his life only eight days ago, but it seemed she'd been here forever.

If he hadn't been so impatient to get Hunter home that first day, he might never have met the outspoken lass. But he had and now...

The flash of her fancy clothes when she hurried around corners, her laughter filling the halls of his home, her delicate manners and teasing eyes, the haughtiness in every move when she was displeased. He couldn't imagine her not a part of his ranch.

Nor did he want to.

Michael wheeled his horse and gently prodded the big paint in the sides to head back to town.

~*~

The back of the stableman riding his horse ten feet in front of her inspired no faith in her present adventure. But then, when did she ever tackle a problem with lethargy? Curiosity and interest kept everything in her world colorful and exciting. Though her school teachers had literally rolled their eyes at her pranks, her friends and schoolmates had voted her the best fun companion for the whole year.

She'd loved the award. Much better than the most improved or the best mannered. She already knew she wasn't a slouch in manners or dress, and she wasn't about to subject herself or those she liked best to boredom from continually fluttering her eyelids and enduring meaningless tea parties or giving in to demands for silly, insipid chatter about nothing important.

Still, a little interesting talk about now would help the mile-after-mile travel go faster.

"Mr...?"

No answer. No movement like he'd even heard her.

"Sir?" Destiny lifted her voice. If he didn't answer now, it wasn't because he hadn't heard her.

"Whatcha wantin'?"

"How much farther?"

"A piece."

At least she knew they wouldn't arrive in the next two minutes.

Destiny tapped her horse's sides. When she'd caught up with the man, she glanced over at him. The brim of his dirty hat was pulled down, covering the top third of his face. The beard covered his mouth, but his jaws moved incessantly, a small dribble of brown juice staining his beard.

Ugh. Destiny slapped a hand at her mouth and shot another glance at the man, but he didn't seem to notice. Good. She hadn't spoken aloud.

"How do you know this Caleb?"

A dirt encrusted hand lifted and swiped at where his mouth should have been hidden under the bush of face hair.

"Call him Leb."

"Leb?"

"Think I heard a time or two his front name was Caleb. Too long pro'bly. Shortened it."

"What does this Leb do?"

"He's a business man, he is." The man grinned at her. "Ma'am."

Relief washed through her like one of those gully washers she remembered seeing as a child.

Destiny brushed back a stray hair and unbuttoned the top button of her shirt. The afternoon sun had warmed the air. If they didn't reach this ranch before long, she was going to be stranded away from town. She didn't relish the thought.

"Do you know how much longer it will be? I have things to do back in town."

"'Taint far now. Just up that hill ahead."

True to his word, when they topped out on a plateau near the top of the hill, a small house huddled half hidden amongst a grove of pine trees. Destiny sat silent, studying the scene before her wishing there was more activity. A couple horses stood tethered to the rail. The porch was shadowed, but a man looked to be sitting on it. There was no other sign of movement. No cattle around. No children. No women.

"Where is everyone?"

The man said nothing. His gaze never wavered from her face, jaws chewing, as if he waited on her next move.

"Is that Caleb sitting on the porch?"

He started to shrug, one shoulder lifting.

Destiny cut him off. "I'm not playing games. I'm serious about finding my friend. If I find out you're fooling me..." She let her words drift off and stared into the man's squinty eyes. "...I'll make sure Hubert Bottoms knows about it."

Why was he averting his eyes?

Destiny drew her mouth tighter. Making fun of her, was he? "And I'm sure Mr. Michael will love to hear how you treated me."

As if a metamorphosis had taken place, the man straightened, his gaze still held hers, but now a definite sulk masked whatever other thoughts he'd had. "Now, ma'am, why would you want to go and do a fool thing like that? I ain't foolin' you any."

She urged her horse forward then tossed back her threat. "See that you don't."

The closer she got to the place, the shabbier it looked. The house had a patch-work look to it. Two windows were boarded up. The door hung lopsidedly. One of the porch steps sagged in the middle, broken.

If this Caleb was a business owner, he must not do business from this place. It looked exactly what it probably was: a hideout for a gang of robbers.

She was close enough to see the man on the porch shift. His tilted chair hit the floor, and a hand moved to the gun on his thigh.

Before she could call out, the man with her hollered. "Haloo the house. We're comin' in."

The man moved closer to the house, and Destiny reined her horse up beside him. He sat his saddle, but Destiny made a move to dismount. His hand shot out and gripped her arm.

She shook her arm, but he didn't let go.

"Stay."

The mumble was low. Destiny glanced at him and wondered if he'd really spoken. She had half a notion to ignore the command, but something about his stillness kept her in her seat.

"Why?"

"You want your head shot off?"

The feistiness that always seemed to raise its ugly head whenever she was crossed urged her to do as she thought best. But a quick glance at the stableman convinced her to do as told. He knew something she didn't.

An eternity later—or so it seemed—the man from the porch called out. "Come on then, if yer comin'."

The man beside her dismounted and Destiny followed his action. As impatient as she felt, she wanted to go ahead, but caution still tugged at her, so she waited as docilely as she could till he moved.

"Barney, whatcha doing way out thisaway? Boss send—"

The man on the porch, who had the longest pair of legs Destiny had ever seen, had finally spoken. Could she ask her question now and be gone from here? He sure didn't look like much of a business man. Destiny cut a look at the man who'd just guided her here. Too late, the thought crossed her mind that she not only couldn't trust this man, but she suspected he was a bad man. A very bad man. Another glance at the one on the porch assured her she couldn't trust either of them. Better get on with it.

"Do you—" She didn't have a chance to finish.

Barney, the stable man spoke up. "This lady wants to ask if you're the Caleb she's looking for."

Surely not. If this man was the Caleb she remembered and dreamed of finding someday—the boy who'd rescued her so long ago, then...

She knew doubt struggled to reveal itself on her face. "Or if you know someone who goes by that name."

The man on the porch shifted his glance back toward Barney.

What was that glance about? Were these two men playing her for a fool?

Not if she could help it.

"We're wasting my time. Let's go." Destiny reached for the saddle horn.

"Hold on. Whatcha bein' so touchy about?" Barney growled.

"Do you or do you not know a Caleb around here? Have you ever known a person named Caleb?" She didn't release her grip on the saddle horn.

"I'm figurin' on studyin' on it a bit." The man on the porch spat and wiped his hand across his thin lips.

Anger surged through her at the time wasted coming here. "No. Either you know or you don't." She gazed at him with the hardest look she could come up with.

"Missy..."

Barney started to speak, but she cut him off. "I'm going."

Swinging into the saddle, Destiny reined her horse around, prepared to gallop as far away from this place as possible.

"You can't take off by yourself. It's late. We can spend the night here and..."

Ignoring his flimsy objection, she slapped the horse

with the reins, and the mare responded as if she couldn't wait to leave.

The sun was getting lower by the minute. That meant Destiny needed to make tracks if she wanted to be back in town before darkness settled down. Leaning lower over the dappled gray horse, she whispered encouraging words in her ears. "Go, my beauty, go. I'll make sure you get an extra handful of grain when we get there."

Eventually Miss Gray, as she'd begun to call her, slowed, and Destiny figured she'd earned the right. She'd gotten away from those two nasty figures. It'd taken a good two, slow-moving hours to reach the shanty, but now Miss Gray seemed as eager to get home as Destiny was. Surely they could make it in the same amount of time. Maybe, just maybe she could beat the darkness.

It was an inspiring, breathtaking early evening. The sky seemed to stretch forever across the span of land. Clear. Clean, and, for right now, innocent of any evilness that resided in the heart of some men.

She'd heard no sounds of hoof beats behind her, so she supposed Barney had decided to stay with Long Legs. She sniffed. Fine by her. His presence had been nothing but uncomfortable.

Destiny breathed in the air, cooling now that the sun was touching the horizon. She hadn't realized how much she loved the outdoors until she'd returned here. And she'd taken off riding as if she'd never been years without extensive practice.

Patting her horse's neck, she looked up just in time to catch a glimpse of a fast-approaching person. She glanced around again, hoping some form of shelter was close at hand. Too late to avoid detection. Whoever the person was, he was headed straight toward her.

A nervous tremor ran up her spine, but it was gone in a second as she suddenly recognized the figure.

Mr. Michael. After her, she supposed. Why else would he be tearing up the land as if demons were chasing him?

He slowed as he galloped closer, circled her until he faced back the way he'd come.

She opened her mouth to greet him, when he spoke.

"Of all the crazy things, what do you think you're doing?"

Some greeting.

And she wasn't about to answer his question.

~*~

Now that was some way to greet a guest when she'd been out doing some worthwhile investigating, although, to be honest, it hadn't exactly turned out that way.

Still, he had no business talking to her as if she belonged to him.

The thought had no more than crossed her mind, when she felt the blood surge to her face. She was tired or else she'd never had such an insane idea. Only it wasn't an idea.

Then what was it?

She snapped the door closed on her inner self-brooding and gave Mr. Michael her loftiest glare.

"What are you talking about? I suppose I can take a ride out of town if I want to. How did you find me anyway?" She was pretty sure no one had noticed them leaving.

He didn't reply right away, only motioned with a hand for her to follow.

The independence in her demanded she whirl and head a different direction, but reason argued she was tired, ready for some supper and rest. Why let him get to her?

"I don't have to answer to you."

An exasperated look was all she got for all of ten seconds, then...

"Why did you need to come into town in the first place, taking my men away from—"

"One man."

"—his work."

"Excuse me. I understood he needed to come into town..."

"Yes, but not for a whole day. One errand to pick up supplies, then he was to return immediately."

Hmm. What was there to say to that? She knew very well she'd hoodwinked the poor guy with her shenanigan plans.

"So you have nothing to say for yourself?"

Was that laughter in his voice? Thought he'd gotten the best of her, did he?

"I have plenty, Mr. Michael. Plenty." With a light kick on her horse's side, she pulled ahead of him and kept that distance the rest of the way into town.

Trouble was, Mr. Michael put no effort into catching up with her.

Disinterest? Or Irritation?

~*~

Destiny's stiff back in front of him sent a smile to his lips. She was a stubborn one and skillful at getting her way. Good thing he'd recognized this early on. He wondered exactly what she thought she was doing? Was there something going on in that sharp mind of hers he had no idea of? If so, he couldn't begin to guess what.

He'd known from that first look at her back on the road when the stagecoach had broken down, that she was pure lady, a feisty one for sure, but still a lady. She seemed so familiar, as if he'd known her previously. And it wasn't as if he'd been around that many young women. But for the life of him, he couldn't place her. At least not right now.

Right now, his priority was getting her back to the ranch safely. If only he could send her back east where she belonged.

But the longer she stayed, the less he wanted to. And that was not a good thing.

Not in the least.

~*~

The sun was setting in a blaze of orange and pink by the time they reached town. She headed straight to the stable, but he pulled up beside her and reached for her horse's bridle.

"Hold up there. Let me take care of your horse. You go on to the hotel. It's much too late to strike out for the ranch tonight. You rest and get refreshed, and we'll meet at the Blue Peacock for dinner."

She flashed him an exasperated look, but it quickly melted to one of satisfaction.

"Fine. Shall we meet in an hour?"

"Let's make it in a couple hours. I have some business

to attend to, and it'll give you more time to primp."

"I don't primp."

Her haughty words had him chuckling. "I don't believe you. That curly hair—"

"My hair, Sir, is naturally curly."

"I'm glad we got that cleared up." He laughed.

"I'm sure you are."

He helped her down, and she turned to leave. "I'll see you then in two hours. Don't be late."

Don't be late, the woman says. Why did she make him laugh? Her unconscious defensiveness over everything, as if she had to always project the image of strength. But throwing that last observation at him—as if men were the ones who primped—made it plain she didn't.

He didn't really need to talk to Jake again, but he wanted to give Destiny time to rest and get ready for dinner. Besides, it wouldn't hurt for him to clean up a bit. After all, he was taking a girl out to eat.

He hurried toward the only business and person in this town he trusted.

Chapter Fourteen

Destiny lay back in the immense tub with her eyes closed. Heaven! It was good to get rid of all the dust from the ride to and from the shack—a trip that had been useless and unrewarding. She should have told Mr. Michael about it, but his attitude had been so condescending. As if she was a child. Or a dimwitted woman who had no creative thoughts in her head.

Ha. What did he know, stuck out on that ranch with few women around?

A ranch she was finding increasingly interesting.

Or maybe it was the...No. She would not go there. Not tonight.

Reaching for the bath towel, she dried herself and wrapped her favorite dressing gown around herself until she did her hair. She chuckled as she thought of Hank's reaction when he'd seen the size of the bag she was bringing. It really hadn't been that many clothes, but it was good she'd had the foresight to bring extra. She walked to the window and studied the town. Dusk had settled in, but the darkness was rapidly taking over.

Close to thirty minutes later, Destiny stepped out of her room, but didn't move. The voices in the room across the hall caught her attention, and she paused.

"I'm sure that's her."

"You haven't seen her in years. She has to have changed her looks."

"No, not that much. Those...eyes. They haven't changed. It's her."

"Keep an eye on her. She may be trouble."

Who were they talking about?

She hadn't any more time to wonder as the sound of footsteps on the other side of the door grew louder as they came closer.

Destiny scuttled back to her room, leaving her door open a crack and hoping to catch a glimpse of the two men from the room across the hall.

And got the shock of her life.

Hubert Bottoms stepped out of the room, dressed in his usual dark suit. To give him credit, there was a frown on his face, almost as if his mood bordered on anger. He glanced neither to the left or the right, only marched down the hallway toward the stairs.

That man—the man in the doorway—looked vaguely familiar, as if she'd seen him briefly sometime in her life. So briefly, she couldn't rememb...

Destiny's mind tumbled back, back, back...

The man with the patch over his eye came from behind the wagon that was overturned. He yelled out to the other two men with him and stared down at the ground, walking slowly until he reached the edge of the trail. Then his eyes—gaze—lifted, and he stared out into the brush.

Right straight at her.

She couldn't move. The little white kitten mewed softly, and she placed a hand over its mouth and wanted to whimper too. But she knew if she did, he'd find her. Find her and kill her like he'd killed Mama and Papa. Her gaze remained fixed on the man with the patch over one eye.

For a long, long time he stared, and then someone had hollered, and he walked away...

At the top of the stairs, Bottoms turned. "Keep your eye on her. She'll lead us to him."

As scary as that comment was, the bigger scare was when the man turned away to shut the door. His gaze rested on her cracked door for too long, and Destiny drew back, fear stabbing at her heart. Had he seen her?

Destiny gripped the door jamb, hands shaking, stomach churning. She wanted to close her eyes, but was afraid to. Afraid her mind would drag her back again to the trip out west with her parents, the horror she'd seen as the brutal men killed her parents, the man with a patch over one eye, who'd stared a forever-minute at her before swinging away on his horse.

There'd been more—much more, but her childish mind had blanked it all out, refusing to see what horrific deeds were being executed. Her terror had lasted for she knew not how long, until a young boy appeared suddenly and had bundled her up in a quilt left behind in the wreckage. Then scooping her up, he'd sat her in front of him on a massive horse and rode slowly to his home.

Destiny shook her head, leaned her forehead against the door for a second, breathing deeply. All of a sudden, she wanted to go nowhere. What if she closed the door and stayed in her room the rest of the evening? All night? What if she ignored Mr. Michael's invitation for supper?

She paced from side to side, reasoning with herself, thinking, thinking, thinking, and finally stopped her pacing in front of the tall window facing the street. She stared down at the few people who hurried, or strolled, depending on their purpose for the moment, and caught the tall figure of Mr. Michael crossing the street. He didn't look up, didn't see her, but she felt his impressive presence even through her closed window.

And that presence settled her nerves, settled the debate inside her. She straightened her shoulders, gave a nod to her image in the mirror on the wall then moved to her door. With a quick glance at the door opposite hers to make sure no one was watching, she locked her door and hurried to the staircase. She might have regained her equilibrium, but that didn't mean she wanted the man with a patch over one eye seeing her.

But now calmer, that conversation did set her curiosity on fire. Had they been talking about her? Why think that? It could have very well been someone else. Or not.

She had no more time to wonder about strange conversations. The man who stood with his back to the staircase—talking with a short, broad man—and who looked every bit as elegant as a high society person back in Boston, was Mr. Michael. But not the ranch owner Mr. Michael. This one was dressed in a suit that would rival any of her men friends back east.

She would not let him know it, but she was impressed.

"I'll be sure to let Virge know." The stranger's voice was low.

"Thanks, Associate."

The unknown man's gaze flicked to her then back to Mr. Michael. If it was a signal, Mr. Michael heeded. He turned, and if Destiny hadn't been staring right into his eyes, she'd never caught the fleeting flash of—well, what was it? Admiration? Shock?

Whatever, she liked it, although she did her best to squash the feeling. He was way too confident to allow him to know her pleasure in his approval.

"I see you managed to be on time."

"I'm always on time, Mr. Michael. I would think you'd know that by now." She flicked a glance at his companion. "And who is your friend?"

For a fraction of a second neither man moved or spoke, then the stranger held out a hand. "Mr. Michael, I didn't realize you had secrets you hadn't shared. And such a beautiful one."

Older than Mr. Michael, he was very short—almost her height, but a tidy and precise-looking man. Destiny held out a hand. "Since Mr. Michael's gone tongue-tied, I'll introduce myself. Destiny McCulloch."

The man nodded, a pleasant smile on his lips, but there was something in his eyes that alerted Destiny there was more to the man than she was seeing. It was a bit unsettling to have him estimating her personality, and that's what he was doing.

"It's mighty nice to meet you, ma'am."

"Destiny, please."

"Destiny." He turned again to Mr. Michael. "I'll let you know if I find out anything. You both take care now."

The man shook Mr. Michael's hand, nodded at Destiny and left.

Mr. Michael stared down at her. "Shall we eat?"

Destiny took the arm he held out, and Mr. Michael led her out the door, to the Blue Peacock where the maître de led them to a table. While he settled, she glanced around, but saw no one she knew.

"Do you eat here often?"

"No."

Her brows rose. "No? Why on earth not? It's a lovely restaurant."

"I'm not in town that often. Three or four times a year normally, unless I have to."

"Not very sociable?"

He ignored the question and continued to study the

menu.

"Oh no, there's Mr. Bottoms." Not really a surprise, but a comment to break the silence.

"Who?"

"The president of the bank here in town—"

"Right." He stood. "Let's go."

"What? We haven't eaten."

He didn't bother answering her, only took her arm again, and against her continual protesting, pulled her toward the door.

She tried to pull from his grip, but he didn't let go, and since fighting against him seemed to be useless, she gave in and sauntered—as much as she could with being hustled—out the door. But that didn't mean she was giving in. Never.

The minute they were away from the door of the Blue Peacock, Destiny whirled on him. "Who do you think you are? You are not my—"

She broke off the sentence, the unspoken words, their meaning, suddenly registering in her brain. Had he noticed what she'd left unsaid?

A quick glance at his face revealed nothing. Either he'd paid no attention to her protest or not understood what she'd almost spoken.

She certainly didn't want him to think she had her sights set on him for a husband.

Her cheeks heated as if she'd sat in the sun way too long. This was outrageous. And nonsense. She was not after any man. Not Richard, Mr. Bottoms, nor Mr. Michael.

But her traitor-of-a-heart pointed a finger at her words, denying what her brain insisted was gospel.

"Where are we going?"

"You'll see...in just a second."

He hurried on, and Destiny almost skipped to keep up with his long-legged strides. In seconds, Mr. Michael turned and walked down a side alley, up to the closest building and knocked on the back door. He'd barely finished when the door swung open and Jake Blackston, the emporium owner, stood before them.

"Mr. Michael? What a nice surprise."

Destiny stared at Jake, at his twitching lips as if he was thinking of a joke but refusing to share it.

"What are you doing in Roaring Springs and at this time of the night?"

Mr. Michael's grin was as big as the Milky Way. "Hoping Miss Destiny and I could cadge some food from you. Happen to know you're one of the best cooks around here."

Jake slipped his glasses down a notch and peered at them for a moment. "Well, I ain't ever been stingy with my food. Come on in."

Mr. Michael stepped back and motioned for Destiny to go ahead.

She stared at both of the men who were still chuckling. Should she confront them? No, it wasn't that important.

Mentally shrugging off her suspicions, she stepped inside the back of the emporium where she supposed Jake Blackston kept residence and was pleasantly surprised at the neatness and homeyness of the place. Small, yes, but no doubt, big enough for one man. "Are you sure we're not intruding, Mr. Blackston?"

He waved away her question. "Just getting ready to enjoy my supper, and it's good, if I say so myself."

"Jake did some fancy cooking back east in his younger days."

"Well, some might not give it that much praise, Mr. Michael, but it is tasty enough to keep a body alive." The man set two more plates, placed a cloth napkin beside each plate and a fork and knife. "I hope you like chicken, Miss. I've been hankering for that and decided tonight was the night. That red rooster was getting to be more trouble than he was worth. Figured he'd feed me for a week at least."

"I love good fried chicken, and if the taste is anything like the smell, then you may not have enough for all week."

His grin was pay enough. "I would have thought you'd had all the chicken and any delicacies you wanted back east."

Had she told him she was from Boston? "Too much so. It didn't take me long to yearn for some home cooking. I remember..."

Her mother's cooking might not have been that fancy, but it was oh, so good! That was what she remembered.

Neither man appeared to notice her unfinished sentence, and it was just as well as she had no intention of sharing memories.

They were midway through the meal before Mr. Michael asked a question.

"Were you able to talk with..." a quick glance at her, then, "...the man I asked you to contact?"

Hmmm. Interesting.

Jake shook his head. "No. Seems he's out—doing a job, if you know what I mean."

Destiny wanted to shake her head and answer, no, she didn't know, but since she was smart enough to realize they were speaking in general terms on account of her presence, then obviously, they didn't want her to understand. "If I wanted to be impolite, I'd talk in riddles too."

"I'm sorry—"

"Don't apologize." Mr. Michael actually smiled at her, though his words were directed at Mr. Blackston.

Or was that a smirk on his handsome face?

Either way, Destiny hated that they were talking without including her.

"Keep sending out those telegrams. I really need someone who's one of the best. And with the things developing the way they are..." Mr. Michael gave Jake another look. "...I'd rather be safe than sorry."

Jake nodded. "I will. But you might have to settle for Virge."

"I guess so. Virge is a good enough guy, but he does everything by the book. And that might not work in this instance."

"You're right about that." Jake shot him a glance. "But he's been your friend for a long time. You know he'd do anything for you."

"I know. I just don't know how all this will play out."

"You still taking precautions with your business stuff?"

"Yeah. You know I don't trust this one."

"I reckon you got good reasons not to."

"Besides, you know there's other issues."

"You've done your best, Mr. Michael. You can't blame yourself."

"I should have taken care of it back then."

"Your dad wouldn't have liked it."

"Look where that got him."

"He died an honorable man, and that's what he wanted his boy to become."

"I've done my best." Mr. Michael laid down his fork. "Hank said there's rumors around town, he's called in Perez."

"It's come to that, has it?"

"Maybe. I hope not. But if worse comes to worst, then so be it."

On what, Destiny wanted to demand an answer. She hated, hated not knowing what they were talking about.

Jake picked up the bowl of sweet potatoes and passed them to Destiny. He nodded at her. "Bought these from a traveling salesman. A little old, but still tasty enough."

Destiny spooned a small amount onto her plate.

"You gotta be careful. You know—that guy from Texas—his reputation, no matter how much you like him. He's been known to take a bribe or two."

Mr. Michael gave him a look. "Never known him to betray a friendship."

"No, but he can be a bit unscrupulous now and then."

"True. But he's the best in the business, and if there's anything out there, he'll find it."

"Just watch your back. You're stirring up a pint of trouble, I'm afraid."

Minutes later, Mr. Michael shoved back his chair and rose. "I'll walk you to your room, Destiny, then I'll be back to talk with you more fully about the problem, Jake."

"I'm not ready to go yet." Destiny stood also but crossed her arms. "I want to help clear up the table."

"Nonsense. You need to rest. We have a long trip home tomorrow—that's if you're planning on returning with me?"

Funny.

Jake turned to Destiny. "You take care, Miss Destiny."

"I will, Jake. Thank you for the meal."

Mr. Michael gave Jake a glance, nodded and opened the door for Destiny. "See you in a few minutes."

"I'm sure Maria is waiting on my return to help her with our upcoming party. Well, that is, if you haven't changed your mind about it?" She cast a sideways glance at him as he led her down the street.

A flicker of a smile flashed across his lips then disappeared. "I'll pick you up at six if you think you can be ready that early."

Six? Why not leave now since he wasn't giving them much time for rest, let alone getting ready for bed? She wasn't used to getting up quite that early, but she also wasn't about to let him know that. "Six? Of course. I love early mornings."

"Are you sure? That would be fine to be able to start out that early."

His enthusiastic response to her sarcasm was not welcome.

She loved mornings, just not quite that early. Eight and nine were more in line with her thoughts of breakfast, early morning strolls and what-have-you.

She wanted to groan, but didn't. She'd got herself into this, albeit unwittingly, and wasn't about to protest now.

Do or die was her usual secret motto, and she wouldn't welsh on it now.

As she started toward the door of the hotel, Mr. Michael swept past her and took hold of the handle. When he didn't open it, she tilted her head to gaze up at him.

He stared down at her and said nothing, but the puzzled frown on his face clued her in. He definitely had something on his mind.

"Did you need something?"

His head barely shook. "You puzzle me."

"I do?"

"You remind me of someone I used to know."

"Really? I believe you've said that before. I'm sure I'd have remembered you if we'd met."

What was she saying? That sounded too much...what? Romantic? Forward?

Mr. Michael shook his head again and turned away. "Good night. I'll pick you up right at six."

Destiny watched as he strolled away. Back to Mr. Blackston, probably, to share more secrets.

Shrugging one shoulder, disdain at his attitude, she pulled at the hotel door, only to stumble backward when it swooshed open. Mr. Bottoms stood grinning at her.

"Where have you been?"

Irritation at his question leaped up her spine. Why did he have to know where she'd been? She bit her tongue to keep from retorting a sarcasm at him. "Have you been waiting here?"

His eyes conveyed he'd gotten the message. "I thought perhaps you'd like a nightcap?"

Destiny glanced at the big cuckoo clock hanging over the receptionist desk. Late, yes. And she had an early start in the morning. But when would she get another chance to question him?

"I could use a drink. Just for a few minutes though. I have an early morning."

"Really?"

He motioned to a clerk who nodded and headed toward another room.

Destiny followed the clerk's departure but shifted her gaze back to Hubert Bottom when he spoke again.

"You're leaving in the morning?"

Why would he think that? She'd given no indication that was the reason. "Yes."

"Why not stay in town longer? The women are meeting this week to discuss our summer festival. I'm sure they'd love to have you join them."

She snuffed the snicker that abruptly erupted from her throat and waited until the server had poured their tea. She looked up when the server didn't leave.

"Ma'am, it's a special tea that our cook developed himself from wild herbs. We hope you enjoy it."

"Why, thank you. That's very lovely to share with me. Make sure you tell your cook that." Destiny smiled at the young girl then turned back to Bottoms when she left. "They don't know me. I doubt they would want a newcomer involved in the planning."

"Newcomer? I was hoping you'd decided to make

Roaring Springs your home."

"Who said I haven't?"

"Spending all your time out at that ranch is not good. Don't you realize people talk?" Bottoms leaned forward.

Why did he have to get so close? Destiny took a sip of her tea. "Should I mind what petty people say? And I honestly don't know how long I'll be here, so why should I care what anyone thinks?"

That should put a halt to his inquisitiveness.

"Because you're a lady, that's why. Ladies set examples. They take advantage of a situation and own it. Make others take notice of their gentility."

Would he be offended if she yawned? Time to say goodnight.

She stood. "I really must go now. Thank you for the tea. I'll see you when it gets closer time to the festival. Good night."

Not giving him a chance to protest, Destiny headed toward the stairs and started to climb when a hand grabbed her arm.

"Don't walk away from me."

Her gaze took in the hand that gripped her arm then lifted to study Hubert Bottoms' face and was taken back by the look on it.

His eyes glittered with a dangerous glint. Nostrils flared. Mouth, a straight line of anger, was barely open as if panting from a strenuous run.

She pulled her arm away, and he let go. "What do you think you're doing? I will go when I want, Mr. Bottoms."

His hesitation told her one thing. He didn't want to let her go and was figuring out in his mind whether to play it safe by agreeing to her demand or get rough by insisting she wait till he'd finished whatever it was he wanted to say.

Either way, she was not in any mood to listen to one more word from him. Not tonight, and maybe never.

"I am tired and want to retire now. Please don't cause an unwanted scene." She wanted to add more. Much more, but figured she'd better not push him. He did have that dangerous look in his eyes, although it'd abated some.

"Very well. When may I see you again?"

"Perhaps when I visit again?"

"I wish you would listen to me. He's not to be trusted."

"Whoever are you talking about?"

"Michael."

"Mr. Michael? I don't believe it. What did he do?" Mr. Bottoms had to be joking.

"Too much to go into detail now, but let me assure you he's not what he seems. You'd do better to stay as far from him as you can."

"Are you serious?" She couldn't believe what she was hearing. Unless she was very, very deceived by the handsomest man she'd ever seen.

"I am very much serious." Mr. Bottoms took her hand and gazed deep into her eyes. "Promise me you'll think about coming into town to stay. Promise."

"I will think about it. I promise. Good night." Destiny whirled away and ran lightly up the stairs, not looking back. She hadn't lied. She would think about it, about what he'd said, just not long.

Mr. Michael might be the most irritating man in the world, but she hardly thought he was—had been a criminal. He was too...decent.

Wasn't he?

Chapter Fifteen

The sun had barely touched the horizon when Destiny slipped down the stairs, her large carpet bag in her hand. She'd heard faint sounds from the room across the hall—as if someone was stirring around for the day—but no one had left the room, at least she'd not seen anyone. Besides, whoever occupied it may not have been interested in her. Just because she'd heard them talking earlier and thought it was about her didn't make it so. Best to forget about it.

After the episode with Bottoms last night, she was anxious to be gone—not that she'd ever admit it to him, or even to Mr. Michael. But she also knew by past experiences, that when she didn't know how to handle a situation, didn't like a situation, and—*admit it, Destiny Rose McCulloch*, she admonished herself—was afraid of a situation, retreat, even temporarily, was the best resort.

She was early—a good ten minutes—so she was surprised when the wagon, with Mr. Michael leaning against it, stood waiting for her.

He pulled out his pocket watch and barely glanced at it. "You're thirty seconds late.

"I am not." Her retort was forceful enough, but the grin on his face was almost her undoing. She held her lips in a firm, disapproving line. Really. This man was the most—most disturbing person she'd ever met.

Handing him her bag, she waited for him to place it in the bed of the wagon. The muscles in his shoulders and arms tightened. He was every bit the man she thought him. At least...

She lifted her gaze to the second story of the hotel and drew in her breath.

Mr. Bottoms stood at the window staring. At her.

And by the look on his face, he wasn't pleased.

Not pleased at all.

~*~

121

Michael didn't look back at Roaring Springs. Never did. It held no fond memories, no hold on him, and if it was wiped off the face of the earth, he'd not miss it. Except for Jake, that is.

He'd wanted to be gone before the towns-people stirred, but he'd forgotten that most of them were hardy souls that rose as early as the farmers on the outside of town did. He wouldn't breathe easily till he was far away from here. This place that'd betrayed his father.

"Why are you frowning so fiercely?"

Destiny's voice shook him from his dismal thoughts.

"Did you get your fill of the town?"

She pursed her lips, tilted her head, but didn't answer.

"I didn't figure you'd be content to leave city life behind, not that that..." he tilted his head backward. "...could be described as a city."

She gave him a haughty glance, but he was almost sure a bit of confusion peeked at him deep within that glance.

"I'll have you know, Mr. thinks-he-knows-all-about-me, that I'm immensely enjoying the country life. Such a breath of fresh air..." Her sigh was the epitome of pure pleasure.

His burst of spontaneous laughter was unexpected. He was even more delighted when she joined him in a hearty laugh.

When their chuckles had subsided, she nudged him. "You could be quite a bit of fun if you'd only forget your fear."

"Fear?" He sent her a scowl. "What makes you think I'm afraid?"

"Oh, I don't know what of for sure, but I do know, Mr. Michael, that deep inside you lurks a trace of fear."

He opened his mouth to argue with her. But wasn't it true? That promise his pa had exacted from him. The temptation over and over to seek the revenge he wanted, and yet held back because of his pa and the promise.

"Something that keeps you from embracing life in its fullness and keeps you from really living in happiness."

If his mouth wasn't hanging open, it sure felt like it. Where did this woman come up with these ideas? Him, unhappy? Fearful? Hogwash!

"Your imagination is even bigger than I figured." He gave a light slap of the reins and the horses picked up their pace a little. "Get all your important business taken care of? Telegrams all sent? Shopping done?"

The shock on her face told him plainly he was right. She'd been so busy with her pursuit of whatever it was she'd come west for, that she'd forgotten her original plans. What did that tell him?

"Mostly. A few had to be left undone because of the demands to leave earlier than I expected."

Was that breathlessness he heard in her voice?

"Really? I thought you were the one—I'll tell you what. We've only come a couple miles or so. I can turn around, take you back. Just say the word."

Michael turned his head a bit and tugged on his hat to hide his smile.

"Oh, would you mind? Since it's no trouble?"

If ever her playacting voice was at its best, today was it. He had half-a-mind to take her pretty little self straight back to Roaring Springs.

Michael gritted his teeth at the sudden, unexpected ping coming from somewhere in his chest. Heart issues?

No, he was healthy as an ox.

Giving a slap with the reins, he started to turn the horses around and caught the quick glance from the woman beside him.

"What are you doing?"

Michael plastered a surprised look on his face. "Taking you back. You did say you hadn't finished your business there, right?"

"Do you take everything I say literally?"

"I thought—"

A rifle blast split the air, and Michael's body flinched even as his hand shoved at Destiny. "Get down."

"What—?"

"Now."

Another couple slaps of the reins, and the two horses sprang into a gallop. Michael's gaze darted, searching for the person who'd shot at them. He didn't let up until he was sure they were out of range of the shooter.

Whoever it'd been, they'd not intended to kill them. A warning shot then.

Destiny looked up at him. "Can I get up?"

He nodded, and she rose, settled herself on the seat again then gasped. "You're shot."

He'd known the shot had winged him, but it wasn't bad. Stung, but he'd live.

What did worry him was being taken unaware. And it was his own fault. He knew the dangers. Knew the man from Roaring Springs who hated him. But he'd been distracted by a pretty face. Allowed himself to forget, for close to an hour, and that could have been a fatal mistake.

A deadly one.

And that brought him around to realizing, whoever had shot, they'd never meant to kill him. A warning, a flesh wound had been their intent, and they'd succeeded.

Very well.

~*~

Destiny's head swam. She wasn't about to pass out and set her lips in defiance. She would not pass out. She would not pass out.

She'd insisted on him stopping once they'd gotten far enough away from the danger. Just enough time to wrap the wound with a piece of cloth she had in her carpet bag. She'd begged him to allow her to drive the team, but he'd refused and scoffed at her idea.

"Do you think they've followed us?"

"I doubt it. If they'd wanted to do real harm, they'd done it back there. That wasn't their intent."

"What was their intent?"

"Who knows? Did you make someone angry at you?"

"No—" What about Hubert Bottoms? He'd been angry last night. Had it been enough to send someone after them?

"No what?"

"Nothing."

"It sounded—"

"It was nothing."

"If you say so."

"I do." Destiny sighed.

"Do you need to stop?"

At Destiny's nod, Mr. Michael added, "Right up ahead is a spring. We'll stop and stretch our legs a few minutes."

Thirty minutes later, Mr. Michael pulled on the reins, and the horses slowed. But a second later, he held up a hand. When she started to speak, he glanced at her and shook his head. He dismounted, tossed the reins over the brake then whispered. "I feel something odd. You stay here while I check it out. There shouldn't be anyone here unless…"

There was no way she was going to be left behind while he had all the fun. "But I want—"

"No. Stay here."

He walked away, and Destiny watched him go, then climbed off the wagon. The day that moments ago had seemed so sunny and bright, suddenly darkened as if his disappearance and suspicions had turned the day into a dense, stormy evening.

She climbed down from the wagon and gave the horses a pat, thinking, listening. Were those murmurs floating through the air? One more pat to the horses, and she made her decision. "Stay here. I'll be right back."

Pulling Mr. Michael's rifle from the wagon, Destiny headed in the direction where he'd gone into the strand of woods. If he was all right, she'd slip back out, and he'd never know. If he needed help…

She had the gun. She'd shot it once and nicked those men who'd destroyed a lot of his wheat. She could do it again, and this time she wouldn't shut her eyes.

The murmurs were getting louder. She took another step, and a branch snapped. She halted, one foot lifted. If she kept that up, both Mr. Michael and the enemy would know she was coming.

When murmurs turned to loud voices, she exhaled and moved forward another foot. Slipping around a huge boulder, she stopped, and it was a good thing. There, not twenty feet away, stood Mr. Michael and two other men, the taller man's black-felt cowboy hat drawn low over his brow. The other man was heavier—the same man who'd talked with Mr. Michael at the hotel when she'd come down the stairs last night. Mr. Michael's gun wasn't drawn, but the tall man held a rifle, albeit in the crook of his arm.

The voices had settled into low murmurs again, when the heavy man walked closer to Mr. Michael, his voice raised in anger.

"I tell you, you need to listen to him. He knows what he's saying. You're gonna get yourself killed off and right quick."

Mr. Michael didn't look too overly upset, but he certainly looked stubborn enough. "Can't do it. I won't have..."

His voice dropped, and Destiny couldn't catch his words.

"Then we'll have to bring you in."

"Associate..."

What were they talking about? No matter. That man—the one who'd talked with Mr. Michael in the hotel last night?—was threatening Mr. Michael, and she wasn't about to let that happen. She didn't know these men, and by the looks of it, they were trying to interfere in Mr. Michael's business.

Wasn't going to happen.

Destiny lifted her rifle and cocked it, all in one move. She allowed a small smile to crack her lips even though her hands were shaking with excitement. Or was it fear?

"You both put your hands up, or I'm going to plug you full of holes."

Their reaction might have been funny had not the tall man lifted his in a split second, aiming straight at her. "You know this woman?"

Before the other man had almost finished talking, Mr. Michael turned.

Was that an exasperated expression on his handsome face? She hoped not.

"Destiny, what are you doing?"

"I'm not about to allow anyone else to damage anything on your property. Or hurt you."

"He's not—"

"Talking won't do the trick—"

"He's—"

Destiny pressed the trigger, the rifle slamming against her shoulder in a savage hit. She wanted to groan, but the sight of three men hitting the ground had her laughing. She was getting good...

Before she could finish that thought, Mr. Michael was on his feet, striding toward her and then pulling the rifle from her grasp.

"What do you think you're doing? You could have killed someone."

His face didn't look too happy. Flushed and angry would describe it much better. She'd only been trying to help, to protect him. And his property. Men didn't appreciate anything.

"That was my intent." Liar.

He gave her another sour glance then turned back to the other two men. She must have missed shooting them because they were picking themselves up, swiping at their pants with their hats. Unfortunately neither looked happy.

"That's a trigger-happy woman you're hanging around. Think I'd be watching my back if I were you." The taller man jabbed at her with quick, irritated glances.

"She is a little crazy, but harmless."

The look of doubt on the other man's face told Destiny he wasn't convinced.

"If you say so."

"Will you please go back to the horses?" Mr. Michael's strained voice seemed to indicate she'd pushed her luck with him.

"No."

"For pity's sake, Destiny, he's a friend. Go now!"

And Destiny went. Not that she was afraid of that tone of his or anything.

Five minutes later, he joined her at the wagon, and without speaking, nodded his head at her to climb into it. He didn't offer to help her, only swung up into his own side, not giving her a glance.

"I'm sorry if I scared you back there. They were threatening you."

"Scared me?" The disgust in his voice told her plenty. "We were disagreeing on how to proceed on certain things."

"Well, you three did bite the dust quick enough. I just

thought—"

He didn't bother to answer her.

Mr. Michael must be really angry at her. Or maybe he was still shaking. She kept a sober face, but inside she was grinning like crazy.

It really had been funny.

Chapter Sixteen

"**M**aria, how many tables do you want set up outside?" Destiny slipped into the kitchen where Maria was making bread. Eight baked loaves lined a side table, filling the room with the savory freshness of home.

Destiny eyed the bread, wondering if she could snitch a slice before Maria could stop her. Maybe. She glanced at the woman who was giving her knowing looks.

Or maybe not.

"I think six will do fine. Mr. Michael has two of his men helping us today, so they'll take care of that. Your job is to pretty up the tables and make sure we have plenty of lanterns ready."

"I can do that with both hands tied behind my back. Where is Mr. Michael today?"

"He and six of his men are out in the fields today, checking stock." Maria patted the loaf of dough into a perfect shape. "He didn't seem in a good mood today. Something happen on the way home yesterday?"

She hadn't seen Mr. Michael this morning. She'd spent the morning making up small bouquets for the women who'd be at the party tonight.

Destiny turned her back to the woman. "Not much. He met up with some men who looked dangerous."

"And he allowed you there?"

Her outrageous tone didn't bode well for Mr. Michael. "Well..."

"A secret meeting then. How did you know about it?"

She might as well tell all. Maria wouldn't stop until she had. "We stopped to rest and drink from a spring, but he took off into a patch of woods and ordered me to stay put. I waited—I really did—for awhile, but when he didn't return promptly, I was afraid he'd run into trouble—"

"You should know better than that. Mr. Michael can take care of himself."

"He is pretty...pretty confident." That he was. And angry.

"So what did you do?"

"I took the rifle from his horse and followed him."

Maria paused in shaping her dough. Her dark eyes widened. "And?"

"In my defense, the men looked dangerous. One was holding his gun—"

She didn't have to explain how she knew that until after she'd taken the gun.

"Did he have it pointed at Mr. Michael?"

"No, but why would he be holding it in the first place? And they threatened him, I think."

"Right. Unless Mr. Michael took him by surprise, and he pulled it quickly."

"Then why not replace it into his saddle holster?"

"Hmm. Go ahead. What happened?"

"I warned them that I was going to plug several holes into them."

"You said that?" Maria plopped the dough onto the tabletop and laughed. "You threatened them?"

Destiny giggled. "Yes, and I shot. You should have seen them hit the ground."

Maria's shoulders were shaking with laughter. "I hope you didn't hit anyone."

"Mr. Michael? No..."

"And the other two?"

"Not them either. But I do think I scared them a little. Their reactions certainly would indicate so."

"Miss Destiny, I can imagine Mr. Michael's reaction."

"All of them flat on the ground. It was funny—"

"What is so funny?" Mr. Michael's grim voice halted—only for a second or so—their giggles.

Then...Maria giggled, and Destiny joined her, shooting the cook a glance.

"Nothing." Their uniform answers were anything but convincing, but Destiny didn't care. Mr. Michael wouldn't dare anger Maria. He loved her too much.

It was time to skedaddle. "I'll go tend to those decorations."

She'd asked Hank last night about flowers for this evening's gathering, and he'd offered to send a couple of the guys to the best place on the ranch where wild ones grew. Now she strolled among the tables, arranging the flowers into bouquets and setting a vase in the middle of each one. Maria had had her spread white tablecloths over each, and with the help from Hank and a couple of the other guys, they strung a multitude of lanterns on ropes around the eating area.

"Everything looks very nice, Hank. Thanks so much for getting the flowers for me."

Maria's niece from a nearby ranch was coming by a couple hours early this afternoon to help Maria finish and serve the meal. Mr. Michael had promised ten of his men the night off, leaving only four on duty. With twelve families accepting their invitation for a social night, it promised to be a wonderful evening. Only a few of the townspeople had been invited, so Destiny hoped, for Mr. Michael's sake, since he seemed to have such an aversion to the community, all went well.

Destiny walked slowly to the barn to give Shyanne a treat. She heard the strumming of a guitar, the whine of a fiddle being tuned and the excitement in the voices of the men as they prepared for the evening.

As she approached Shyanne's stall, she murmured softly and held out the carrot. The horse nibbled it, nodding its head occasionally in approval. "Good girl."

"Howdy, Miss Destiny. Spoiling that horse, I see."

"Hi, Hunter." Destiny continued petting Shyanne. "She deserves it. Such a good girl, aren't you? Why aren't you in there with the rest of the men getting spruced up?"

"Plenty of time. Just making a last minute check on everything. Don't want any hitches."

"Surely there won't be."

"You never know."

He looked so serious, Destiny grinned. "You have a girl coming tonight?"

"Now, Miss Destiny, why would you ask a question like that?"

The boy's—why did she insist on calling him a boy when he was as old as she?—face had grown red. She really shouldn't tease him. "I'm sorry, Hunter. You're nice looking, strong, and a hard worker. Any girl would be proud to be your girl."

"Ah, thanks."

If she didn't know him better, she would think he was squirming a little.

"Fact is, I do have a young lady I'm hoping to court."

"You do? Who?"

"Maria and Hernandez's niece, Rosita."

"The girl coming to help Maria this evening?"

"That's her."

"Hunter, that's wonderful. I'm pleased for you. Very much so. I hope she'll have time to socialize with you some."

"Mr. Michael said he'd make sure."

"I'm happy for you. Now I have some things to take care of and if I don't go and make myself presentable, I'll have to stay in my room all evening while the rest of you are enjoying yourselves."

"You always look like a lady, Miss Destiny. Don't you worry none about that."

She gave him a smile and headed to her room. Now for a long soak in the tub and a leisurely hour of dressing.

~*~

She needed clean towels and stopped at the huge upstairs hallway closet to grab a couple. The towels were on the top shelf. Way too high for her to reach any.

She needed a stepstool and knew where to get one. Mr. Michael had one just inside his door, and he probably wouldn't be in his room yet. That would work.

Hurrying down the hallway, she stopped at his door, listened, then gave it three raps.

No sound.

Softly, she opened the door and peered in. Still nothing. She pushed at the door, and it widened. One step in, she stopped dead. There, in his huge chair, sat Mr. Michael, hands clasped behind his head, eyes closed.

"Did you need something?"

She sure didn't, not right now, not with the blood running straight to her cheeks, red hot. "I'm sorry...I didn't think...well, actually, I did...what I mean is..."

What a mess. Be quiet and back out of his room as quickly as possible and hope she would never see him again would certainly be the best thing for her to do.

She slipped him another glance and wanted to moan. He'd opened his eyes, now staring straight at her.

"Did you forget which room was yours?"

"To be honest—"

"Please do." His mouth widened in a teasing grin. He stood.

Panic struck. Unfortunately, it was her on the verge of fleeing and not him. Was he headed her way? What made her think of the crazy idea to go to his room after anything?

"I just wanted to borrow your stepstool."

"Why didn't you just say so? What are you doing?" He picked up the stepstool and handed it to her.

"Thanks. I wanted to get some clean towels from the closet, but I'm too short to reach them." She grabbed at the stool, and tossed her answer back at him as she sped down the hallway.

She tossed down the stepstool, which promptly turned over. Irritated, she stooped and settled it back on its pudgy legs, then stepped up on it and reached to the top shelf.

She had no trouble reaching the towels now, but while pulling two of them from the stack, several others decided to topple to the floor.

What a mess.

She started to climb down to pick up the fallen ones and dropped the two towels she'd been holding.

"Why don't you try asking for help when you can't do something?"

Destiny jumped, teetered and felt herself going backward. She stretched, reaching for the sides of the closet door—anything to stop her toppling backward when...

Two firm hands clasped her waist and lifted her up and off the treacherous stool. For what seemed like an eternity, those hands held her suspended, then slowly, painfully and slowly, they settled her back on the solid floor.

She didn't give herself time to breathe again. "You startled me."

The grin on his face did nothing for her confidence. Did he think her falling was amusing?

"Just trying to keep you from breaking your neck."

"Really?" She made a big pretense of looking at the stool and the floor. "I'm not thinking it would have hurt me much."

Without an answer, he lifted the pile of towels, straightened them and replaced all but two on the shelf. Then he handed the two towels to her. "There you go."

She couldn't speak, way too embarrassed.

He studied her for a minute, the smile disappearing. "Perhaps you wouldn't have been seriously hurt. You're strong and young. But I'm thinking I wouldn't want even a small bruise to darken that lovely skin of yours."

Mr. Michael turned on his heel and started to leave.

What had just happened? Had that really been a compliment or was it understated sarcasm about her clumsiness?

"Mr. Michael."

He turned around to face her. "Do you need something else?"

"Uh...uh, thank you." What was she thinking? His words had probably meant nothing. A general observation.

His puzzled expression showed plainly he wondered about her sanity. "You're welcome."

And then, in seconds, he was shutting his room door.

Destiny stood staring down the hallway for a moment, then hurried to her own room and shut the door. Hopefully that would keep out images of good-looking men.

~*~

Michael shut his door softly and strode to his window overlooking the barn and his land beyond. He never grew tired of gazing at it, thankful his father had had the foresight to choose the right place to raise him. In spite of the problems they'd experienced through the years and losing his parents, he loved this land like he'd loved few other things.

If only his pa was still alive. If only those three men weren't dead.

But they were, and nothing he wished would make it

different. There wasn't any going back.

He couldn't go there today, not with that party Maria and Destiny had worked so hard on. As much as he dreaded it, as much as he'd been tempted to head to the hills, there was no way he'd disappoint them. He glanced at the suit Maria had pressed and hung on his closet door. Almost time to dress, but before that, he had one more thing he wanted to do.

Michael took the stairs two at a time, stopped briefly in Maria's sewing room, grabbed her shears then stepped out on the front porch. Twenty feet to the east of the house, was the rose garden his father had planted in memory of his wife, Michael's mother. Every year he'd added another plant until the garden was a colorful rainbow.

Now, with three quick snips of the scissors, he cut three roses and a frond of the dark fern that grew beside the nearby creek. He'd have Maria tie these together and deliver them to Destiny before she came down for the evening activity.

He had no idea what she'd be wearing. Whatever it was, she'd be the belle of the ball, and as much as he wanted to deny it, she was attractive. She was also stubborn, strong-willed and seemed to know her own mind.

So why was he so drawn to her?

Chapter Seventeen

Destiny finished dressing and studied herself in the mirror. The dark rose material of her dress highlighted her blondness. She was her mother's daughter for sure and knew her mother would approve of her looks, whether she agreed with her actions or not.

If only Mr. Michael approved.

She shook her head. Why was she worrying about Mr. Michael when Richard was waiting for her in Boston? Just because this place was exciting and there were two handsome men around, that didn't mean she had to stay, did it?

She checked her thoughts. What she meant was, Mr. Michael never gave her any encouragement that he was interested. Mr. Bottoms did, decidedly, but his rather rough actions that last night in Roaring Springs were disturbing, to say the least.

Why had he acted so strangely, anyway? She hadn't done anything untowardly to him. If a woman was supposedly tired and wanted to retire, it was generally accepted—back east. The men always enjoyed their smokes and drinks and talks without the women present.

And the women would congregate in a sitting room, genteelly sipping their personal drinks and usually talking on such boring subjects, she'd escaped every chance she had. She'd much rather have been arguing on subjects concerning politics or business, giving her opinions whether they were right or wrong.

Truth be told though, her favorite activity had been the walks and strolls in the park with her dog, when she had one, or enjoying a good book outdoors, the sun threading its way through the branches of the oaks and maples.

Sigh. She wasn't in Boston now and had no desire to return anytime soon. She'd been so busy lately she'd had little time to read, but—she vowed to herself—tomorrow she'd borrow one of Mr. Michael's legion of books in his library and find someplace quiet and secret to enjoy it.

Loud voices, laughter and the screeches of laughter from children intruded into her thoughts, and Destiny went to the window and looked down on the activity below.

Judging by the number of people scattered below, most everyone had accepted their invitation. The fun beckoned, and Destiny headed out of her room.

She'd dawdled long enough.

~*~

Michael stood under a nearby oak talking with the best neighbor he had, Miles Anderson. One who was pleasant, unobtrusive and easy to get along with. The man's wife was quiet, smart and pretty, their children fairly well behaved and trained to work. They were also one of the few ranchers in this part of the country who had, besides himself, employed several people. Maria and Hernandez's niece worked there. She and Hunter stood close to the rose garden talking.

But when he caught Anderson's attention on something besides himself, he turned slightly to see what it was.

It wasn't a what, it was a who.

Destiny lingered in the open doorway, glancing around, a smile tilting her lips upward. She looked like one of the climbing red roses bordering the entryway. On her shoulder was the bouquet of pink roses he'd cut for her.

"I see my guest of honor has joined us. Excuse me, Anderson, while I go and introduce her to everyone." His gaze swept over the group of party visitors then fastened on Destiny again. He spoke before he even reached her.

"I see you've decided to join us. A late entrance is always so..."

She tilted her head toward him. "So what?"

"So noticeable?"

"That's not a nice thing to say. The plain noticeable seems so...so common. You do know that can be thought of in different ways."

"I do know that. What about dramatic?"

"Better, but not much. You speak as if I'm trying to gain attention."

Her pout was adorable but didn't suit her.

"How's this? You look positively ravishing tonight."

Her frown deepened. "You're determined to make me angry, aren't you?

"Why would you think that when I've tried to compliment you?"

"Have you?"

Her eyes gave her away. She was still embarrassed about entering his bedroom.

"Then would exquisite suit you better?"

"Much. Thank you."

"Then that's how I would describe you. Would you like to meet our neighbors now or refresh yourself with a drink?"

"Oh, let's meet your neighbors. I'm so excited to do so."

He slid a glance her direction. "Just watch out for any amorous gentlemen."

"Is that supposed to be funny?"

"No. It's a serious warning. Not many of them have seen as pretty a woman as you."

"I'm not certain whether to be angry or pleased."

"I'd much prefer you to be pleased." He stared down at her as he handed her a glass of Maria's homemade apple cider.

~*~

It'd been a breathtaking and fun two hours of socializing. Three of his cowboys had done him proud with their skill on a guitar, fiddle and harmonica, filling the air with music and giving the company of people time for laughter, serious conversation and much-needed socializing. Hunter and Hernandez had supervised several children and young people's games, causing laughter to highlight the evening.

A couple of the neighbors' sons had spent as much time with Destiny as they could reasonably do. And all the time she'd laughed and enjoyed their company, she'd been aware of the dark brown-eyed gaze from Mr. Michael.

It was only when she'd walked away from the handsomest young man in the group of attentive pursuers that she realized Mr. Michael had disappeared. Could be he was off talking cattle with one of his neighbors. Or maybe he'd struck up a deal with someone needing work. Or maybe...

Something was going on. Something interesting. Something she was missing out on by flirting with men she had not the least interest in.

How could she have missed Mr. Michael's disappearance? And the number of his men had dwindled by two in the last few minutes. Hunter for one, given that Rosita was desperately trying to ignore a young man determined to win her attention.

And, an abandoned guitar gave convincing evidence that Hank had abandoned his musical post.

Hmmm.

She set her glass down on a nearby table, cast a quick glance around to see if anyone was watching, then slipped around the corner of the house. Pausing, she listened and studied the surrounding area. Where could they have gone?

Out to the fields? No, unless there was a real emergency, Mr. Michael wouldn't have left the party.

Then where?

The barn? Why the barn? Was an animal hurt? She'd check, just to make sure.

The barn was on the far side of the house, away from the party, so Destiny knew she'd probably not be seen. Still, she searched the area for any wanderers. No sign of anyone, and she hurried toward her destination.

The voices stopped her.

She crept closer.

A deep voice spoke. "You know, don't you, he's out to get you?"

Sounded like someone she didn't know.

"We already know that. Anything new?"

Was that Jackson?

"He's ready, in position and financially. He has the loyalty of his followers and has placed the fear of God in the others that will keep them quiet and pacified."

"I'll never understand how anyone can harbor a made-up grudge for years."

Mr. Michael for sure.

Who were they talking about? The shiver that ran up her back caused her to clench her teeth to keep from chattering with the sudden fear. Was someone trying to hurt Mr. Michael?

"Yer pa was a reasonable man. If any fingers need to point, it would be yers."

Was that Hank again?

"It should be over and done, Boss. No disrespect, but you need to forget it."

Definitely Hunter. She'd know that voice anywhere. But what were they talking about? And to whom?

"Yeah, I know all that. Gone over it in my mind a million times, but if only I could have stopped it. We'd not be in this mess... I blame myself."

Destiny pressed her back against the barn wall. What were they saying? Sounded like Mr. Michael had done something wrong. Something bad.

Something very bad.

~*~

Michael held up his hand, silencing the protests of his two best hands. No, they were more than that. They were true friends who'd proven to be loyal. If anyone had his back, these two did.

He glanced at the other two men who'd joined them. Though he didn't count them as friends, like Hank and Hunter, they'd been decidedly dependable when needed the couple other times he'd sent for them. And he'd known them a long time. That meant something.

He cocked his head as another snap of a twig sliced the air in a minute sound. Someone was definitely outside the barn. Someone having a romantic moment? More like someone—a spy in his midst?—maybe. Someone he hadn't discovered?

Whatever. Something, or someone, was outside. Listening? Passing by? Strolling around, being nosy or wanting a break from the socializing as he had?

He slipped to the partially-opened doorway and peeked out, aware that the tall man—Virge—had headed toward a rear door.

Nothing.

Edging outside, he scanned the immediate area then farther afield. A motion caught his attention, and he shifted. Was that...

A blur of pink swirled around the far corner of the house.

Virge walked up to him. "Looks like your girl is sticking that cute little nose into business where it doesn't belong."

"Afraid so." Michael sighed.

What had she been doing? Was she really the one who'd been snooping around the barn? And worse, what had she heard?

~*~

Destiny pressed her back against the wall of the house, breathing in and out, in and out. Stop shivering. Stop panicking. *Just because it sounded...bad, doesn't mean it is.* They could have been discussing something totally innocuous. Mr. Michael was a good man.

Breath back to normal, she peeked around the corner, back at the barn, and saw a tall, long-legged person striding toward her, letting no grass grow under his feet.

Mr. Michael.

She grabbed two handfuls of her skirt and ran toward the front of the house. She couldn't talk with him—and ran straight into the broad chest of Mr. Michael's nearest neighbor's son, Adam Isaac.

She didn't suppose anyone could look so delighted at the collision.

"Miss Destiny, now this is what I call a right-nice meeting. Who are you running from?"

"I'm not running from anyone, Adam."

"Adam Isaac, Miss Destiny, and it sure looked like it, but never mind. I'm just right-down, plum grateful it was me here to catch you. Could be a sign..."

"A sign?" What on earth was he talking about? She cast a glance back at the other end of the house and jumped at the sight of a strong, tall shadow of a man standing there, staring at them. She whirled away from the sight and grabbed onto the boy's arm to hurry him around yet another corner and back to the party.

Caleb's Destiny

Adam Isaac was still rambling on, about a sign, she thought. Why on earth was he talking about signs? Couldn't he see she was upset?

Glancing upward at the young man, she realized he couldn't see she was upset.

It was then *she* realized there would never be anyone else for her but...

Richard's handsome face floated in front of her. Smiling. Beckoning.

Was it a sign that it was time to return to Boston? A time to settle down with Richard and forget her insane idea to find the boy Caleb? To forget her increasing interest in this area, this ranch? To forget Mr. Michael?

Her head pounded, and she pressed a hand against her heart. "I think I need a cool drink, Adam Isaac. Would you...?"

"I'll be glad to do that for you. Here, sit right here. It's quiet and away from the chatter of everyone. I'll be right back."

It was an ideal place to hide out for a few minutes away from the crowd of Mr. Michael's neighbors and friends. But her mind refused to release the conversation she'd heard minutes ago.

What had they said?

Who was out to get whom? Mr. Michael was out to get someone? No, more like someone was out to get Mr. Michael. But that raised the question of why anyone was out to get him. What had he done that was so bad someone was out to get him? It made no sense.

Someone who was ready both in position and financially. One of his neighbors? Ready to do what? Mr. Michael was financially well off, or at least it seemed so. Position, what did that mean? Settled?

Destiny shook her head and shut her eyes, the better to block out her thoughts.

It all circled straight back to the words, *I blame myself.*

A dark shadow suddenly blocked out the light of all the lanterns strung earlier. Destiny opened her eyes.

The tall man Mr. Michael had talked to on the ride home two days ago, when she'd threatened to shoot him, stood in front of her, staring as if trying to figure her out.

Or maybe planning her demise. He'd get off the hook for sure, seeing as he'd claim justifiable revenge. Destiny felt a misplaced chuckle threatening to spill from between her lips, but forced it back. Now was definitely not the time for levity.

"May I help you?"

Her voice shook a trifle, but maybe he'd not notice.

"No need to be afraid. That's if..."

His voice trailed off as if considering what he'd just said. Was he re-thinking his comment?

"That's if what?"

Was that really her voice sounding defiant and brisk? She peeked a glance at him. Hmmm. His face was shadowed. But was that a trifle hardening of the facial muscles?

He leaned forward, just enough to place his face even with hers. "If you can keep that pert nose of yours out of other people's business. Can you do that, Miss?"

What? How dare he? Who did he think he was?

She drew back. "Who do you think you are? I'll have you know, I'm—"

"Miss, I'll have you know, I couldn't give an owl's wink who you are. Stay out of business that doesn't concern you, for your own good. You got that?"

She could feel it coming. That anger and stubbornness that always seemed to get her into trouble. She knew it, but didn't care. That's how it went every time, and every time, she plunged straight into that trouble, forgetting—or not caring—that she'd pay the consequences later. Either through punishment—such as disapproval or dis-appointment—or her own accusing conscience.

So be it.

"Are you threatening me? I don't think Mr. Michael would care for your tone or words—"

"Are you sure about that?" The tall man straightened. "If you're as smart as I think you are, you'll curb that nosiness. I'm sure your Mr. Michael would like that."

"How would you know that?"

She was talking to his back as he strode away and didn't look back, as if he hadn't heard her last taunt, or didn't care.

What a mess.

Another long sigh, and she straightened. She smiled at Adam Isaac as he delivered the drink to her hands, talking all the while.

Mr. Michael had said he was a friend. But was he really? But then maybe he was a friend, all right. A gunslinger friend.

But why would Mr. Michael need a gunslinger? Was his feud with Bottoms that bad? Were the two men out to kill each other?

Adam Isaac's hand was outstretched as if he wanted her to place her hand in his. She dutifully obeyed, and he tucked her hand into the crook of his arm, as well-mannered as anyone she'd ever met.

She gave him a smile, but all the while her mind seethed with unanswered questions. And all of them pertained to that tall man—and Mr. Michael.

Chapter Eighteen

Michael stood at the corner of his home, watching that rose-pink dress disappear around the opposite corner. Destiny. It had to have been her spying. What had she heard? Too much? At least, enough to cause her to question what was going on.

And that wasn't a good thing. He wanted her far away from his problems. From the danger that possibly might be brewing.

He'd thought he'd had it over with years ago. Thought things had been forgotten, smoothed out, but no.

Hank had worked with Michael's father and Michael had grown up thinking Hank was his real uncle. And Hank knew Michael had done his best.

And as far as Hunter went, he'd been a very young child when Michael had gone through all this trouble. So what Hunter knew was only because of what Hank had shared with him. He'd tried to shield the boy. Didn't want him growing up with the internal battles he himself had suffered through.

But every man had to come to the place where he decided for himself how his life would go. And Hunter had reached that point.

One thing about both his top men: Hank and Hunter were loyal. He knew they were. They wouldn't betray him. Not them.

So what to do about Destiny? Talk to her? Tell her what was going on and see if he could convince her to back off?

Nope, that wouldn't work. At all. So what then?

Send her back east? His heart pinged. He doubted she'd go unless he hogtied her, and he couldn't imagine that would succeed.

He'd have to be more vigilant than ever. Keep her close. Maybe even assign Hunter to stay close by her. She'd have questions, but he'd have to come up with some kind of vague reason for Hunter's sudden attention.

He hated to do without Hunter's expert help. He was young, yes, but reasonable, strong as an ox but firm enough to handle even the rowdiest hand he had.

That young man didn't know it yet, but he had plans for him. Big plans, although he truly hoped they'd come to pass quite a bit in the future.

Michael frowned at his own reasoning.

Maybe he'd just have a talk with Destiny. Reason with her and explain. Maybe it'd work, but he doubted it.

He headed back to his party visitors and Destiny.

~*~

Hunter hurried back to the party area. He'd gotten only a few minutes with Rosita. He was hoping she'd be allowed to spend a couple of days with her uncle and aunt, but with it being late spring it was up in the air whether it would happen or not.

His gaze scanned the immediate party area. Everyone looked relaxed and happy, enjoying the music, games, and conversations. Too bad there wasn't time for more of this stuff. Of course, Mr. Michael had never been one to socialize much, and for good reason. There were few in these parts to be trusted. And he sure wasn't overly friendly to many.

Rosita was gathering up dirty dishes but glanced at him. Her mouth widened in a small smile and she held up a hand, her fingers widening to signal five minutes.

Good. He'd have just enough time then to talk to...

He caught sight of Miss Destiny surrounded by three young men, each vying for her attention. Her mouth kept its smile, but her eyes betrayed her.

She was troubled.

Hunter headed her way, but before he could reach her, shots rang out. One sent a lantern flying, the glass shattering across a table. Another clipped a nearby tree branch causing it to split and fall near Miss Destiny.

Bodies dove for cover. Hunter swept the area beyond the edges of light but could see nothing. Rosita was on the ground, but Miss Destiny still stood, staring down at the front of her gown. Hunter sprang toward her when, from the corner of his eye, he saw Mr. Michael reach her and drag her behind one of the large trees.

Hunter veered toward Rosita and fell to the ground beside her. It was only then that he spotted the blood covering the front of her dress and apron.

~*~

"She's hurt. I think she got shot." Destiny was babbling even as Michael sheltered her in his arms.

"Quiet." His gaze took in the dark beyond the lights, yet nothing illuminated the person targeting him and his friends here. Five minutes passed, and there were no more shots.

Loosening his hold on her, he stared down at her. "You could have been shot. Why did you just stand there?"

"Let me go. Let. Me. Go. Rosita was shot." She squirmed away and ran toward the girl still lying on the ground, Hunter hovering over her.

Michael sped after her and shoved Destiny aside. "I need a couple of you men to help get her inside. Someone head to town and get the doctor."

"I'll go." Hunter stared down at Rosita even as he spoke.

"You sure you don't want to stay here with her?" Michael motioned to two of the other men who'd run over to help. "Let's try not to move her unnecessarily. Ready? Lift."

"Mr. Michael?"

"Go, Hunter. Be safe, but hurry." He nodded at the young man.

They'd just entered the doorway when Michael heard the pounding of horse hooves. Pray God, Hunter didn't break his neck. Or that he didn't run into the person who did this. "Destiny, get Maria. She'll know what to do until the doctor gets here."

They'd barely carried Rosita to the extra bedroom upstairs before Maria hurried in, Destiny following, and both ladies carrying cloths tucked under their arms and pans of water.

"Mr. Michael?" Maria's face was white, her voice trembling.

He knew how dear this niece was to his employees,

knew they considered her as a daughter after the girl had lost both parents in Mexico over a war between clashing families. Heartbreak wouldn't begin to describe their emotion if Rosita died. Devastation would be a closer description.

"Easy, Maria. I need you to be strong here. You and I will do what we can. Hunter's gone for the doctor..."

Maria straightened, drew in a long breath and nodded. "You are right. Everyone out except for Mr. Michael. Destiny, stay close, please, in case I need you."

Carefully, the woman who'd been a lighthouse to him through his early years cut Rosita's clothes from her and examined the wound.

"Lots of blood loss, but a clean shot. The bullet, thankfully, went straight through her side."

Maria nodded even as she dipped the cloth into the warm water. "I'll get her cleaned up. You can send Miss Destiny back in. I know you have things to do." She shot him a glance, letting him know she knew what he needed to do.

"Right." He gave her arm a quick squeeze and left the room.

"How is she?" Destiny stepped up to him the minute he exited.

"Serious, but she'll pull through. Maria will see to that. You all right?"

"I'm fine. What happened out there?"

Michael stared down the hallway, feeling the fear again for what was happening. Not for himself, but those visiting his home, enjoying their evening, for his hands and employees, and...for Destiny. His insides trembled again at the fear that had pierced his being when he saw her standing there while the bullets whizzed by her. Surely no one had intentionally planned to shoot her.

Him? That was the better explanation, and one that didn't bother him. He was used to being threatened, although, if he was being truthful, he hadn't really had to worry about it recently. But now...

"Maria needs you if you can help?"

"Of course." She turned to step into the bedroom, but looked back for a second. "Be careful."

So she did realize the danger they'd just gone through,

the potential danger ahead. He shook his head as he left the house. He reckoned he'd never forget the sight of her outlined there in the light as a so-far-unknown assailant had endangered his guests...and her.

"Boss?" Hank stepped out of the shadows.

"You find anything?"

"Hard to tell in the dark. Virge is still out there. Says he'll be on the alert. I sent a couple other guys out to keep watch."

"Good. If you see Virge in the morning, I want to talk to him before he leaves. Make sure of that, Hank."

"Got it."

"All our guests gone?"

"Yeah. Figured they'd best be headin' for their homes. A few offered to help if we needed them, but didn't think there was anything we couldn't do."

"Good thinking. Get some sleep. We'll do some searching in the morning."

"Right."

Michael watched as Hank headed toward the managers' quarters, but his mind was on what he couldn't see. Hernandez and a couple other guys were clearing up after the party—something Maria would have done had she not had to attend to Rosita. Hernandez' back was hunched as if carrying a burden. Poor man. He must be worried sick, yet Michael knew the man trusted his wife implicitly to do all she could for their niece.

He could do nothing else here for the moment and headed to the barn. Whistling softly, Jasper answered with a snort. Time to ride out and see for himself what had happened.

Morning would come quickly. He wanted answers.

~*~

Destiny woke with the sun brightly shining into her room. She stretched then remembered the night before. Sometime in the wee hours of the morning, Maria had sent her to bed, once the doctor arrived, insisting she'd be fine with watching over Rosita.

She dressed quickly before standing in front of her east window, watching as three men rode slowly back to the ranch house. Mr. Michael, it looked like, and two of his men, unknown to her.

She ran down the stairs and headed outside. Mr. Michael dismounted as she walked up to him. "Are you all right? Do you want something to eat?"

"Yeah, let me clean up a little, and I'll be in in a minute or so."

Twenty minutes later, Mr. Michael joined her in the breakfast room. "Smells good."

"Well, I can't cook like Maria, but it's filling. I'll get you coffee." She poured a cup full of the dark liquid and carried it to him. "I'm sure you're tired."

"I'm fine. Thought I'd get a couple hours sleep then head back out."

"Did you find out anything?"

"Not much." He spooned eggs and a steak onto his plate. "Footprints indicate possibly one man out there."

"Shooting at us?"

"Yes. Could have been a couple more farther out, but only one came in close enough for a few shots. Whoever it was had to have a sight mounted on his rifle to be shooting as far away as he was."

"What does that mean?" Destiny studied his weary face.

"Could be someone—someone who knew what they were doing."

"Don't most men know how to handle a gun?"

"Yes, but some men—some men shoot as a business."

"Meaning?"

He stared down at the fork that held his last bite. "Meaning a hired gunslinger just might have been out there last night."

"Mr. Michael, are you sure?" Someone had hired a gunslinger to shoot at Mr. Michael's ranch? At his visitors, or was a particular person the target? Surely not quiet Rosita.

He didn't answer, but his mouth set in a distinct frown that allowed no more questions. He shoved back his chair. "I'm going to get that rest now. Tell Maria I won't be home for supper tonight."

"Where are you going?" Destiny stood when Mr. Michael did.

"We've got our hands full checking our land today.

Later I'm headed to town. I want to talk to someone."

Destiny grabbed his arm. "Take me with you."

He looked down at her. "I can't take you."

"Please...I promise to stay out of your way."

"That's not the point. It might be dangerous."

"Then don't go. You don't have to, do you? Is Hunter or Hank going with you?"

One side of his mouth crooked up. "You wouldn't be worried about me, would you?"

She jerked her hand off his arm. "Of course not. Whatever made you think that?"

"That cute little frown between your eyes gave me a clue."

She laughed. "That cute little frown might mean I'm angry at you for refusing me."

"It might."

"And?"

"The answer's still no, but..."

"But what?"

"I have a surprise for you."

"You do. What is it?"

"I can't tell you."

"Then it's not much of a surprise."

"It will be."

"How?"

"After I leave, Hank will take you to it."

"What?"

"Yep, that's if you're a good girl and no more coaxing."

"I'm not a child."

Mr. Michael walked to the doorway before looking at her again. "Then stop your coaxing. You're not going."

~*~

Really? He thought she was childish? What did he know about insatiable interest in everything? Nothing, obviously.

Destiny stomped her way out of the room, but relented when it came to checking on Rosita. Her own grievances with Mr. Michael didn't come into play when it came to this gentle girl—probably her own age.

Peeking into the room, she realized Rosita was awake, staring out the window, her face pale but her eyes alert.

"Rosita?"

The girl turned her head. "Miss Destiny, please come in."

"How are you feeling?"

"Alive." The faint smile widened her lips.

"And we're all so very thankful for that. Can I get you anything?"

A dry chuckle escaped Rosita's throat. "No, Tia Maria has waited on me hand and foot. Plied me with way too much food. If she keeps on, I will be so plump no young man will look at me."

"I seriously doubt that a certain man on this ranch will ever be able to take his eyes off you."

Rosita's face reddened, but her mouth widened again even as she protested. "I'm sure I don't know who you mean."

"I'm sure you do. I saw Hunter briefly this morning. He seems to be wearing a permanent worry-frown."

The girl dropped her gaze and fiddled with the coverlet on her bed. "Do you like Hunter, Miss Destiny?"

"I do. He's a fine young man."

"He hasn't been in to see me. Not once. If he cared..." Her voice whispered the words, the tears edging them with emotional impact.

"He hasn't? I'm surprised. He seemed devastated with worry."

Rosita said nothing.

"He's probably resting, as is Mr. Michael, I think, but I imagine they're heading out afterwards. Would you like me to send him in later if they get home in time?"

"Oh, no. Please don't ask him to come in. If he really wanted to see me..."

She didn't have to finish the sentence.

"Then would you like me to read a little to you this morning? Mr. Michael has some very good books in his library."

"Would you?" Rosita's eyes sparkled.

"I would." Destiny stood. "I'll be back in fifteen minutes. I know just the book I think you'll enjoy."

Chapter Nineteen

Destiny hurried down the staircase straight to the library. She was always a bit awed at the immense stash of books Mr. Michael owned. His collection was as impressive as any owned by many of the society people back east. She wondered, as she randomly ran fingers over the titles on one shelf, how he'd managed to attain such a vast array of books.

She knew what book she was after, but enjoyed the atmosphere and smell of printed books. A magical world waited in libraries, and it was one she was pretty fond of.

Her fingers stopped at the book she was looking for, and plucked it from the row. Running her right hand over the cover, she smiled, imagining Rosita's reaction to the poignant story.

She laid it on a nearby table and kept gazing at the titles as she slowly circled the room. She stopped abruptly when she faced the glass-covered cabinet. Destiny tugged at the two doors, but they were locked, and she pressed her face close to see what the few journal-type books were, but there was nothing to give her even a clue. Worn and tied with two—what probably had been red at one time—faded ribbons, the books begged for her to open them and read.

One shelf held a delicate, flowered, gold-rimmed teapot with four cups and saucers close by. Had Mr. Michael's mother owned them? Drank and served from them? Another shelf held a worn Bible lying open on a yellowed doily.

Two pictures stood nearby. In one, a sober toddler sat in an ornate gold frame while the other was a simple silver-plated frame surrounding a young man and woman, both posed stiffly. Yet something in their eyes— or was it their hand positions? Was it because of his lying lightly on her shoulder and hers covering his lovingly? As if...as if they were in love? Mr. Michael's parents? Perhaps.

And on the very bottom shelf laid items that no doubt had been owned by Mr. Michael's father. A pistol and a long-bladed knife along with a beat-up metal coffee pot and cup and well-worn hat shared the shelf. All the items looked used but well kept.

In a corner of the very top shelf stood several carvings that caught her attention. A wooden dog, a small rabbit, and a horse were among the ones that stood out to her. A lump the size of a small apple suddenly seemed to lodge in her throat as she tried to swallow the emotional response her body felt at the sight of the handmade carvings. She laid a hand on the glass, yearning to bust open the door of this cabinet and touch, no, hold, these cherished toys that Mr. Michael's childish hands had held and loved.

So much like holding her own carving of a kitten that she'd owned since a child.

He'd been a boy who'd been loved so much.

Whatever, this cabinet held priceless, precious items obviously or Mr. Michael wouldn't keep them under lock and key. Something he cherished, no doubt, so it had to have been his parent's items. His memories.

Destiny swallowed and straightened. She cast a last, longing glance at the glass cabinet, picked up the book she'd read to Rosita, and exited the room, shutting the door as if it was a hallowed spot.

Walking slowly up the stairs, the book in her hands, she smiled. Rosita would love *Great Expectations*. And she didn't mind one little bit another glimpse into Pip's world again.

~*~

Destiny stood in the doorway of Rosita's room watching as Maria set down the bowl—of soup probably—she'd been feeding the girl, and lifted a napkin to wipe her mouth. She was crooning, and when Rosita gave her a feeble nod, the woman turned to replace the napkin with a cup and caught Destiny hovering at the doorway.

"Come in, Miss Destiny. Rosita just finished the nourishing soup I made special for her. But do you think she would eat it all? No! She did not. Only a few spoonfuls, and she says she doesn't want more." The woman shook her head. "She will not gain strength by not eating."

Destiny smiled and winked at Rosita, when Maria wasn't looking, and the girl gave her a feeble smile, although her eyes sparkled with laughter.

"If you'd like to leave the bowl, perhaps she'll eat more in a bit." Destiny held up the book. "I've come to read."

"Now, Miss Destiny, she needs her rest—"

"No, Tia Maria. I dearly want to hear Miss Destiny read. Please..."

Maria propped hands on her hips and frowned at first Rosita, then Destiny, but she finally raised her hands in defeat, shaking her head, then marching from the room, muttering.

Destiny scooted a chair close to the bed.

"She doesn't mind, you know." Rosita's soft voice was like a soothing ointment on a bad burn. "She makes a fuss, but that is the way in Mehico. She means no harm but won't show that she is happy you are spending time with me."

"I know. It took a little time for me to realize she has a heart as big as a horse."

Rosita giggled. "I'm anxious to listen. Please read."

"Good." Destiny opened the book and flipped to the first page and began. In seconds she was lost in the words, carried away by her imagination and the book to a vastly different world. It was nearly a half hour later that she glanced up and realized Rosita had fallen asleep. Closing the book, she placed it on the stand beside the soup bowl, adjusted the cover on the bed and laid her hand softly on the girl's forehead. Cool. Good.

She started to pick up the tray holding the uneaten bowl of soup then walked to the window to look out instead. The cloudy sky threatened rain, but no rain was falling as of yet.

"I'm bored now," she whispered to herself. "I'll go for a walk this afternoon after I get my chores done for Maria. That should be interesting enough to keep me out of trouble."

Nodding, she scooped up the bowl and spoon, left the

room, and pulled the door closed after herself.

But the day led to one thing after another. She'd insisted on helping Maria hang clothes on the line and then offered to help bake cookies for all the hands on the ranch. Maria had confided to Destiny that she had the habit of baking cookies at least once a month for all the hands, and the men didn't take it kindly if she tried to skip. Maria had laughed, delighted they loved her baking.

By the time she'd finished her work, it was headed toward late afternoon. If she didn't start soon, she'd not be able to get her walk in. It was time for an adventure. It might not be grand and exciting, but then, who knew what might happen?

It was a warm late afternoon, the breeze blowing lightly against her skin but the weather promised a beautiful summer. What would happen when summer was past? Would Mr. Michael insist on her leaving?

Right now, though it had looked like rain earlier, the storm had held off. She had plenty of time, she figured, to get in a walk before the rain began. She walked slowly around the ranch house, trying to decide where she should go. She could check out the fruit orchard or maybe ride to the top of that mountain where she and Mr. Michael had watched those men destroying his wheat crop. But both of those were too long of trips for today. Maybe...

"Miss Destiny?"

Destiny turned. "Hank."

"Mr. Michael asked me to show you something." He gave her a gentle smile.

"A surprise?"

"Yes, ma'am. Come along. It's in the barn."

What could it be? A new colt? A baby calf whose mother wouldn't take to it? Destiny strode alongside the tall man beside her, him not saying another word.

He led her to a ladder and pointed. "It's up there."

"So I'm to climb the ladder to see what my surprise is."

"That's what he said. You want me to go first?"

"No, I'll be fine." Destiny hitched her skirt a fraction and started climbing. At the top, she heard the cutest sound in the world and hurried to climb into the hay-strewn loft. The soft sounds of mewing led her straight to where a mother cat was feeding her babies. Destiny plopped down and looked up at Hank who'd followed her up the ladder.

"They're adorable, Hank. May I hold them?"

"Go ahead. They're old enough. Mr. Michael said you are to have whichever one you want as your pet. The others will be barn cats keeping down the never-ending supply of rodents."

Destiny picked up one after another, murmuring words of endearment, cuddling the soft, helpless creatures as Mama Cat watched her.

"They're all so cute." She set down the black and white one and picked up the snow white one. "This is the one, Hank."

"Are you sure?"

"Positive. He—she—which is it, Hank?"

"It's a girl cat, Miss Destiny."

"She reminds me of one I had when I was little. Yes, this is the one. May I take it to the house? Will Mr. Michael care?"

Hank chuckled. "No, Miss Destiny, I'm shore Mr. Michael isn't going to mind if you do that, and it's old enough now to leave its ma. You might have to stay clear of Maria for a few days. She's a right down stickler for cleanliness and no messes. I'm thinkin' that little critter is going to be spoiled rotten and makin' plenty of messes to be cleaned up."

~*~

After Destiny made sure her kitten was tucked safely and comfortably in its new box in her room, she headed outside again. It was time for that walk she was wanting before the rain started.

Why not walk straight to the area where those bullets had come from and see if she could uncover some clues? After all, back in school, she wasn't teased about being nosy for nothing. She'd earned that reputation justly.

She cast a quick glance back at the house, the barn and hands' building, but saw no one paying any attention to her. Destiny picked up her pace.

Caleb's Destiny

The land was beautiful, hilly, and flat in some areas, with patches of forest and plenty of wildlife, including edible plants—if she knew what was what. But she could learn. She took her time, studying the land, keeping a close eye on the way she was walking. She for sure didn't want to get lost and have Mr. Michael upset and sending someone to find her.

She paused after a half hour or so and climbed up on a large boulder to rest. It was on a slope, so it did give her a bird's eye glimpse back the way she'd come. She could see part of the immediate ranch property, minute from her view, but still cozy and nice. She'd grown so used to the place she almost felt like she was...home.

Whatever that meant.

Because, although she wasn't entirely sure he would do it, it was always a possibility Mr. Michael would get tired of her being around and try to ship her back east. But the longer she stayed, the less inclined she felt to go back east. And what about Richard? He was fast becoming a memory instead of the real live person he was, at least back in Boston. Here? Not so much.

What was she going to do about him? It wasn't fair to leave him hanging when she'd communicated very little to him about herself.

A twig snapped close by, but Destiny ignored it. She leaned her head back, eyes closed, and allowed the breeze to cool her face.

"Now if this isn't a beautiful sight."

The softly-spoken, but somehow disturbing voice intruded on her thoughts, and for a minute, Destiny wanted to snap at the person destroying the atmosphere.

"Really? I'm trying to relax here." She turned as she spoke and gasped. She knew this man. Had seen him somewhere. Roaring Springs? No... Yes. It was...it was...

"You haven't forgotten me, have you?"

The man standing there grinned, but somehow it wasn't a friendly one. Somehow it seemed...sinister? Though his words seemed innocent enough.

"I'm thinking we ought to get better acquainted."

"What are you doing here? This is Mr. Michael's property." He was standing right in the middle of the trail. There was no way to go around him, and she certainly couldn't climb down the steep incline behind her. That would be more like a tumble down the bank.

The man stared at her, his one eye unblinking, dull and dead-like. But worse than the eye, was his smile.

A shiver ran up her back and Destiny screamed. Long and loud. Ear-shattering.

The man took a step forward, not breaking his eye contact, although amusement flicked across his lips as they tilted even higher in a disturbing grin. "I like to hear a woman scream. Makes her more...interesting."

"Go away. There'll be someone here in minutes, and it won't go well for you when they find you here."

Her threat rolled off him like he was covered in oil.

"Do you think so, Miss McCulloch? I dare say you wish it was so, would like me to believe that's so, but you see, I'm smarter than you think, and much, much more dangerous than you thought."

Destiny seldom felt fear. Excitement. Interest. Amusement. But seldom fear. Especially not like the fear coursing through her body right now. What was the man saying? That he was going to kill her? Or something far worse? He'd have a fight on his hands to try anything. Unless he killed her. She swallowed and hoped he couldn't see her doing so.

Snarling her lips at his suggestion, she cast him a don't-you-dare-try-anything glance, but she wasn't ignorant. She was in a possibly serious situation and had better come up with a plan more than screaming. It was doubtful anyone from the ranch heard her scream, so it was up to her to rescue herself. She cast a glance at the immediate area looking for anything she could use as a club for defense.

"Are you afraid of the big bad wolf, Miss McCulloch?" He held out hands that looked as if they'd never done a day's work. "Be good now, and you won't get hurt."

She sent a scorching glance his way, but he only laughed. Softly, which made it that much more sinister to her.

He sobered as quickly as he'd laughed. "I'm thinking it's time you and I have some fun. You attracted me from day one when I first saw you. I'll confess, Miss

McCulloch, that I'm smitten with you. Be a good girl."

"Never! I'm going nowhere with you."

He sighed. "I've always enjoyed my women a little fiery. That always seems to make things a little more fun." He advanced toward her a few feet, his gaze never leaving her face.

Destiny jumped up and took two steps backward.

Too close. Too close. She was too close to the bank. He was too close to her.

"Come on. Be reasonable. You know I'm going to win this battle between us. I'm much stronger, you see. Women can't ever beat a man. Too weak, they are." He eyed her and took another few steps.

She refused to answer him, although she seethed inside at his words. Blathering idiot, he was.

He must have thought he'd won the battle. As he stepped within touching distance of her, Destiny lunged toward him, shoving with all her hundred fifteen pounds at the man who not only outweighed her, but who was much stronger. He gripped her arms and would have jerked her toward him to be clasped tight in his grip, but at that moment, she kicked him—hard, and he stumbled backward, letting go and gasping at the pain. Moaning in agony.

He wobbled, bent almost double, and then as if God himself had sent a miracle, his feet slipped, and he stumbled backward. Straight toward the ground. Straight toward the boulder she'd sat on minutes earlier. Landing hard.

The solid thunk interrupted his groaning, and blessed silence filled air.

Destiny stared at him, lungs heaving, relief flooding through her body at the close call. He wasn't moving, and she stepped closer. He looked...

She shivered, and edged around him to flee back the way she'd come, not stopping, losing the light shawl she'd carried with her. Running. Running. Straight back to the ranch.

The trip from the ranch had taken twenty minutes, dawdling, stopping to take in the scenery. Now, she made it in much less. She burst onto the immediate grounds of the ranch and saw Maria walking to the side door of the house as if returning from an errand.

"Maria! Maria! Help! Help!"

The woman turned, and Destiny plowed into her, clinging and babbling. Maria wrapped her arms around her, soothing, then scolding. "Tell me, Miss Destiny, what is wrong. Tell me. Now."

Destiny lifted her head to stare at the woman and realized she was crying. She swallowed back her sobbing and gasped, drawing in her breath before she could speak.

"He's dead."

Chapter Twenty

Michael and Hunter rode into Roaring Springs early in the evening.

"Hunter, I need you to keep watch while I talk with Bottoms." Michael spoke as he dismounted and tied his horse to the rail.

Hunter didn't speak, but moved to a spot where he could watch Bottoms' banker office and the Blue Peacock.

Michael walked straight to the office, but when the door refused to open—locked—he strode to the Blue Peacock and stepped inside. He spotted the man immediately near the back. No doubt, if he'd been watching, he would have seen Hunter and himself ride in.

Shaking his head at the waiter, he headed to Bottoms' table, all the while keeping an eye open for any of his employees who might be hovering close by, to keep at bay those Bottoms didn't want to talk to.

When one man rose, Michael shoved him back into his seat and bent to whisper in his ear. "Don't move. Got a man watching for the likes of you, and he's handy with a gun, and trigger happy at that. Hate to see you meet your maker before you turn thirty."

He straightened and the young man settled back into his seat, his face red as his plaid shirt.

"Smart boy." Michael patted his shoulder and walked away.

"What do you want?" Bottoms didn't bother looking up, only continued to cut his steak. He lifted his fork, placed a piece into his mouth and chewed.

"Bottoms, where were you last night?"

The man raised his gaze, his mouth a widened display of sarcastic delight. "Right here in Roaring Springs. Ask my man sitting at that table two down."

Yeah, right. As if that young clown would tell the

truth. "Uh, huh. And I suppose you have no idea who was out at my ranch, shooting an entirely innocent young girl?"

Bottoms sobered. "Miss McCulloch?"

"No, although she was in danger. Maria and Hernandez's niece was shot last night. We're fortunate she's alive."

"I see." He picked up his fork again and started to lift another piece of steak to his mouth.

He didn't have a chance. Michael slapped at his hand, sending the fork flying across the table.

Bottoms half rose, his face an angry mask, then settled into his seat again. "You asking for trouble?"

"I think you already have." Michael lowered his voice. "If you, or any of your men, come near my ranch again, you'll pay the price—"

"That's rich coming from a thief like you."

"Your pa got more than his share. If he hadn't been such a greedy, thieving murderer, none of this would be happening now."

"I aim to pay you back. One by one. One way or other. Watch your back." Bottoms stood slowly, staring straight into Michael's eyes. His words were so softly spoken, Michael wondered if he imagined them.

Bottoms sat again and gestured to a waiter. "I seem to have dropped my fork. Another one."

Michael started to turn, to walk away, but spoke over his shoulder to the man. "You've been warned."

And then he did walk away.

He should have dealt with him here and now. The man wouldn't stop, and Michael was certain Bottoms would attempt to carry out his threat—as he'd said—one way or another.

Glancing at Hunter, Michael headed to Jake's Emporium and small living quarters in the back. When he knocked, Jake Blackston answered, motioned for him to enter. Hunter settled against the wall of the building.

"Been to see Bottoms, have you?"

"Yeah, for all the good it did."

"He'll never change. You know that. Right or wrong."

"I don't care what he thinks about me, what he plans

on doing to me because of his made-up reactions to the past, but when it includes hurting my people, that's another story. I won't allow that to happen again."

"I heard about Rosita getting shot. How's she doing?"

"She's weak, but conscious and strong. She'll pull through."

"Good to hear. She's a lovely young girl." Jake lifted the coffee pot toward Michael.

"I'm hoping this can be resolved quickly before anyone else gets hurt."

Jake was quiet for a moment. "Not if Bottoms has his way. You need to stay away from Roaring Springs for a spell."

"Maybe, but that won't keep him from causing trouble."

"I'm afraid you're right on this one." Jake poured coffee into his cup, but if the expression on his face was anything to judge by, Jake was anything but happy that he was right.

~*~

Hubert Bottoms stared down at his now-cold dinner. The anger inside him was like burning acid, eating away at his very inner being. With a sudden motion, he knocked his plate and silverware off the table, hearing the crash that somehow did nothing for his mood, and ignored the shocked glances cast his direction. He wanted to hurt someone, and that someone wasn't in the Blue Peacock at the moment. The anger that fueled his actions wouldn't be eased until he killed that someone.

Lifting a hand, he sneered at the waiter who rushed to his table. "Get me another plate of food and make sure it's hot this time."

The waiter started to speak, thought better of it, and nodded before rushing back toward the kitchen.

Bottoms ignored the man and motioned for his man, who shoved back his chair and hurried to him.

"Do you think you can follow him without getting caught? Report back to me when you find where he's gone."

"Yes, sir." The man shifted from one foot to another.

"What are you waiting for, idiot? Go."

He wasn't used to showing his anger or his frustration

when his plans were waylaid. Not that they were now. Just because his enemy had thrown down the gauntlet, so to speak, meant nothing to him. Nothing did till he made his one-time friend, now enemy, pay.

And pay he would. Dearly.

He shook his head as he watched his man hurry out of the room. The town was going to pot. He was going to have to do something about that.

~*~

"Jake, you think you can keep an eye on things here a bit longer? I don't want you discovered being involved with me and then having to go up against Bottoms or his men." Michael sipped at his coffee, but kept his gaze fixed on his longtime friend. What would he have done without the encouragement the emporium owner had passed out all these years? From the time he'd been barely a teenager to now, the man had stood firm in his friendship and done it without arousing too much suspicion from others who weren't so trustworthy. The man was a gem.

"I can. So far no one's suspected our friendship, and I plan on keepin' it that way."

Michael nodded but didn't speak.

"Havin' a bank account here in town keeps our banker happy, and I've sought Bottoms financial help a few times on minor issues. I think it keeps him pacified."

"For awhile, maybe, but Jake, if they got suspicious...it wouldn't go good with you. I wouldn't put much past most of the people in this town."

"I know you don't have faith in the people here, but you've got to remember, they're under thumbs that haven't been overly understandin' with those who disagree with the, uh, rulers here." Jake lifted another biscuit, allowed the honey from a jar to dribble its sweet goodness on it, then crammed a bite into his mouth. "Hmm. That's good. You ought to try one, even if I did bake them."

"Not hungry, Jake, although if I remember correctly, you always could bake up mouth-watering biscuits. And don't you ever tell Maria I said that." He set down his cup and stretched. "You may be right on the citizens here, but don't ask me to trust them. So far, they've given me no reason to."

"You 'bout to take off for the ranch again? You're always welcome to get a few hours of shut-eye."

"I reckon I'd better go. Don't want the ranch to be without both me and Hunter too long. Hank does a fine job, but he is getting older." Michael stood. "You sure about that bank account? I hate to see you lose all you've saved through the years because of me."

Jake snorted. "Don't worry none about me. I've got enough sense to not keep all my eggs in one basket. Same place you go to is where I keep the majority of mine."

"Good for you. You always were a smart man."

"My ma never raised any stupid children."

Michael slapped him lightly on the shoulder and laughed. "I'm afraid I'll have to agree with you on that one."

When Michael turned to leave, Jake stopped him. "Sure you won't spend the night here? You could leave before daybreak and still be home fairly early. I'd feel lots more comfortable with that plan."

"You could be right, but I won't rest easy till I'm home again to make sure all's right."

"Then be careful on your ride home and keep your senses about you. I wouldn't put it past your real enemy to try anything, and especially at night. They are not forgivin' people and will do anything to take you down. I'm surprised they've waited all these years to do so. Be very careful."

"I will." Michael stared at him for a long moment. "Anytime you want to live in the country again, just come on out. I'm sure you could get a good price out of this place."

"Not yet, but maybe someday. Right now, I'm where I'm supposed to be."

Nodding, Michael opened the door, listened, then stepped out, placing his big hat on his head as he did so. The door closed behind him, locks snapped shut, and Michael hesitated, allowing his vision to adjust to the darkness. "Seen anything?"

"Not much. Some movement. Me and that guy who

tried to follow us had a right nice talk in the stable. He decided he'd best be headin' out of town before he got into too much trouble."

Michael could tell Hunter was grinning.

"It's dark as pitch out here but if you head on out of here, I'll keep watch and make sure anyone who has the notion of followin' us is occupied for a space. I'll meet you outside of town."

"Good job, Hunter. Be careful. Don't want to lose you."

Hunter grunted. "They'll have to be smarter than that runt to take me down."

"I'd say you're right about that, but I'm sure there's more where that kid came from. Don't be late and make me worry about you." Michael swung away from his manager, but he heard the soft comment Hunter threw after him.

"Don't make me worry about *you*, Mr. Michael."

He smiled. His manager was a sassy person, but invaluable. Michael would definitely do what Hunter had advised.

Chapter Twenty-one

It was raining when Destiny woke the next morning. The threatening sky from yesterday had kept its promise and brought the rain. Just the thing to enhance her mood. And to remember yesterday's horror.

She stared out the window, the depressing dark clouds and rain-streaked window urging her to cover her head and drown herself with depression. She tugged on the cover, preparing to do as her mood suggested when a knock at her door interrupted her. She waited, hoping whoever it was would go away and leave her alone.

She gave another tug on her quilt, squirming to settle more comfortably. A knock exploded into her room again.

"Go away."

"No." Another pounding, open-the-door knock.

Mr. Michael. Ugh.

"I said, go away. I'm sleeping."

"It's ten o'clock."

"I don't care. Go away."

"I'm not going away. Get up or I'm going to drag you out of that bed. Come and face the music."

That didn't sound good. Maybe silence would make him leave.

Seconds ticked off, one by one, but a minute hadn't passed before the door handle jiggled.

He was coming in.

Destiny threw back the covers and yelled as grouchily as she could. "Stay out. I'm up. I'll meet you downstairs in fifteen minutes."

"Very well. Not a minute longer."

He was threatening her? Must be really angry.

Thirteen-and-a-half minutes later, she paused in the doorway of the library and peeked in. Mr. Michael stood at the window.

"I'm here."

"Sit."

Rebelliousness rose like an angry wildcat. Forgotten was her depression, her fear he'd drag her out of her room to answer his questions. Who did he think he was? He didn't know that—that man yesterday had threatened to kidnap her and maybe worse. She'd barely escaped...

Mr. Michael turned to face her. "Tell me what happened yesterday."

His voice was so quiet. Too quiet. It sounded dangerous, and Destiny drew in a deep breath, preparing herself.

"What on earth were you doing outside the perimeter of the yard?"

"I thought I would take a short walk. I didn't realize there was still danger."

He said nothing for the longest minute she'd ever endured.

"Will you please sit down? You're making me nervous." She hadn't meant for her voice to be as scared and soft as it sounded, but it did, and there wasn't a thing she could do about it.

"As you very well should be."

"You are not my boss."

"I'm still responsible for you."

"I can take care of myself."

"Such as yesterday?"

"Exactly. I averted a kidnapping and possible, uh, other unpleasant situations."

His sigh was a heavy one, long and drawn-out. "I'm sorry. My only excuse was the worry I felt for you late last night when I learned what happened. I do think you should have thought before wandering off without knowing it was safe."

"I'm sorry I didn't think. I wasn't going to go far, but it was so nice to be outside before the storm. I quite forgot the time and possible danger with enjoying your land. I *felt* safe."

"But you weren't, as you found out quick enough."

Destiny shivered. How long had that man stared at her before revealing his presence? "I—I..."

"For what it's worth, he wasn't there."

"He was. I should know."

"Yes, but when we got there early this morning, he was gone. Whether he recovered enough to escape or his body was moved by someone, he was gone. And the rain has washed away any footprints or blood that was there before."

"I do wish I knew which way he disappeared. I won't feel safe until I know he's gone permanently."

"I want you to promise me you won't take any more walks away from the house. It's not safe, Destiny. I can have Hank on guard to go with you if you find it necessary to wander around a bit more."

"I don't need a watch guard."

"I think you do."

His words were tart, but the slight, crooked smile on his lips was teasing, then he sobered again.

"Destiny, there are things that happened in my past life that are causing trouble now. I don't know how dangerous it will get, how things will play out, but I want you to know this. If you want to move into town, that's fine, or even go back east, at least until this is over, one way or the other."

"Are you in danger?"

He hesitated. "There's always danger when there's feuding, but I don't go into it thinking of that. Those thoughts can get you killed."

"Can't you settle this like gentlemen? Peacefully?"

Mr. Michael's dry chuckle wasn't amusing. "Don't you think I've tried that? I've bent over backwards to make people happy, but when they're determined you've done them wrong and refuse to see their own—errors, then there's nothing else to do but protect your own."

Destiny studied his face. It was haggard as if he was tired, or maybe it was worry that had lined his face. Whatever, she should have been more accommodating. He was running a large ranch, after all.

She stood. "I'm going to check on Rosita then, if you're done with me."

He nodded and scrubbed a hand across his face.

At the door she stopped and turned back. "Mr. Michael?"

"Destiny?"

"That man."

"From yesterday?

"Yes."

"What about him?"

"I've seen him somewhere else."

"Where is that?"

"He was in the hotel room across from mine." There was no way she'd bring up that he'd been one of the men who'd murdered her parents. "And I saw him talking to Hubert Bottoms late one night."

"Can you describe him?"

"He was tall and thin-like and had a patch over one eye."

"Perez."

"Perez?"

"He's a gunslinger and very, very dangerous."

"Then I had every right to be afraid."

Mr. Michael slowly nodded but didn't speak, so she started to leave again.

"Destiny, you're all right? He didn't hurt you?"

She smiled. "He didn't have a chance."

And that brought a laugh from him.

~*~

She looked like one of those bluebonnet plants that bloomed in the spring. Her blue dress draped softly around her curves, the ribbon in her loose curls sat like a crown on her head, and her deep blue eyes were like sparkling sapphires, glowing with laughter and fun and joy in life—a promise that all would be all right.

Normally. Today they were more somber, but still carried the promise, albeit dimmed for the moment.

Michael didn't smile as Destiny left the room, but his heart warmed. What a difference she'd made here on the ranch. A ray of sunshine.

But a magnet for trouble.

Everyone adored her from the ranch hands to Maria and Hernandez so there was no thought of sending her home even if he wanted to. But how dangerous was it for her? Would he regret allowing her to stay on when the men after *him* would do anything to destroy him?

They'd killed his father, and he would have had his revenge had it not been for *his* father.

Michael would have killed them all, had it not been for his father's pleading words. His hatred had been strong enough, mad enough to blindly follow his emotions. But his father's last words had done the trick. They'd kept him—child that he was—from committing murder.

Yet their good intentions to keep him safe and happy didn't resolve the guilt he felt for not stopping the killings. He should have known, even though a child, that Bottoms wouldn't stop until everyone of the men were killed.

He really should have killed the man.

Still, after his father's death, one man had been the saving of him. Well, Hank *and* Maria.

She'd taken the reins of his person and bossed him, rebuked him and loved him to adulthood. He'd loved her like a mother, and she'd returned that feeling, scrubbing away some of the loneliness and anger inside him with her love.

And Hank had guided and shown him how to grow into a real man. He'd not allowed him to slack, but made him start from the bottom and climb up the hard way. Even though Hank had been unlearned in schooling, he'd insisted on Michael learning his manners as well as learning the ranch and managing all the money he'd inherited from his father. And when he'd whined and rebelled, Hank had had no trouble bringing him down a notch or two.

As he stood, the words from his mother when he was just a child reverberated in his mind as he remembered her standing in the doorway of their cabin, watching three of the partners on the porch argue and nearly come to blows over their differing opinions.

"Gold is the devil's special tool to use against men."

She'd been right, as she'd always been. Loving and sweet, born into society, she'd hardly been prepared for the life she'd jumped into when she'd married Pa. But not once had he ever heard her complain about her lot. Her face in his memory had faded over the years, but her words of wisdom had not.

That gold his father had found, right before his wife's death, had been a blessing and a curse. Murder, anger, jealousy and hatred had sprung way out of proportion, and now...

Well, now he had to deal with it.

He wasn't a youngster anymore. It was time to put an end to this feud.

Hopefully, for the last time.

~*~

His boss was in trouble, and Hunter didn't like it. Not one little bit. He had to do something about it.

Hunter propped one foot on the bottom fence rail, watching the horses enjoy the warmth of the day, then at the sky with the clouds scurrying east as if being chased by a bear. The rain was over for today, he reckoned. The sun would be popping out any minute now.

Remembering his mother was impossible. There were no pictures in his mind, no loving memories of her...at all. But Pa...that was something else. The man had been honorable, and Hunter reckoned there wasn't much of anything bigger than being honorable.

Pa and Mr. Michael's pa had been friends. That he did know. Good friends. Trustworthy friends. And they'd both been shot down dead. It wouldn't have been so bad if it'd been a fair fight, but it hadn't been. Being dead cause of a shot in the back by a double-crossing, coward of a man—well, that was the lowest of the low.

Worse, the coward had gotten off scot free.

And that was all he remembered. That period of his life was blank, dark and gone.

But he'd had Hank. When Mr. Michael had refused to talk about the past, Hank had stepped in.

Hank had shared a thing or two about the past, about what had happened back then. Hank had explained about the shootings, the caution—the promise—Mr. Michael's pa had exacted from his son. Mr. Michael's high standards came because of his pa.

Hank had filled in some of the blanks when Mr. Michael wouldn't. Not because he wanted to go against Mr. Michael. Hank loved Mr. Michael like a son. No, he'd never go against him, but he understood him and knew why Mr. Michael wouldn't talk about the past.

He'd explained in his quiet way the jealousy and distrust that finally led to the killings.

But even with Hank explaining, he wanted to know more. Something inside him urged him to get to the bottom of it. He knew that someday, he'd need that information. That someday, he'd have to make things right.

Nope, even though Mr. Michael hadn't talked about the past to him, the boy ten years Hunter's senior, and barely out of childhood himself, had made him his ward, his friend and finally his ranch hand boss. It'd been the grounding of Hunter to have someone to look up to, someone to answer to, and someone he could trust wholeheartedly.

So now Mr. Michael was in trouble, and Hunter figured it was up to him to settle this everlasting, ridiculous feud, once and for all.

But first...first he was going to go see Rosita.

~*~

"What was it like in Boston, Miss Destiny?" Rosita, cheeks pink and far from the paleness of the previous week, pled with her to describe her life in Boston before reading more of *Great Expectations*.

"It's a beautiful, blooming town, and I don't mean just in looks. Immigration is bringing many people to our country—lots of the Irish who are loud and fun and determined to find a home in a new country. The ships that dock are big and full of interesting items. There is a lot of life at the ports, and it draws me like a good-luck charm. Of course, I try to be discreet because that area can be a bit dangerous."

"Miss Destiny, you didn't really go there, did you, by yourself?"

"Yes, I did, many times. Sometimes I had a companion go with me, but few of my friends were as fascinated by the scene as me, so I went alone more times than not. All the more exciting."

"I wish I could be that brave."

"Then sometimes I would sneak into the university halls and out into the parks where the students would debate and occasionally a professor would lecture on the newest ideas of the day."

"You did that? Oh, Miss Destiny? What if you'd gotten caught?" Admiration and fear fought for dominance in the girl's eyes.

"But I didn't get caught." Destiny laughed. "And what if I had? What would be the worst thing to happen? Thrown out? Now that would be an exciting event!"

"How did you have the courage?"

"I'm not sure I thought about courage that much. I was interested in what the students were learning. I was curious, so I followed that instinct to learn more."

"I'm not sure I could have done that."

"I think you're stronger than you think."

Rosita was quiet, her gaze on the coverlet that spread across her lap. "I think—I think I would love to visit, someday, that city. Do you think that would be possible for someone like me, Miss Destiny? Am I wrong to even think something like that?"

"Nothing is impossible. We live in a wonderful country, and I think if it's your dream, your passion to visit Boston, or anywhere else on the earth, then you should do it. You have to decide what you want and go for it. I didn't know what I wanted until the last six months, and I knew I had to come west."

"I'm so glad you did." Rosita leaned forward a little and placed her hand on Destiny's arm. "Would you mind reading a little to me now?"

Destiny opened the book to the marker and began reading, doing her best to bring the story to life for Rosita. After only fifteen minutes of reading, she glanced at the other girl and saw her attention fixed on the door. She turned.

Hunter stood there.

"I'm sorry to intrude, Miss Destiny. I wanted to check on Rosita, but I will go—"

"Oh, no, please stay. We've had a nice visit, and I'm sure she'll love to visit with you now." She closed the book, placed it on the stand and rose. "I'll see you later, Rosita."

The girl nodded and smiled, but her attention was fixed on the young man who walked into the room slowly, hat in hand.

As Destiny left, the sound of their low voices followed her.

Chapter Twenty-two

Later that afternoon, as Hunter left the house, Michael approached him, and they walked toward the barn. "Hunter, I'm counting on you and Hank to keep things safe while I'm gone for a few hours. Won't be long, but I need to talk with Virge, and today's the day we're to meet."

"You and the Marshal decided to keep in touch cause of Bottoms, I suppose?"

"Right. We figured we'd better meet half way between here and town at least once a week so he can keep me updated on what's happening in town." Michael glanced at the clearing sky. "Keep an eye on Destiny so she doesn't get into any more trouble."

It'd been close to two weeks days since the party for Destiny but seemed forever. Michael hadn't been to town nor had he or any of his men seen anyone suspicious on his property since he had warned Bottoms to stay away the day after Rosita was shot. That didn't mean his enemy had forgotten his grudge or given up trying to kill him. He knew though all was quiet for the moment, he'd best not let his guard down.

"That's a mighty big assignment you're passing on to me, Mr. Michael. Don't rightly know how I'm to keep Miss Destiny reined in. She's got more spark than those mustangs you like so well."

Michael laughed. "Don't I know it, and it's a big chore, but you can do it and I'm counting on you."

Hunter heaved his britches up a notch. "Then that's what I'll do. You can count on me."

"Right." Michael swung onto Jasper's back, touched his hat and nodded at Hunter. Whirling away, Jasper broke into a canter, then slowed to a steady pace.

It took him a little over an hour, as always, to reach the spring where he'd met Virge before. Few people knew of this out-of-the-way place and a place for him or his men to stop briefly to rest before beginning the last hour of the journey to his own ranch. He'd met Virge here only a few times, but it was a quiet spot away from the concerned glances of his own ranch people. No need to upset his own over his personal matters.

At least, he hoped this mess would stay personal.

He turned right several hundred feet away from his usual stopping place and wound his way through the underbrush and trees to the actual spring. Neither Virge nor his horse were in sight, but he figured he was close by. He'd never known the man to be late for anything.

He was right. Seconds after he'd dismounted Jasper and swung the reins over a branch, Virge appeared from behind a large boulder.

"Figured you were around somewhere. Any news?"

Virge said nothing, but the grin on his face told Michael he was pleased to see him again. He wasn't much of a talker, more of a doer, but he was worth his weight in gold for giving what was needed.

"The girl pull through?"

"Rosita? Yes, she's fine. But—"

"I know. Dirty trick shooting an innocent girl. You have a right to be angry."

Somehow that statement didn't convince him to feel happier.

"I have some news." Virge stooped to tear off a leaf of the peppermint that grew beside the spring then thrust it into his mouth. "Nothing beats the taste of mint. Reminds me of my mother's fudge she'd make. Always put a drop of peppermint in it."

"Your news?"

"Yeah, that." He chewed another ten seconds. "Figured I'd have Associate sneak into Roaring Springs yesterday on pretense of needing help with some legal work. Being a fairly new marshal, he wouldn't be recognized yet."

Didn't sound like much, but Michael knew not to question his friend's methods. The man always seemed to know what he was doing.

"I'm fairly well known in these parts..."

"But not overly loved," Michael taunted.

His friend glared at him for a moment. "I'd say you're loved even less, if you want to get down to the nitty-gritty details."

"You're right about that. Go ahead."

"I can get by with hanging around some, as if I'm passing through, but too much time in any town raises questions why a marshal has nothing better to do but eating and drinking. People get suspicious, you know. So I told Associate—he's smart—to talk to the attorney and ask for the best available land to buy. I don't suppose you want to take a guess what his answer was?"

"No, I can't."

"Referred him to the bank. Said the bank manager could give him a few ideas."

"Bottoms. So even the town lawyer is in cahoots with him. But if Bottoms thinks he can get his hands on mine, he's badly mistaken. Maybe some of the land farther west?"

"Guess again. He wouldn't give Associate any clear idea of what he was talking about, but seems he knows of some land that he possibly can get his hands on by fall."

His land for sure then.

"Think he's serious about killing me? He's made the threat enough times over the last few years."

"I've got more. My associate..."

Virge always talked about his partner, who worked with him more often than not, as *associate*.

"...talked with a few of the men around town. They tried to be discreet talking about Bottoms, but the rumors are that the prestigious banker in town has big plans to take over this part of the state." Virge eyed him. "We knew he was hiring a gunslinger—had our suspicions, you know—but seems he's brought in the worst of the worst. The one we figured he'd use, if he could get him. You know who that means. The man who'll do whatever for a price. Bottoms has plenty of money. He can pay for the best."

Michael stared at the clear water from the spring. "I know my men are good. Better than good, but they're not killers. I don't expect them to go up against this type of man."

"Every one of your men would stand with you in a heartbeat if you ask."

"I know that, but I don't want to ask. This is my fight."

"You can't do it alone. Associate and I will stand with you, but we have to do it legally."

Michael nodded. "I understand, and it's what I prefer."

"Right now Associate and I can moderate what's happening in Roaring Springs. I can also, if you give the word, call in a couple other marshals, although I prefer not to do so—" Virge raised a hand, his gaze suddenly alert.

Michael drew his gun, his own gaze searching the land before him. "I suggest we move to a more secure place."

"I agree."

Both men dove for their chosen hiding places. Only moments later, Virge spoke.

"Not crazy waiting on someone else to take the initiative."

"Nor I. I'm going to see if I can locate our unwanted guest. Cover me."

"Let me do that. You have more to lose than me."

"Are you saying you'd miss me if worse came to worst?"

"Not so much, but I fear Maria's wrath."

Michael snickered. "Coward."

"Yeah. Go, if you're going."

Taking a deep breath, Michael headed, in a roundabout way, toward where both he and Virge sensed another person was sneaking up to them.

There was plenty of brush and bushes and a healthy stand of trees, so moving to where he wanted to go wasn't that difficult, but not knowing who or how many were out there was another story. If he let down his guard even a fraction, it might end up being the last thing he ever did. He wouldn't put anything past Bottoms, or whoever he'd hired, to take him out.

He was carefully feeling his way around the spring and back toward his goal, when he almost stumbled on their target. Crouched behind a large tree trunk was a man. He didn't look like a hired killer, but who knew? He wouldn't take a chance.

In a calm voice, he spoke. "We've got you covered. Hands in the air and turn slowly around."

The man stiffened, raised his hands and turned. From behind the man, Michael saw Virge stand and walk toward them.

"Who is he?"

"No one much, only a little trouble. 'Fraid he followed you from town. He goes by Ernie."

"You think Mr. Bottoms trusts a stranger who rides into town askin' legal questions?" The man sneered at Virge, but when his hands inched down, Virge waved his gun at him, and the man reached for the sky again. "He'll just send more men. Yer done, mister. Whatever you did to him, figure yer done in these parts. I'd ride on out if'n I was you."

"You're not me, and I'm not riding anywhere except back to my ranch." Michael's retort sent an angry red to the man's face. "I thought I told you not to come near my property again. Why are you following Virge?"

"I've got nothin' to say. Jest 'cause there's two of you don't mean nothin'."

"Looks pretty overpowering, if you ask me." Virge muttered. "I'll have my associate take him in. No use letting him loose where he can annoy the daylights out of everyone."

"Sounds good, but before you do that..." Michael turned to the man. "What's Bottoms planning?"

"I ain't talkin' anymore."

"Who was the person who shot the girl on my property?"

The man pressed his lips together. "Ain't talkin'."

"I think it was him." Michael eyed their captive. "But then, I doubt he has the guts to shoot anyone."

"I'd say you're right about that," Virge added. "Still, might be kind of fun to just go ahead and string him up—"

"Whatcha wanna go and do that fer? I ain't hurt nobody. Now Cain, he might be the one yer lookin' for." His gaze shot from Virge to Michael.

"Guess he might have something useful for us after all." Michael grinned.

"Nah, not him. He isn't high enough on Bottoms' list

to know much of anything. Just an errand boy, if that. Let me take him. Of course, if he doesn't make it to the jail..." Virge shrugged.

"I know a'plenty."

Michael kept a straight face as he ordered. "Then you'd best get to talking. I'm not sure how long I can hold this man off."

"Bottoms did send some guy to cause some trouble at yer place. I reckon it was him that shot that girl."

Michael felt his face going stone cold. Some might call it anger filling his very being, but it wasn't. Nope. It was worse. Much worse. The same emotion that had swept through him when his father had been murdered.

And it scared him.

He didn't get this deadly coldness inside him often, but he knew how much the emotion could cloud a man's judgement, and he had too much to lose to allow that.

"What's his name?"

"Only know him by Cain."

"Cain Wilson?" The marshal jerked his gaze back to the man in front of him.

"I reckon that might be him. Seen him a time or two through the years. He was on the stagecoach—you know, the other man you ran off yer place."

"Do you know him?" Michael's sharp question was aimed at Virge.

"Yeah. He's a sharp-shooter, not in the same league as some, but still good. Is he the one who accosted Destiny?

"He's one of the men who was on the stagecoach, along with this man, when Destiny arrived. It broke down, and I allowed the people to stay at my ranch for a couple nights." Michael swiped a hand through his hair.

Virge motioned to Ernie. "You seen any other new men in town that Bottoms hired?"

"I reckon not."

"You better not be holding anything back."

"Yeah." Michael glanced at Ernie. "You haven't told us much. What else do you have? I have a notion to let this guy string you up just for the fun of it."

"Don't know nothin' else."

"Virge, you still got that long rope on—?"

"Wait." Ernie interrupted Michael. "This is the last thing I know. So if yer gonna hang me, then you might as well git at it."

"Go on then. Virge, I'm sure, will let your judge know you helped out here."

"Perez is in town. You know who he is, doncha?" At Michael's nod, Ernie went on. "I ain't skeered much of anyone, but that pedro is one skeery man. I heard he shot a man dead cause he stared at him too long, and one time he hung a dog just cause the dog sniffed his pant leg. Don't wanna tangle with him. He's a mean, crazy pedro."

"Get to the point."

The man looked at him as if he thought he was crazy too. "Well, I reckon there's only one reason Mr. Bottoms calls in someone like him. He's plannin' on killin' you."

~*~

Late that afternoon, Michael met Hunter and Hank out by the barns. "Virge and I caught one of Bottoms' men today—Ernie that you escorted off the ranch. Bottoms sent Ernie out to follow Virge to find out what a marshal was doing in Roaring Springs, and Bottoms has, for sure, hired Perez to take me out."

"Well, we figured that, but it's good to know for shore." Hank shook his head. "Sounds like war. What you gonna do, Boss?"

"Not sure we can stand up against that man and the rest Bottoms will send as back up."

"Don't you worry none, Boss. We'll be waitin' on the varmints." Hunter punched at a fence post. "We can take 'em."

"What I can't understand is why Perez is waiting around. He's known to be a fast worker, doesn't piddle around." Michael stared into the distance, wondering if, even now, someone out there, beyond his vision, was watching, waiting.

"I reckon there's a definite reason he ain't tried to kill you yet, Boss. Could be Bottoms has another project more important or could be Perez has something on his mind. Some plan or idea." Hank slapped the rope he carried against the fence over and over again.

Agitated, the man was. Or worried. Hank might not be

a learned man, but he was definitely intuitive. He knew how to read men, and Michael figured he was right on target this time. Perez was acting out of character, and that was troubling. And dangerous.

Hunter shot him a worried glance. "You don't reckon he's thinkin' of Miss Destiny, do you?"

"I reckon he better not be." Michael shot Hunter a worried glance in return. "I want you two to be on high alert. Warn the other hands and don't take any chances. I'd like all of you to go in twos when you're away from the ranch. I prefer none of you head into Roaring Springs, at least until this it settled."

"Got it, Boss. We'll make sure the boys understand what you want." Hank switched the twig he chewed on from one side of his jaw to the other. "You know you kin count on us. Ain't never been afraid to confront the wrong, and not about to start now."

"And Hank, I'd like you to ride out to our Indian friends over on the north side of the property to keep their eyes open. Ask them to make sure no one stampedes the cattle we have out there and let us know if they see anyone who shouldn't be there."

"I'll go right now, Boss."

"Thanks, Hank. Appreciate that. I don't expect anyone to take chances. Don't want to lose any of you if we can help it."

Hunter said little, only stared into the distance as if thinking. Michael knew the boy was older in experience than years, but he hoped he wasn't planning anything foolish. And anyone who went up against Perez thinking he was going to be an easy take-down would be courting a death wish.

"You find out who shot Rosita?"

Michael studied Hunter. "You're not planning on doing anything foolish, Hunter?"

"You know I never go at anything half-cocked, Boss. I jest need to know."

"Virge did say Bottoms sent Cain Wilson out here to harass us. He probably didn't mean to shoot someone, but..."

"Doesn't matter his plan. He did shoot someone, and I

don't plan on letting that go, Boss. I can't. You know I can't."

He didn't want to agree. He wanted Hunter to stay away from the likes of Cain, but he wouldn't. With or without his approval, Hunter would do what he thought was the right thing to do.

And he couldn't fault him for that.

Minutes later, Michael found Destiny in the kitchen helping Maria bake pies. "Those look delicious. Don't suppose I could sample a slice to make sure they're fit for consumption?"

Destiny laughed, but Maria slapped at Michael's hand when he reached across the table to grab a piece of crust. "You know better than that. You'll spoil your supper."

"When have you ever known me to turn down your supper, Maria? Come on, just a smidgen. I'm starving."

Maria's dark eyes stared at him for a moment. "I can't tell whether he is really starving or just teasing to get what he wants."

Destiny rolled out the crust for the last pie. She shot a glance at him, a smirk on her face. "He's fibbing, Maria. Look at that twinkle in his eyes. Any time a man has twinkling eyes, you know he's lying or about to, to you. I never trust a man with twinkles in his eyes."

"You're making that up so I can't get a piece of pie. I don't have twinkles in my eyes." She thought it was funny, did she? Two could play that game. "How many slices of apple did you eat when Maria wasn't watching?"

Her quick glance at Maria assured him his hunch was correct. "I was going to invite you for a special walk after supper, but since you're so determined to be mean...well, I'll go by myself."

Ha. That would get her goat. See how fast she switched her tune now.

"A special walk? Where would that be?"

"Wouldn't you like to know? Since you won't be going—"

"Maria, maybe we could share one little piece with this man since he's so hungry."

Michael laughed with Maria, and Destiny joined in as the cook handed her boss a big slice of the apple pie.

Twenty minutes after supper, Michael waited in the library where Destiny was to meet him for their evening walk. He was about to think she'd decided not to come when she appeared in the doorway, a shawl lightly wrapped around her shoulders.

He made a pretense of looking at his pocket watch. "You're late. Again."

"Sorry. I stopped to see Rosita for a few minutes and couldn't get away till Hunter showed up. He really cares about her, doesn't he?"

"Yes, he does. I think he has matrimony plans for the future." He motioned for her to precede him into the hallway and picked up a large bouquet of flowers. "He wants to get established first before making any declarations to her."

"Meaning a home?"

"Yes, that and some extra savings. I don't think he'll have to worry much about that, though."

Destiny's gaze searched his face. "Why not? He is your overseer here, and I suppose it's a good job, but it takes a lot of work and money to make a real home. I would think there are always some unexpected incidents that take money to hurdle. Will he be able to do both within a reasonable time?"

"Hunter is young, but he is mature in his thinking. He doesn't rush into things, listens when he's instructed, and quick to learn. I've always planned on sharing part of my land with him when the time comes. I have more than I need, and, if he wants it, it's his. I'll also see that my hands and I give him all the help we can in building his first home. I think he can have his own place up and running within a year or two."

"You have his life all planned out."

Was that a bit of an edge in her voice? Possibly, but she didn't know the circumstances. Didn't realize who Hunter was.

"No, not exactly, but it's my duty and desire to help him all I can. He not only deserves it, but he's entitled."

"Whatever that means."

When he refused to take her bait, she went on.

"What do you mean by entitled?"

He was quiet a moment, deciding how to answer that. He should have been more careful in how he worded his response. Only he, Hank and Maria and Hernandez knew the depth to that answer.

"He's been with me since a kid. I owe it to him." A good enough answer without a lot of depth, but it would do. "Let's not talk about all that anymore. I want you to enjoy the scenery. Look."

Chapter Twenty-three

The valley opened up below them in a scene Destiny had seldom seen before. It hadn't been too much a climb to reach the spot, but she stood rooted, taking in the sight. "It's magnificent. I've seen some beautiful sights on your ranch, awesome even, but this...this is so breath-takingly lovely, I want to cry."

"Crying makes me nervous, so please don't."

Mr. Michael's voice had such a touch of panic in it that Destiny had to laugh.

"Well, I'll certainly try not to, since crying sends you into a panic. But you did spring this on me. No warning whatsoever that it would take my breath away."

"I did tell you it was a special place."

"You did, but not how special. Do you come here often?"

"Only a few times a year. I'm way too busy to come often, but it's my favorite spot on my land." He hesitated. "And there's another reason for it being so special. Come." He took her hand and led her to the right.

There, not fifty feet ahead was an enclosed area built of large rocks that formed a fenced-in cemetery. Inside were two wooden crosses, and Destiny turned to Mr. Michael, not speaking, but the question, she was sure, was clear in her eyes.

"Yes, it's my parents' graves." He lifted the flowers. "Hence these."

She'd noticed them, of course, but they'd been so busy talking, she'd not given herself time to ask about them. Truthfully, she'd thought perhaps, maybe—hoped?—he'd planned to give them to her.

What was she thinking?

"The flowers are beautiful. May I go in?"

"Of course. Come." Leading her to a small opening, he stepped close to his mother's grave and laid the flowers on top of it. For several minutes, he stood there, saying nothing, his head bowed. Abruptly, he stepped closer to his father's grave and laid a hand on the wooden cross, standing quietly even longer.

"He was such a good man. Strong and brave and good-hearted. What good did that do him? Backstabbed and murdered in the end."

"Really, Mr. Michael?" How sad. What else did she not know about this man she'd grown to respect and to—

"Yes, really. Sometimes, in the past more so than today, I've been bitter and wanted revenge on the murderer. But of what use is that? It won't bring Pa back, and it's surely not going to ever heal my hurt from losing him." He shrugged. "I think he deserves retribution, but who am I to do so?"

"I suppose we all, at times, want to wreak revenge on our enemies, but I agree with you, it really does little good. And sometimes, I think, more harm than good." Destiny hesitated a second wondering if she asked about the pictures in his library, if he would think her too curious. "Those pictures in your library, are they your parents?"

He nodded. "The only one I have of them. That's why I keep it locked up. It was taken before I was born."

"I understand." That didn't explain the other items locked in with the picture. What of them?

He took her arm and guided her out of the enclosed area.

"Let's head back. Would you like to walk alongside the stream? It takes a little longer to walk back following it, but well worth it."

"I'd like that."

The storm clouds had passed through, leaving behind warm weather, yet not too hot, and with the evening shadows, a light shawl was a welcome addition to her outfit. Destiny tightened hers around her a bit even as she took in the three deer across the stream, in the meadow. She pointed. "Look."

"If you keep your eyes open, you'll see quite a few wildlife. I walk this trail sometimes when I want to ponder life and be by myself for awhile. I've seen coyotes, elk, deer and even a time or two bears."

"Does that happen often?"

"Not enough." He touched her arm and pointed. "See the owl?"

Midway up in the trees right above them sat a great horned owl. Even from where they were standing, Destiny could see his blinking eyes and the slow rotation of the head as he took in the surroundings. She laughed and glanced up at Mr. Michael.

His gaze was fixed on her. They were too close, but he still had his hand on her arm and to step away would seem—overly cautious? Perhaps. If she didn't then, she realized, she'd be so caught up in that intense gaze of his, she'd be hopelessly lost.

Was his face moving closer?

Was he going to *kiss* her?

~*~

Destiny's face was filled with wonder, so near to his own, so tempting that it was almost Michael's undoing. He'd never wanted anything so much as to kiss this girl who stood beside him, with uplifted face, lips as moist and soft as the dew on an early morning, eyes lit with joy and a small smile that widened her pink lips, staring upward at the creature in the tree.

He leaned closer, tempted beyond measure, and she looked at him. He saw the sudden understanding and the hunger in her eyes. She tilted her head, the desire for the kiss blatantly obvious.

Michael dipped his head, his lips almost—almost touching hers, and—

"Whoo. Whoo."

He jerked backward and then laughed at the surprise and disappointment that registered in her eyes. Her laughter joined his as the tension from the second before dissipated.

The flutter of wings drew his attention upward again.

"He's gone."

"He didn't enjoy the moment as much as—"

"Us?" Her question was breathless and tentative, but laughter again edged her voice.

"Probably." He took her hand and guided her around a large rock. "I wanted you to see the flowers up ahead before we reach the house."

"I love flowers."

What had he done? Given her the idea he was interested? That he wanted to be serious in pursuing her when he knew he couldn't? Not with what faced him in the near future.

A fight? No doubt. Ruin. He hoped not. Death? Possibly.

One thing he knew, he wasn't about to go down without a fight.

After that...

Michael glanced at the woman beside him.

After that, well, time would tell.

~*~

When Michael stepped into the breakfast room of his home early the next morning, he caught sight of Virge standing at the serving table filling his plate with some of Maria's buttermilk biscuits and gravy, two sausage patties and heaped-up, brown-fried potatoes.

"Are you trying to eat me out of house and home?"

Virge didn't bother glancing at him. "Gotta get my wages somewhere and figured Maria's fine cooking will fill the bill very well." He paused long enough to send an amused glance at him.

"What are you doing here on such a bright and sunny morning? Just saw you yesterday."

Virge's glance said a lot, but he didn't speak. He sat at the table situated in front of a large window and dug into his plate of food. It was only after half was gone that he laid down his fork. "You and your men still on alert? Not letting your guard down?"

"Minimum duty with our normal chores. Hunter, Hank and the rest are rotating guard duties on specific areas of my land. Our Indian friends on the north side are covering that area. Of course, we can't be everywhere, but we've got it covered as good as we can. What's up?"

"Associate said Perez killed a man the other day, said he heard it was a fair fight. Sounds to me like Bottoms is tightening things up a mite in Roaring Springs. Once he has that accomplished, you know what he'll push for next. Perez won't tarry. He's known to be a fast worker and gets the job done."

"He wouldn't be in demand if he didn't."

"Michael, you tell those men of yours to be careful. He won't blink twice about taking them out if they stand in his way, or even for no reason."

"Understood." Michael hesitated. "I know there's nothing you can do yet…"

Virge shook his head. "Not yet. He's got a lot of suspicions hanging around him, and a few notices for his arrest in different towns, but no one, and I mean no one, has seen or caught him actually doing the killing. And those suspected of hiring him do no talking."

"Makes it hard to arrest him."

"He's like a ghost. I can't say it any stronger. Watch your back. This guy doesn't care how he kills, fair or not."

"I understand."

"Then I've got to go. I'll be back in a day or two." Virge paused a moment at the doorway, nodded at Michael, and…

The explosive crash of a window breaking sent both men to the floor as the shot blasted through the air like a lightning strike. Michael drew his gun, crouching near the window. He drew a breath and gave a quick gander out the broken window just as another shot whizzed past him. He jerked back.

Whoever was out there had a scope or was close to the house. No one shot with accuracy like that without one or the other. Although some he'd known had come pretty close.

"You hurt?" Michael called out to his friend.

No answer.

"Virge?" He swung his gaze around.

Virge sat on the floor near the doorway, his back against the wall. Blood spread across the man's shoulder, his face white as the sheets Maria washed on Mondays.

"Virge!" On his belly, Michael squirmed for the doorway, and once there, he realized the man was still conscious.

"I'm all…right. Hand me my gun."

"Sit still till I examine your wound." He pulled open the man's shirt and examined his wound. He'd lost a lot of blood but seemed lucid, although hazy. He reached up to pull off the cloth covering the serving table—metal dishes clattering as they fell—and pressed it against Virge's shoulder. He squirmed into the hallway and called out.

Maria came running.

"Mr. Michael, I heard a shot. What's—"

"Will you be able to get him to a room?"

She paused as her gaze caught sight of Virge. She didn't speak, only ran back toward the kitchen area. Seconds later, Hernandez and Maria hurried toward him, Maria carrying cloths.

Michael and Hernandez both crouched and pulled the man into the hallway, away from the doorway. When Michael stood, he looked at them both. "Can you two take care of him?"

"Yes, Mr. Michael. You do what you need to do. We will take good care of Virge." Hernandez nodded.

"Good." As he started to leave, he placed a hand on Maria's shoulder. "Don't let him die, Maria."

She looked at him. "He will not die in my care, Mr. Michael, not with a shoulder wound. He will live."

Nodding, he turned and started down the hallway to his living area when he heard Virge's grumbling behind him.

"Don't need no coddling. Hand me my gun. Mr. Michael, don't you go out there alone."

Michael heard and smiled, but ignored him. A shoulder shot wouldn't keep that contrary man down. He'd be up in a day or two, demanding to be let out of the house.

Inside the library he took his rifle down, from the pegs on the wall, and grabbed the bullets he needed. Then moving to the front door, he listened, his gaze fixed on the distance. The man had shot from the east, so somewhere, he'd gotten off the trail and crossed Michael's land to get to the spot he'd shot from. He hadn't targeted the barn nor the ranch hand building. Just the house. Meaning, he wasn't after anyone else but him. Or maybe the marshal.

There was still no sight of him, no more shots, so perhaps he had gone.

Or not. Lying in wait, knowing Michael wouldn't sit it out. If he knew anything about him—and Michael was sure Bottoms had laid it all out to him—Perez would guess he wouldn't hole up. He'd go looking for him. So Perez would be alert and ready. He was no fool.

A thought struck him. He should have reminded Maria and Hernandez not to allow anyone in the house to go out. He whirled and headed back down the hall. "Maria."

She rushed out of a side room. "Mr. Michael?"

"Don't allow anyone—anyone, do you understand me, Maria?—to leave the house. Make sure Destiny understands that, and no matter what she says, don't allow her outside."

"She'll listen to me. You go, Mr. Michael, but don't you come back to me dead. Do you hear *me*?"

"Yes, Maria. I hear you and will do my best." He didn't waste any more time, but trotted back to the door, gave the outside surrounding area another cursory study, and then slipped out the door and headed for the nearest tree. Just as he rounded it, another shot rang out, clipping his chosen tree but missing him. Thank God.

If Perez was as smart as all the tales about him were reported to be true, then he wouldn't wait on Michael to get to him. No, he'd be on the move and not running from him. He wasn't a coward, whatever else he might be.

He knew the path he wanted to angle toward Perez, full of shelter with trees and rock boulders that would shield him from Perez's sight. Pulling in a deep breath, Michael crouched and ran toward his next target with no gun shots following or hitting him. He didn't pause long, but kept on the move, slowly, methodically, advancing toward *his* target.

He kept his eyes peeled, and his ears alert, acknowledging again that the man would already be on the move. He wasn't about to be caught unaware.

Moments later, Michael paused to give his surroundings yet another study and didn't see anything, not a movement, not a—

There. That flicker. Off a rifle scope. No. Perez wouldn't be that stupid. It was a trick. He'd bet his shirt on that. He'd better utilize extreme caution if he wanted to live through this.

He needn't have worried. Two gunshots rang out at the same time, and Michael froze. Two?

He moved then, cautious, but not wasting any time. The two simultaneous gun shots could only mean one thing. Someone else was out there shooting.

Who?

~*~

Hunter knew as soon as he heard the first gunshot what was happening. Someone was after Mr. Michael.

His hero—Mr. Michael—wasn't a novice. No sirree. But he was alone in this fight against a known killer, and Hunter wasn't about to let that happen, no matter what Mr. Michael wanted. He'd die for the man who'd been like an older brother to him.

He picked up his rifle and headed toward the door of the manager's ranch cabin.

It was time.

~*~

Destiny was sitting with Rosita when she heard the first shot and the crash of glass downstairs. Pausing, she turned her head, listening.

"What's happening, Miss Destiny?" Rosita opened her eyes.

"That was a gunshot, and close." She laid down her book. "I'd better go check and see what's going on."

"Miss Destiny..."

"I'll be careful, Rosita. And I'll come back and let you know what's going on."

Destiny kept walking straight downstairs where Maria caught her standing in the doorway of the breakfast room. "What happened, Maria?"

"Someone's shooting outside. Mr. Michael went to investigate, but he warned us to stay inside. The doors are locked, and as soon as it's safe, Hernandez will board up the window in here. Right now, I could use your help. Come."

Destiny caught Maria's arm. "Is Mr. Michael safe?"

Maria's solemn gaze held hers. "I don't know. I doubt it, but we will pray. Now come."

"Should I go check on him?"

"No, we must do as he says. No one can be outside roaming around with a shooter. Now stop your fussing and come."

Destiny followed the woman, but her heart lent wings to her spirit straight to the man teasing death outside in the hills.

~*~

Hunter slipped through the woods, silent as a deer seeking refuge. Mr. Michael, Hank and even a few of Mr. Michael's Indian friends had taught him to hunt, to walk through the woods undetected, to learn sign and look for herbs and wild edible food. He wasn't afraid, just cautious as he sought the man trying to harm Mr. Michael.

Mr. Michael would be out here somewhere and Hunter for sure didn't want to run into him, on purpose or accidentally, but he wanted to get to the man causing harm before Mr. Michael did.

He had a pretty good feeling where the man would be. He'd have to be there to shoot out the dining area window.

Hunter adjusted his stride, slowing, moving carefully. Those rocks up ahead...He edged softly around the biggest boulder and caught sight of the man's bay. He blew out soft breaths of air, warning the horse, to make sure he didn't nicker, then he was close enough to rub a hand over its back.

He lifted his gun as he stepped closer and caught sight of the man, back to him, kneeling with his gun aimed the opposite direction from Hunter.

"Mister, drop your gun."

The man started to turn, but Hunter spoke again. "Toss that gun away if you want to live to see the sun set tonight."

The gun landed on the ground feet away from Hunter. The man raised up, slowly, slowly, legs staightening...then...

With one quick swivel toward Hunter, his hideout gun

was blasting.

But Hunter had been waiting. He'd seen enough poker players—and other men—to know some of them carried a hidden gun, and this man wasn't any different. Hunter was shooting barely a split second behind the other man, even as he felt his own body recoil at the shot that struck him. He stumbled back.

But he didn't fall. Not until he made sure the other man—the man who'd shot Rosita—had fallen and wasn't getting back up. Then, body weaving, a dark funnel swallowed his mind, and he dropped to the ground, gun still in hand, but unconscious.

~*~

Michael took it slow getting to where he figured those gunshots came from. Not knowing what he'd find or who would be waiting was reason enough to continue taking care. The shots had been so close to simultaneous they almost seemed as one, but they weren't. He was close enough, he could tell from the sound of them, they had come from two different guns. Definitely not from the same gun.

Another three hundred feet, he smelled the gun smoke. Edging through a strand of tall trees, he spotted two figures.

Both on the ground.

Michael walked closer to the man farthest away from him and felt shock race through his body. It wasn't Perez, for sure. It was the man—Cain—from the stagecoach, not moving, the bleeding wound on his chest telling the story, and all he needed to know. He was dead.

Moving away from the killer, not giving him another glance, he hurried toward the other body—and got the shock of all shocks. He dropped to his knees as his gaze took in the sight of Hunter, his shoulder blood red.

He pulled off his shirt and pressed it against his manager's wound, turning as he did so to glance once again at the figure of Cain lying twenty feet away, eyes open and staring at nothing.

He turned back to the young man lying still as death. He had to get him back to the ranch where he could get more help.

"Boss?"

Michael saw Hank step out into view from behind a tree.

"Heard shots and figured I'd better check it out." Hank looked down at Hunter. "The kid hurt bad?"

"Yeah."

Hank glanced over at Cain. "That the killer?"

"It is. Let's get Hunter to the ranch house." Michael walked over to where Cain's bay horse was tied, ran a hand quickly over the horse's neck then led him over to Hank. "Can you send Jackson after the body later? Have him take it into Roaring Springs."

"Will do, Boss."

With Hank's help, he lifted Hunter up onto the saddle then swung up behind Hunter and wrapped arms around the young man.

Without another glance around, he headed home. To Maria, who'd do her best to save Hunter.

~*~

Michael opened his eyes, surprised at the sun shining through his window. It was early, and by the looks of it, another warm, sunny day was in store.

Yesterday had been the hardest day of his life. Watching Hunter lying in his bed, restless and fighting to get up for most of the day. Maria had shaken her head more times than not, pondering, he knew, why Hunter was so agitated.

He threw back his covers, surprised that he'd slept all night. First things first. He was assuming Hunter was still alive or Maria would have woken him. With the strict orders he'd given her last evening, she wouldn't have ignored his demands.

The knock on the door broke into his thoughts. "Come in, Maria."

It wasn't Maria. Destiny walked in as if she owned the place. "I've brought you breakfast. Maria said to tell you she'd better not see your face until every last bite is gone."

He chuckled. The woman was too bossy for her size. "I need to check on Hunter."

"I already did. He's not conscious yet, but he's holding

his own." Destiny pulled a stand close to his chair and motioned for him to sit.

He nodded then scooped up a bite of his scrambled eggs and lifted a piece of the bacon to his lips. "This is good, as usual."

"What's Maria saying about Hunter?"

Her hesitation told him all he needed to know. Shoving the stand aside, he stood. "Never mind. I'll go check for myself."

"But Maria said for you to eat every bite."

"I'm not hungry."

"You're going to be in trouble..." she called after him as he left his room.

"I know." He spoke over his shoulder as he hurried down the hallway.

Right now, all he cared about was Hunter. The boy had to live. He just had to.

Chapter Twenty-four

"**I** must go to see him, Miss Destiny. I must." Rosita threw the cover off her lap and started to stand.

"No, you mustn't. Maria would never have allowed you to roam the house if she'd known you would want to try to assist her." Destiny hurried over to her and laid a firm hand on the girl's shoulder.

It'd been three days since Mr. Michael and Hank had carried Hunter into the ranch house. Rosita had been wild with grief, and it'd been all Destiny could do to keep her away from the man.

Now, Rosita was on the point of rebelling.

"But I must." Rosita looked up at Destiny. Big tears like sparkly diamonds hung at the edge of her eyelids then rolled slowly down her cheeks. "I really must. Tia Maria is being overly protective. It's not right. I want to be there with Hunter."

Destiny's heart beat with pity. Wouldn't she have felt the same if it'd been Mr. Michael?

What was happening? First Rosita, then Virge, and now Hunter. It was frightening, when she had time to think about it, but thankfully, she hadn't had that time.

Maria had instructed Destiny in no uncertain tones, days earlier, that Rosita could roam a bit about the house, but she didn't want to catch her coming near Hunter's room. She was too afraid of Rosita relapsing. Of course, when Rosita had heard the restriction, she'd wanted to ignore Maria's orders. It wasn't fair, she'd said. And Destiny had agreed. Wholeheartedly.

But Maria was the law in Mr. Michael's house, and no one, in their right mind, crossed her when she was worrying herself over everyone.

Thankfully, Virge's injury hadn't been nearly as serious as it had first looked. He'd climbed from his bed defiantly and left against the protests of Maria. Still hurting, with an arm in a sling, but insisting he'd been in lots worse shape in times past.

But poor Hunter. Two nights after being brought home, he'd grown weaker in spite of the constant attention from Maria and Mr. Michael. Destiny had tried her best to be there, if either needed her, but those two were like well-oiled stagecoaches that never encountered a bump on any trail.

Earlier tonight, Maria had shaken her head, a sign she doubted he'd make it to sunrise. In spite of her best effort, the wound had gotten infected, giving Hunter a seriously high fever.

They'd kept it a secret from Rosita, fearing a setback, but the girl was smart. She'd known, and only remained in her room because Mr. Michael and Maria had marched into her room and threatened to send her home if she stepped foot outside her bedroom door.

She'd obeyed, but grudgingly. And angrily.

Now, Destiny feared Rosita had reached the end of her rope.

Dropping down beside the chair, she put as much cheerfulness as she could in her voice. "Rosita, let me go talk with Maria. I think I can get her to allow you to see Hunter. With Mr. Michael's help, he can help you get there. Would that do?"

Rosita stared at her for a long minute, her eyes giving away her doubt. "I trust you, Miss Destiny. Please make Tia Maria see. Otherwise..."

Destiny stood. "I will do my best. I promise."

Casting her a last glance and hoping Rosita would be good, Destiny hurried toward Hunter's room. He was still way too sick to move to the managers' cabin, so the room off the kitchen, that Maria used as a room to rest in when necessary during the day, continued to be his recovery room.

She peeked into the room. Mr. Michael sat close beside the bed, head bowed, and silent. Drawing a deep breath, she tiptoed inside the room and spoke. "How is he?"

"Stable right now. Maria thinks there will be a crisis tonight."

Destiny stepped closer. How could she bother this

man with Rosita's request right now when he was so burdened down? She opened her mouth to speak, but he beat her to it.

"Destiny, I don't know how I can go on if—if something happens to Hunter. I've practically raised him. He's been like a brother, a son to me. He hasn't lived yet, hasn't had time for a life of his own, to propose to Rosita and settle down..."

"No, but he's had you as a mentor, someone to look up to, and I'm sure he's loved you for all you've done for him." She wanted to weep at the sadness in this man's voice, but swallowed back the tears. "I will pray for him."

He nodded. "Thanks, Destiny. Right now, God seems far away."

"I know. I know." She knelt down beside him. "Let me sit with him a bit please. You can stretch your legs. Besides, Rosita is begging to see him. I'm afraid she will do something rash if we don't allow her to come down. She is feeling so much better and is only a little weak."

"Do you think she should?"

"Yes, I do. She is not a child, and I've grown to love and respect her. She is strong in spirit, but sweet, and will be good for Hunter." Destiny cast a quick glance at the figure lying so death-like in the bed. "She might even be able to reach him when no one else can. Yes, I do think it would be good for her and Hunter."

Mr. Michael stood. "Then I will talk with Maria. If she agrees, I will bring her downstairs for just a few minutes."

Destiny sent him a smile, hoping it would cheer him a little, but he seemed not to notice as he turned to leave. She settled into his chair and picked up Hunter's limp hand, stroking it, preparing to speak soft words of comfort and encouragement to him—if he could even hear her.

But a familiar voice behind her interrupted her thoughts.

"Thanks, Destiny. Knowing you're here, helping where needed, caring for Rosita and Virge while Maria's so busy with Hunter has been a blessing. I'm glad you're here."

Her back was to him, and she didn't turn around, but

she didn't need to. Mr. Michael's words warmed her heart and sent tears to her eyes. Knowing he recognized her presence and the little she was doing was worth all the sleepless nights and worry she'd endured the last week. Maybe, just maybe things would work out after all, and she'd never have to leave this place.

Destiny looked down at her left hand and smiled at her crossed fingers.

~*~

It was late. Destiny rose from the bedside chair she'd sat in, after reading for half an hour, and talking with Rosita much longer, then listening as the young girl murmured until, at last, she slipped off to sleep. How long, was the question, but surely longer than a few minutes.

Maria had refused to allow Rosita to see Hunter, afraid it would set her back physically. Rosita hadn't cried, hadn't thrown a fit or even tried to sneak down on her own. Destiny knew her friend was heartbroken.

She herself was aching to go check on Hunter. Yes, Mr. Michael and Maria were at his bedside doing the little they could do, so her presence there wouldn't be necessary. But her heart yearned to run as fast as she could to Mr. Michael's side with what little encouragement and hope she could convey to him. His agony over possibly losing Hunter was unbearable.

She had so many unanswered questions. So very many things she needed to know, yet the last two weeks had been filled with trauma that had left all of them unsettled and on edge. She had no time to look for a little boy from her past named Caleb. No time to even wish she could find the thief who'd stolen her mother's locket even though she knew it would be a hopeless task. It was long gone by now. Probably around the neck of some girl who'd never treasure it like she had.

Tiptoeing toward the door, she stopped when Rosita's soft whisper reached her ears.

"Miss Destiny, will you come and get me if Hunter gets worse?"

Destiny turned back toward Rosita and the bed. "I thought you were asleep."

A faint smile slid across her lips and disappeared.

"Almost. Promise me you'll let me know if he's worse."

Destiny didn't want to promise. How could this precious girl—a girl she now considered a friend—handle the news if—God forbid—Hunter was worse? Or died?

How could she bear it if it had been Mr. Michael who lay in bed close to death?

"Please?"

"I will, Rosita. I will come and get you. But don't give up. We've got to trust that Hunter will pull through this."

Rosita nodded, and Destiny turned to leave again.

"I will say prayers, Miss Destiny. That is the only hope I have."

Rosita's voice was barely a whisper, but Destiny heard. She didn't stop walking, but hurried to the room where Hunter lay.

Dying?

Destiny hoped not. She really, really hoped not.

~*~

Michael stood at the only window in the room where Hunter lay. His heart was so heavy he felt it was almost dragging the ground.

An occasional hand stirred to handle the late evening, but necessary tasks. Most, though, congregated closer, lanterns nearby, waiting with him, hoping with him, and some, no doubt, even praying for the crisis to pass favorably.

He wanted to cry at the possibility of Hunter dying. He wanted to, but he wouldn't. He was a man, and as Pa used to say, men don't cry.

The moon was low in the sky, climbing steadily, with only a few twinkling stars helping to dispel the dark. Michael's men outside the house kept vigil, some sitting, some moving quietly about, but all waiting. With him.

The sound of a footstep came from behind him, but before he could move, a warm arm brushed his. The soft, barely-there touch, the warmth from her hand on his arm steadied his emotions, and he felt the heaviness ease within him. Not much, but enough he didn't feel that smothering awfulness inside him.

She didn't speak, only stared out the window as he did, and maybe like him, looked upward into the

203

heavens, hoping, praying God would hear their prayers.

When Maria entered the room and went straight to Hunter, Michael didn't move, and neither did Destiny. He waited, and so did she.

Minutes later, he heard the rustle of Maria's dress as she straightened, and her deep breath before she spoke.

"The crisis will be tonight. Not yet, but soon. I suggest you both get some rest. I will send my husband for you when I know more."

"I'm staying."

"No, Mr. Michael, go. I don't want any anxiousness in this room tonight. I will take good care of him. I will send for you when it's time. Go now."

He didn't want to listen to her. Didn't want any suggestion that Hunter might not pull through, but he knew she was right. He was dead from lack of sleep and worry. If he could rest, even for five minutes, he'd have better control over his emotions—if...

He loosened his arm from Destiny's light clasp and left the room. Not for long. Just enough that Maria would think he was listening to her.

Then he'd be back. He, as a young teen, had taken the boy under his wing, and he wasn't about to leave him alone for long now.

~*~

Destiny peeked through heavy lids as the sun laid warm beams on her face. Where was she? Not in her cozy room here on Mr. Michael's ranch—

She sat upright. Maria leaned over Hunter's bed, checking his temperature with the back of one hand. Mr. Michael stood on the other side, his face still, his brow wrinkled with worry.

Maria straightened, and like the rising sun sharing its brightness, Maria's face brightened. "He's past the crisis. He's made it. He'll pull through."

Destiny moved to Maria and hugged her, but Mr. Michael didn't move. His face lost its worry-lines, his body relaxed. When he lifted his gaze from Hunter to Maria, Destiny saw the gratefulness in his eyes.

"Thank you, Maria. Thank you."

That was all, and he turned and left the room.

Maria returned Destiny's hug, then thrust her away.

"Why are you crying? This is no time to cry, but rejoice. Our prayers have been heard."

Destiny laughed. "I know. I know. You did it, Maria. You pulled him through."

"No, not I, you silly girl." Maria shook her head and flapped a hand at her. "Now you must go and inform Rosita of this good news. Run, child, before she takes it in that stubborn head of hers to descend the stairs on her own."

And Destiny ran. Not only because she'd been ordered by this woman she'd come to cherish dearly, but because she was overcome with joy at Hunter's sure recovery.

She burst into Rosita's room and stopped short.

Rosita sat up in bed, not moving, her gaze fixed on her. Expectant. Hopeful. At peace.

Destiny didn't have to speak. Rosita gave a slight nod and opened her arms. Destiny went to her and the two friends hugged, the happy tears sliding down their cheeks.

~*~

"Mr. Michael." Destiny stepped into the rose garden.

"Destiny. Thanks for coming."

It'd been two weeks since Hunter had passed his crisis. The worry about Bottoms and what he would try next hammered him. The potential of harm to Destiny, or any of his people, dogged him continually.

"Is something wrong?"

Her anxious tone prodded him to get to his point.

"No, that's not why I asked you to meet me."

"Why then?"

He motioned her to sit on the garden bench and then sat beside her. "Now that things have quieted down a bit, I felt I needed to ask you if you're desiring to return to Roaring Springs? Or would you like for me to arrange transportation for you back to Boston?"

"Is that what you want?" Her gaze searched his face.

"Well, I'm not sure I'm comfortable with you spending time alone in Roaring Springs, given all that's happened here. I couldn't forgive myself if something happened to you because of my enemies' hatred of me."

Her face was so still, her hands folded and refolded

the handkerchief in her lap. "I'm not afraid."

"But I am. You don't realize the danger."

She raised her gaze again to his face, and her brows were drawn together in a frown. "What danger? Why would I be in danger because of you?"

Why was she being so stubborn when all he wanted to do was make sure she was cared for? If she was tired of being here, tired of all the drama and wanted to go home, then he'd like to make sure it happened swiftly and comfortably for her.

"Why is there danger now? After all, we haven't had any incidents since that man who tried to kill you died, so you should be all right, shouldn't you? Am I right?"

"Are you being serious, Destiny? That killer was hired all right, but he wasn't to take me down. His part was only harassment. If anyone got in the way, then so be it. The man behind all of this is still alive. And he's not finished trying to ruin me." He knew a trace of irritation rode through his words, but for the life of him, he couldn't help it. Women. They could be more contrary than that stubborn mule Pa used to own.

"Well, who is this behind-the-scenes-man? Why don't you go and take care of it?"

Her flippant reply did nothing to ease his irritation. "Do you think I haven't tried? I've bent over backward, trying to appease this greedy person. He's determined to ruin me."

"I think you're over-reacting." She shrugged and turned slightly away from him.

"I am not. You're not listening. The man behind this is dangerous, and he will do anything—anything, I say, to ruin me. That's even destroying my land, killing those close to me—"

"Who is he? I want to know his name."

"You know him. Bottoms, who pretends he's a banker in town. The greediest man in the whole state."

Her eyes widened. "Really? I think you're mistaken. He was very pleasant to me."

Well, mostly.

"Really?" It was his turn to project sarcasm in his voice. "You are acting like a stubborn child who's unwilling to listen to reason. All I want is to make sure—

"

Destiny stood. "I won't listen to any more of your—your suggestions. If you really want me gone that much, since I've been such a hindrance, then I'll be packed and ready to go to Roaring Springs in the morning. Early. Please ask Hank if he'll have the wagon ready."

She flipped her skirt away as she swiveled away from him. He let out a sigh. He'd really, really messed that up. Whatever was up her craw, he couldn't figure it out.

But what had he expected? With the tensions going on for the last two weeks, no wonder she was a bundle of nerves. He should have been gentler with her. Women, he figured, needed a soft touch, and he'd come across as a horrible boar. He should go after her and explain.

He stared after her retreating figure, but the definite slam of the side door was proof enough for him that any explanation would be better off at another time.

Destiny McCulloch was in no mood to listen.

~*~

Destiny rose early. She figured she might as well, seeing she'd not slept a wink all night. After Mr. Michael's definite—well, almost definite—statement that she should leave the ranch and go back to Boston, she'd been devastated. Truthfully, her emotions were still in high gear from all that had happened in the last week, so she might have been a little—hmmm, overly agitated at his words.

Still, he could have been more generous. A lot more generous. She'd felt unwanted, just when she'd begun to feel appreciated and welcomed as a member of his household.

So much for that thought. She closed her carpet bag. Hank had already come for her trunk minutes before, so all she had to do now was head downstairs, but she didn't.

Gazing around her room, she felt tears prick her lids. She did not want to leave. Leave Maria and her husband? Rosita, who'd she just lately come to count as a friend? Hunter, who was healing nicely, but who still had a long way to go? Hank, and his fatherly, gentle ways?

And Mr. Michael. She wanted to smack him for his unfeeling words, his attitude toward her and most of all, his disregard for what she'd thought of as the beginning of...

What? Romance? She scoffed to herself at her own foolishness. He'd never once given her indication he cared in that way. Not once. She'd imagined it. Silly her.

She strode to her window and looked down. Hank stood by the wagon, checking out the wheels—her heart leaped. Perhaps there was something wrong, and they wouldn't be able to leave.

No, he was nodding and walking toward the hitched horses, so all must be fine.

There was no sign of anyone else. Not Maria, or any of the other ranch hands. Not Rosita, who was beginning to stray from her room quite often.

And not Mr. Michael.

Destiny angrily jerked away from the window.

And all the time she'd been here, she'd found out nothing about the boy Caleb. She should have, but she'd been so interested in weaving herself into the household, she'd allowed her main goal in coming west, to languish in the back of her mind. Almost forgotten.

She sighed. As much as she didn't want it, as much as she wanted to run away from it, she had to go. There was no way she'd allow Mr. Michael drag her down the stairs and toss her on that wagon like a sack of grain. She'd walk dignified and genteelly down those stairs and never give this place—or him!—another thought.

The stairs were a mile long, but her descent took no time. Too soon, she handed over her carpet bag to Hank. Too soon, he was holding out his hand to help her into the wagon.

But she turned and studied the ranch house one last time. No one stood at the windows waving. No Mr. Michael came running out the door, yelling he'd made a mistake and didn't want her to go.

Stretching out a hand blindly, because of the tears clouding her vision, she allowed gentle Hank to help her into the wagon and adjust her skirt. So much for appreciation. She bowed her head and refused to gaze back as Hank slapped the reins and headed to the gate at the end of the lane.

She would not look back. She would not look back...

Hank scrambled out of the wagon and opened the gate, and Destiny picked up the reins to urge the horses through it. When Hank had refastened the gate and climbed back into the wagon, Destiny gave up.

She looked back and realized the truth.

No one cared that she was leaving the ranch.

Chapter Twenty-five

Michael stared long after the wagon disappeared from his view. He'd wanted to go after her, to stop the wagon and tell her not to go. But he hadn't.

He'd thought long about the best and safest method of keeping her out of harm's way, and the only thing he could come up with was sending her away. The shootings had been the tipping point. As long as she was in Roaring Springs, away from the ranch and not associated with it, or if she decided to head back east, then, he figured, she ought to be fine. Bottoms wouldn't touch her.

Destiny was angry and hurt. He'd not been in any windows or doorways watching her leave. There was no way he'd allow her to see him. It would have been the undoing of her and maybe stop what he wanted to accomplish.

No, he hadn't been watching from the ranch house. But he'd stood behind that big tree at the gate watching, and he'd seen her. He'd been so close, he'd caught the longing glance back at the ranch, the slump of her shoulders, and even the tears that gathered in her eyes. She hadn't seen him, but Hank, he was sure, had.

He'd allowed her to leave, thinking he was using good judgment.

He hoped he'd decided wisely.

~*~

Two days later, Destiny strolled down the street of Roaring Springs and opened the door of the emporium. Jake, behind the long countertop, looked up, and a smile lit up his thin face.

"Miss Destiny, what are you doing here in Roaring Springs?"

She opened then closed her mouth. No way would she tell him she'd been sent away from the ranch like a misbehaving child being punished. "I needed some town life."

That ought to do. She bent over his row of soaps on display and sniffed. Hmmm. The lavender one was nice. "I'll take this."

Jake nodded and reached for the bar. "Haven't seen much of the ranch people for a few weeks. Everything all right out that way?"

"Fine. Fine. Do you have any linen? I'd like a yard to hem into handkerchiefs in my spare—"

"How long you in town for?"

Would the man never quit asking questions she didn't want to answer? "I don't know. Your festival is coming up, and I sort of promised Mr. Bottoms I'd attend with him."

"You did? That's still a few weeks away."

The look of shock on the man's face had her questioning her own judgment. "Is there some reason I shouldn't go with him?"

He looked at her, but said not a word.

"Well, I've got other business in town. I'll stop back by after lunch and pick up my items. Oh, and add some white thread to my order, please. Good day, Jake."

"Good day, Miss Destiny. You be careful out there who you 'ssociate with. Not everyone is as they seem."

She stared at him a moment, then nodded. "I'm always careful, Jake, and can take care of myself. Good day."

Giving him no more time for warnings, she shut the door firmly behind her back. She'd barely taken two steps when the door opened again. Jake Blackston stood there.

"Miss Destiny?"

What now?

"Yes, Jake?"

"We need to talk."

She didn't want to talk.

She really ought to send another telegram to Richard. But she didn't want to do that either. It'd been so long, she'd almost forgotten what he looked like.

Lunch at the Blue Peacock sounded good, but then

she'd run the chance of meeting Bottoms. Meeting Mr. Bottoms wasn't something high on her list, and she knew hardly anyone in the town. Maybe she could visit each of the other stores, chat a little with the owner and see if any of them might know of a grown Caleb.

Eyeing the multiple stores lining the street where she could possibly find information about Caleb, she wondered if it was a waste of time. She started to glance down at her mother's locket and remembered it'd been stolen.

I can't do this today.

Her room beckoned, and she wanted, oh, so much to obey, wanted to run to get to a sanctuary where she didn't have to answer questions or avoid people she had no desire to talk with.

And most of all, she wanted to go home. Not to Boston, but to the ranch. To Mr. Michael.

None of these things was going to happen.

She heaved a sigh of disappointment. Blinking back the tears that threatened to fill her eyes, she looked at Jake, standing patiently—or so it seemed—waiting on her to answer him.

"Should we go inside?"

"Please." He held open the door.

Sighing, she reentered the emporium again. Probably to another batch of questions. Or advice, which was even worse.

Jake went behind his counter and fiddled with something beneath it, then pulled out a piece of paper. Only then did he speak again.

"Destiny, what was yer mother's name?"

What? Why on earth did he need to know that? He didn't. She opened her mouth to object, but he beat her to it.

"Please, Destiny. If what you say is what I think you'll say, then it's important. At least to me."

She studied him. She did like Jake. A lot. And he was Mr. Michael's friend after all. Just because she was hurt and upset didn't mean she ought to take it out on him.

"It was Shannon."

"I thought so. From Boston, she was, right?"

"Yes..."

"Why?"

"Because yer mother was my sister. She was comin' west to meet me. I heard she got killed, but didn't know she had a girl child."

"But that means…"

Jake was grinning. "Yep. Yer my niece, and I'm yer uncle."

~*~

Michael couldn't believe how Hunter had bounced back. Although Maria wouldn't hear of him being up walking around, let alone sitting up, he was alert and restless, telling everyone who dared enter his recovery room that he was sick all right, but of being coddled.

Maria let it go in one ear and out the other, but the men shied away from lingering too long in the room, loathe to argue with his persistence. Fleeing was the word the cowhands teased each other with, and none denied it.

That was why when Hunter got word Michael was having a meeting with his closest hands and Virge, he insisted they hold it in his room or he was getting out of his bed and the room one way or the other.

Hernandez had conveniently dragged five chairs into Hunter's room, and now, Virge, his associate, Hank, Jackson and, of course, Hunter, listened as Michael talked over the situation with them.

"Heard you took Cain Wilson out." Virge sipped his coffee then nodded at Hunter.

"I did."

"Reckon it was worth takin' a bullet to kill that swine."

"Worth it to me, and more. He needed to be dead, anyone shootin' a girl." Hunter's tone didn't permit any argument. He meant what he said and wouldn't take it back.

"He had it comin'. You'll get no trouble from me over it." He glanced at Michael. "What's your plan? You can't go riding into town shooting anyone who stands in your way. I'd have to bring you in."

"Not planning on it. But so far, reason hasn't worked. I've talked until I'm done talking." Michael ran a hand through his hair.

"He's been more reasonable than I would have been."

Hunter's grumble was only a slight bit more agitated than Michael felt.

"Might as well go over it again so everyone'll be knowledgeable about what happened."

He didn't want to. At all. But he figured he might as well.

"Years ago, my pa, Hunter's pa, Bottom's pa and another man went together in business. It was a bad set-up from the beginning. The man back east was backing our adventure with his money, Hunter's pa and mine were doing the work, and Bottom's pa kept the books."

"Never liked that man even as a kid." Hunter scowled.

"Neither did Pa, and I figure Bottom's pa was the least trustworthy, given what happened afterward."

"What did happen?" Virge leaned forward.

"Bottoms' pa constantly badgered Pa, constantly accusing him of cheating, crooking him, but Pa was smart if unlearned. He knew how to handle the man and most times it was settled peaceably. But when Bottoms' stole the gold Pa was taking to town to have assessed, Hunter's Pa tried to stop him, and Bottoms's pa killed him."

"Was there anyone else there to verify the killing?" Virge stood and paced a couple of times before sitting again.

"Only one person." Michael looked over at Hunter.

"Hunter? He had to have been a kid. Maybe he was mistaken or they both shot?"

"I was not mistaken. Nor blind. And Bottoms's pa wasn't shot. He killed my pa, shot him in the back. What kind of man does that?"

"Hunter's right. Pa and I found Hunter, and his father who didn't have his gun on him at the time."

Virge nodded and motioned for Michael to continue.

"Here's where it gets crazy. Bottoms took the gold, and there was a lot of it, thinking he'd gotten it all. Pa thought the vein was nearly gone, so I figure Bottoms decided he'd take it all. My thinking is it's what he had planned all along."

Michael sneaked a quick glance at Hunter, but the young man was staring out the window as if disinterested.

His mind flashed back to the four-year-old boy sobbing over his dead pa night after night. He'd seen, now and then, glimpses of the bitterness and anger that stayed for the most part hidden inside Hunter. That little bit of hardness that made him into the marksman he was today.

Michael was good with a gun. Very good. But Hunter? If he hadn't taken the boy under his own youngster wings and raised him as a little brother, Hunter would have turned out much worse. A gunslinger?

Possibly. The young man's only redemption was the gentleness and loyalty that was instilled deep within him—traits he'd definitely inherited from his pa. That and himself had been the saving of a young life that could have gone bad.

Michael acknowledged it. Hunter's eyes carried, so much of the time, the sadness inside him. He could be angry at the young man for killing Cain, but he wasn't. That sadness told him all he needed to know. Hunter would keep his bitterness and anger under check. Maybe not forever. But definitely not something he'd allow to rule him.

Knowing that made Michael realize more than anything else that Hunter was a man. And had every right to make his own decisions.

Virge was staring at him, wondering, probably, why he stood there without speaking.

"What Bottoms didn't know at the time was Pa had laid back the money from what he'd already had assessed earlier. He hadn't told Bottoms knowing he'd want his share early. Pa wanted to wait till the fourth partner got here to split it evenly."

"And?"

"What Bottoms stole was more than the other three partners were to divide. He took the money and left town with his family. None of us heard anything from them for years. It was only five years ago that we found out our new banker in town was the son of Billy Bob Bottoms. He came back, looking rich and important, and has fooled the town's people into thinking he's a good man ever since. But from the research I've done, he's a troublemaker. Hops from town to town, overruns it through crooked deals, then hightails it and leaves the town broke. But no one—or I should say—few of the town's people will listen."

"But why does he badger you now? His pa got more money than his share."

"I don't know how he found out about us. Like I said, his father's was much larger. I think it's just he's greedy. Never happy unless he has the upper hand."

"And upper hand means he's determined to control the town, one way or the other. Including you, though you're not actually a part of the town." Virge swiped at a fly that buzzed around his head.

"Sounds about right. I didn't see the shootin' of Hunter's pa, but I knew Bert Bottoms' pa. Never trusted him nor what I've seen out of young Bottoms. Wouldn't put it past his lyin' about the banker bit. Anyone can do a might of studyin' enough to pass off as a learned person. That don't make it so." Hank handed Hunter a glass of water. "Drink, lad. Maria said—"

Hunter grabbed the glass, and a bit spilled onto the blanket covering his legs. "And not to dispute everyone's comments, but Billy Bob Bottoms wasn't just greedy or crazy, he was mean as a rattlesnake. I saw it in his eyes time after time, and being a little kid, he scared me, but when he shot Pa, that's when I saw the same dead look as those snakes. There was no soul in that man, and I reckon he done passed it on to his son."

For a long moment, no one spoke.

Michael stared at the boy he had practically raised. His own pa had been shot soon afterwards by the same hand that had killed Hunter's pa. Michael had had to grow up fast. And it had only been because of Hank that he was who he was today. He swallowed down the emotion.

"The vein ran out, and though I found a small vein on some additional property I bought, it was a separate deal from the partnership and much later in time."

Hunter sat up a little. "When he appeared in town one day and set up shop as a banker and found out Mr. Michael had settled outside of town and was doing good, he was so jealous, I think it's eaten away any little bit of decency that might have been hidden somewhere inside his gut, which wasn't much, if you ask me." Hunter flopped back against his pillow again.

"Don't be fooled. He's a powerful man in town and has most of them wrapped around his little finger. They're blind, and whatever Bottoms says goes around here." Michael motioned to Maria when she appeared at the door with another pot of coffee.

"That's why you stay away from the town for the most part." Virge held out his cup for a refill.

"Exactly. I'm not one to go looking for trouble."

Virge sipped at the brown liquid in his cup. "I reckon you have a plan."

"Not really, but I have to do something. I can't let these shootings continue."

"And who's to say he won't take it into his head to bring in more gunslingers?" Hank's words were so quiet they were that much more grim.

"I reckon now's as good a time as any to tell you what I've learned. I wanted to get your versions of history between all of you and the Bottoms' family."

Michael gave him a sharp glance. "You know something we don't?"

"Yeah, I do. Here's the gist of it.

"Bottoms' pa only died a year or so before young Bottoms headed west. Seems his crooked ways caught up with him, and someone—the sheriffs back east could never find out who did it—shot him in the back one night. They found him two days later in an alley in a bad part of town."

"Are you serious?"

"I am. He died in such a similar manner as your fathers—it makes me almost question how it could be without involving—"

"Virge. Stop right there. None of us could have done this. You know this."

"You didn't let me finish. If I didn't know you better and you vouched for Hunter, then I might have doubts, but I do know you. You're solid gold, my friend. I believe you."

Michael gave him a nod of appreciation for that trust.

"There's not much I can do unless I have proof of something. And everyone I've contacted in other towns have no definite proof. Seems all he has done is done in a way that nothing can be pinned on him." Virge gave his head another rub. "He's smart all right."

"And that's the heart of it. The deals he pulls off, the people he pulls into his schemes either suffer by being charged for the crime, pay with their savings being taken by him by what seems to be, legitimate means, or by being forced to give up their property by inability to keep their agreements, again by him."

"Then it's hopeless. We'll never be able to get him goin' legitimately." Hunter's frustrated words echoed what they all were feeling, if their expressions were anything to go on.

"We need someone to go in who can trick him into believing them, but will catch him in the act. Know someone who could do that?" Virge tapped the arm of the chair he sat in.

Michael glanced at each of the men. No one spoke or offered up a suggestion.

"Well then, what about that gal of yours?" Virge stared intently at Michael as if to force his agreement.

"My gal? Who are you talking about?" He should have kept quiet, because not only did Virge crack a grin, but the rest offered sly grins at his response.

"Yeah. Yours. Think she's got it in her to pull something like this off?"

"Are you talking about Maria? No way—"

"Come on, Mr. Michael, you know who he's talkin' about." Hunter's grin just about split from ear to ear.

"Are you talking about *Destiny*?

"Why not? She's smart and good looking enough to catch Bottoms' attention. Think she'd do it?"

"Absolutely not. Do you see her anywhere around here? She didn't exactly leave thinking highly of me, I'm sure, and I doubt she'd do anything I asked her to do." Michael jumped up and strode to the window and back twice before anyone interrupted his agitated march.

"Why not, Mr. Michael? She's got spunk and loves adventure." Hunter sat up again and leaned on an arm to support himself.

"'Cause I said so, that's why. I will not have her involved in this. Why do you think I sent her away? It's bad enough we've had three people shot on my property because of this mess." He sat, then jumped up again. "I'll give up everything before I allow her to do something like this."

"You're wrong, Mr. Michael." The quiet voice spoke from the doorway, filled with confidence and determination to sway him. "Miss Destiny's not fragile. She's full of life and courage and love for her friends. She'd jump at this, and not carelessly, but with thought and determination to succeed."

"Maria?" Michael turned and stared at his cook.

"Yes, it's me." Maria walked into the room and right up to her boss, staring into his face. "Miss Destiny is a strong woman. You do her wrong by insisting she shouldn't help. You know that. You broke her heart by sending her away when all she wanted was to make her home here. Do you think you have all the answers? Do you think you know her? Not so much, Mr. Michael, if you don't know that she loves you."

Her words had descended into a whisper, but Michael heard, and he felt as if his heart had stopped beating. Did Maria even know what she'd just said?

He'd thought of Destiny as nothing more than a distraction. Attractive, alluring distraction, to be sure. Tempting, even. But to think she loved him? She was way too...

What? Young? Independent? Stubborn? Well, what was wrong with that?

"I don't want her in danger, and this suggestion sounds like she would be." Could he really be considering this?

Virge looked at each of the men in the room and then at Maria. "It seems she's our best shot at pulling Bottoms in. I think we ought to seriously make plans on how to do it."

"I don't know—"

"Michael, I agree with Maria. She's no fragile flower petal. Talk to her. If she's willin', then go for it. If it makes you feel better, I'll stay in town and keep watch over her."

Hank's offer was sincere enough, but Michael still hesitated. And he knew why.

"No, not you, Hank. We don't need Bottoms suspicious. He doesn't know Associate or me, at least not well, and he may wonder why we're around so much, but that might take his focus off of Destiny. Associate and I will keep watch over your Destiny, Mr. Michael."

Virge's words were sincere, and he knew the man meant what he was saying. But...

Michael stood still, staring into the night. He'd never been one to be afraid, but had just accepted what had to be done and what would be done, regardless of what he wanted. Yet tonight, his body felt as if he was on fire with fear.

And he couldn't put that fear out, no matter how much he tried to douse it with hollow assurances, that all would be all right.

~*~

It'd been a week since Destiny had been dumped in Roaring Springs, and it had been a whole week of misery. Bored out of her mind, discouraged by the unfriendly people—but then she hadn't put herself out any to make friends. She'd avoided the Blue Peacock, not wanting to run into Bottoms.

Destiny sat at her window upstairs in her hotel room late one night, staring out onto the dark street below. The street was almost empty save for a few people hurrying toward their homes and a few men staggering, arguing to themselves or to anyone who happened to be loitering nearby. Lifting her gaze heavenward, the stars were bright, with one, probably the brightest, twinkling at her, and she gave it a look of approval. A bit of hope in her dismal world right now.

That and the fact she had a real live uncle living in the same town as she was. That fact eased the lonesomeness a bit, but not much.

Uncle Jake—sounded odd to say it—had urged her not to talk to anyone, including Mr. Michael, about their relationship yet. He figured—he said—he needed to be careful. If Bottoms found out they were related, he might somehow use it against either one of them. Anytime, he reckoned, Bottoms would come after him.

And she'd agreed to keep quiet for awhile.

In spite of that good news, she was still discouraged. That was what she was, and maybe a tad sad. Or was she plain out feeling sorry for herself? She shrugged. Didn't matter. Why had she allowed Mr. Michael to run her away? She could have called on Maria to side with her. Even a fake illness could have stopped his easy dismissal of her presence.

She'd thought herself valuable during all the shootings, to him and his household, but obviously not enough to keep her close.

Perhaps she should go back to Boston. At least there her school friends and others valued her—

The sound of several soft knocks on her door jerked her attention from her own pity party. Who would be knocking on her door this time of the evening?

She'd seen no sign of the men who'd occupied the room across from her's when she was last here. Easing out of her chair, she tiptoed across the room and pressed her ear against the door. No sound. Wait. Was that a slight scuffling of feet?

"Who's there?"

A soft voice answered. "Miss Destiny. This is Virge, U.S. Marshal, and Mr. Michael's friend. May I talk with you?"

What did she have to do with a marshal? And that one in particular. The same one who'd tried to give her orders at Mr. Michael's party.

Fumbling with the lock, she finally managed to get it undone and opened the door a crack. Two men stood outside, one of them holding out a badge, and she studied it. Looked legitimate to her.

She opened the door and motioned them inside. "I know you."

"I reckon. Nearly shot me."

Destiny smothered her sudden giggle. She'd forgotten about that. No wonder he'd been so unpleasant at the party. "Why are you here?"

"Mr. Michael needs your help." Virge shoved his badge

into his shirt pocket.

Her heart skipped a beat. "What's wrong with him?"

"He's not sick or injured, but someone is trying to kill him."

"I figured as much. With three people getting shot while I was at his ranch. He told me Mr. Bottoms is after him. Is he? And why do you think I can help?" Did they expect her to reason with the man?

"May we sit down? This might take awhile."

Destiny glanced at the one chair in the room. "Well—"

Virge chuckled. "I see. Well, we'll stand then. You sit."

"Take the chair, your friend will have to sit on the floor, and I'll sit on the bed. How's that?"

Virge nodded. "Here's the plan..."

Chapter Twenty-six

In the morning, Destiny headed to the desk in the front of the hotel where a young woman worked. She was a pretty-enough woman, or she would have been had she'd dressed a tad bit better. And her hair could have stood an updated hairdo. But she looked friendly, although tired. She'd never engaged her in a real conversation, but now...well, now, it was time to make friends. This woman would work fine for the plans.

"Excuse me. I know you're busy..."

The woman was reading some kind of book so she couldn't be that busy. Obviously.

"...but could you help me with something?"

The red-head looked at her and straightened. "Of course."

"Could you recommend which store has the best hats? I've heard there's a lady who doesn't have a store but who makes them identical to the best back east. I'd love to buy one for the upcoming fest."

"Oh, yes, Delia's my dearest friend and very knowledgeable about the fashions back east. I hardly think you'd be disappointed with her work." She leaned in close. "She makes them to order, you know."

"She sounds just like the person I'd love making my hat." Destiny frowned. "I don't suppose, no I couldn't ask it of you...I've noticed how busy you are."

The woman laughed. "Sometimes it is hard to keep up. My husband and I own this place, and we do good business, but he's not one to hire more employees than necessary. Thinks I can do everything, almost. And then he's out of town so much. But I do love him. He's very smart."

Really? And leave your poor wife here working herself to death because he didn't want to pay for more help? Destiny held back the sniff of sarcasm.

"But I'm rambling. Please go ahead and ask."

"I hate to ask it, seeing you're so busy."

"Please, do."

"I wonder, do you suppose you could get someone else to work this afternoon so you could go with me to visit your friend? And didn't you say your husband's out of town? Why not have supper with me at the Blue Peacock afterwards? It would be nice to have a friend."

For a moment the woman stared at her, the blankness in her eyes giving her away. She'd never done such a thing, possibly ever. Destiny's heart melted a little.

"I'm not sure Henry would be pleased. He trusts me to handle the hotel."

"With no rest? No time for yourself?" Destiny frowned the tiniest bit to convey her own confusion. "Perhaps it's time to let Henry know there needs to be some slight changes."

The troubled look changed quickly to confusion, then hope.

Destiny threw in the clincher. "I'll buy your supper. Perhaps that would help smooth over his—his objection?"

"I think it would." She mumbled the words, then straightened her shoulders. "I'll do it. Perhaps it is time for Henry to learn I'm not his housemaid. What time would you like to leave?"

"Four?"

"Four it is."

~*~

At four that afternoon, Destiny descended the stairs of the hotel and looked around for the woman. Why hadn't she asked her name? She didn't see her anywhere—wait. Was that—it couldn't be.

The woman turned from the desk and glanced at her, smiled and lifted a hand.

Destiny hurried over to her. "You look lovely."

"Thank you. I figured if I was going to do this, I'd do it right. I haven't dressed like this since—I don't remember when. I've forgotten how to look like a lady."

"Well, you certainly look like one now. Shall we go?"

"We shall." The woman smiled. "It's on the other side of town, a bit out of town actually, but not far. A nice walk."

"Sounds perfect. By the way, I guess we should introduce ourselves if we're going to be friends. I'm Destiny McCulloch from Boston."

"Boston? How nice. I'm from Philadelphia. And my name is Ruby Harlow."

"Really? I've been there, with friends. Why did you come west?"

"I fell in love. Henry came from a nice home, but had no interest in his father's business. He wanted adventure, and so did I if he wanted it. We married and headed west. Ended up here where he could begin a new business. We had enough for a down payment on the property, borrowed the rest, and have been going strong for two years. We should have it paid off in two more years."

"That is exciting. No children?"

Ruby's face fell. "Not yet."

Destiny patted her arm. "You've got plenty of time. They will come. I'm sure of it."

"I hope so." She motioned. "There's her house. You'll like her."

~*~

Two hours later, Destiny and Ruby entered the Blue Peacock. She knew exactly what table Bottoms insisted on when he ate at the Blue Peacock. She should, as she'd dined there with him before. She requested the nearest table to his. He was already seated there with his back to her, so it was easy—so far—to put her plan into action. She didn't want him to notice her too soon and kept her voice low until the right moment. Then when Ruby asked a question, she knew it was time.

"Do you have friends around here?" Ruby picked up the menu. "I haven't had chicken for awhile. I think I'll go with that. They don't have it often, you know."

Destiny propped her chin on her fist, raised her voice in as melancholy manner as she could. "I did have. I had someone I was very fond of."

Ruby's eyes widened. "That sounds—"

"Sad? I guess it is. He's a handsome man, wealthy and well known around here. You might know him?"

"Who?" Ruby's question was a gasp of interest.

"Mr. Michael. I thought so much of him. I think—I think I was falling in love with him." she paused, waiting that fraction of a second to increase the tension. "I will say it. I loved him."

"Destiny. You say 'loved.' Did something happen to him?" Ruby laid down the menu and leaned forward. "Did he *die*?"

"Oh, no. He's very much alive, but there's another girl out at his ranch, and though I think I was very helpful to him when he was having some...some troubles, he sent me away without any encouragement that he returned my love. And before you think I imagined it all, he did make me think he cared. I just don't know what I'm going to do now."

Ruby sat back in her chair and fanned herself with her hand. "I really didn't know him, but he always seemed such a gentleman the few times I ran into him. I'm so shocked I hardly know what to say."

"There's nothing to say. The thing is, I really don't know what to do now. Stay for a bit, which is what I want to do, or go back east."

"Only you can decide, dear Destiny, but I sincerely hope you won't leave just yet. We've only become friends, and I hate to lose you so soon. It's been such a lovely few hours."

"I feel the same way." Destiny reached across to grip Ruby's hand when the other woman's gaze lifted.

"Miss McCulloch."

Destiny gasped, but her insides smiled at her success. The man she was fishing to snag with this scheme stood beside their table. "Why, Mr. Bottoms. Are you dining here tonight?"

"Yes, I am. I couldn't help overhearing a little of your conversation. It sounded as if you are troubled. May I see you tomorrow? Perhaps talking with an old friend might help?"

With him being the 'old friend'? She didn't think so.

"Of course. I'd love to see you again." She bowed her head in mock modesty.

"Lunch, say one?"

"I'd like that."

Bottoms tipped his hat then and excused himself, and Destiny watched his departure, her mind only half-listening to a rambling Ruby.

~*~

Rosita's chair was pulled up close to Hunter's bed. She held a book she was reading from, her voice light and soft as a spring breeze. The book was interesting, but not as much as the emotions that flitted across her face, immersed as she was in her reading.

She was beautiful, so much so that she took his breath away. Did he even stand a chance with this exotic person who didn't know how lovely she was? He stretched out a hand until his clasped hers, and she laid the book on her lap as her gaze lifted and met his.

He didn't say anything at first then whispered the three words. "I love you."

She stared at him, not a crack of a smile on her face, and he held his breath. Had he been wrong in thinking she returned his love? They'd never spoken of it, but she'd given every indication she enjoyed his attention. Maybe she had her sights set on some Mexican lord who'd set her up as a regular lady? With him, all she'd get was work and his love.

She pulled her hand away then slapped at his, tears pooling in her liquid brown eyes. "Why did you take so long to say it? Did you think I'd wait forever for you? What if I'd—"

He reclaimed her hand and tugged until she bent over him, and slowly, teasingly, he kissed her.

By the way she responded, he was pretty sure she was enjoying their first kiss as much as he was.

Time to talk to Mr. Michael.

~*~

Lunch day with Bottoms. Destiny dressed in a yellow, sunshiny dress, to meet him. He'd encouraged her weeks ago, when they had been on friendly terms to call him Bert, and she was determined to remember to do so. Better to further the plans.

She had seen no sign of Virge and his partner, Associate, as Virge insisted on calling him. Gathering a handkerchief and her bag, she glanced around her room to make sure she hadn't forgotten anything then carefully locked her door after exiting.

She was early, which she'd planned to be, but was surprised to see Bottoms loitering at the bottom of the stairs.

"What are you doing here?" Bert Bottoms snarled at the woman opposite him.

It was the disagreeable woman from the stagecoach when Destiny had first arrived. Lucy. What was she doing here with Bottoms?

"I followed you. On purpose. I mean to talk with you whether you like it or not." She gripped his arm when he tried to walk away.

Bottoms jerked his arm away, causing Lucy to lose her balance, but she recovered quickly. She was a tough woman, Destiny gave her that.

"When your father threw me out—after using me for his purposes—I waited and didn't forget. But when he ruined my parents by stealing all they had, and killing them, I vowed I'd get back what he stole. I'd get my revenge. That's why I'm here. I've talked to a lawyer, and he's drawing up papers to go to court. You can give me what I want and deserve or I'm spilling the beans. All of it, the theft and the killings. I ain't takin' no for an answer. I intend to get what was promised to me."

"So Patchey..."

Patchey?

Then light dawned. Could it be the man with the patch over one eye? Perez? Destiny shivered.

"...was right. He did see you."

"Who else? Your family owes me, and I told your old man back then, I'd not forget. I want my share. Your father promised..."

"Shut up!" Bottoms glanced around the room. "Keep your voice down. I'm meeting someone."

"I won't. I'm down on my luck, and tired of it. It's you and your family's fault I'm in this business. I need some money and need it now."

"You'll not get a cent out of me."

"I deserve it." She searched his face. "Or else."

"What do you mean by that?" He grabbed her arm. Hard. "Don't you threaten me, you little—"

"Stop it, you're hurting me." She glared up into his face. "I will tell everyone in this town who you are. What your family was. What they've done."

"I'll kill *you* first—"

Destiny couldn't hear the rest of his words.

Lucy jerked away from him. She tossed back the words as she ran out the door, not even trying to keep her voice down. "You've been warned."

Destiny shivered. Who were these people? If Bottoms' father had really done all that to Lucy's family and killed poor Hunter's father and Mr. Michael's—she couldn't bear to think about it all. It was too much. She could not go down these steps and pretend to flirt and like this person.

But for Mr. Michael?

Destiny closed her eyes and felt the tears trying to squeeze from between her lids. She straightened. She *could* do this. For Mr. Michael, she could do anything.

She called out as she descended. "Bert, I thought we were to meet at the Blue Peacock?"

His smile was friendly enough, but something—some emotion—was it distrust?—lurked deep within his eyes.

So he didn't trust her yet. It was understandable. They hadn't parted on the best of terms. She'd make sure to remedy that.

Holding out a hand, she smiled as if totally delighted to see him but didn't speak, waiting on him to give her an answer.

Being early indicated he had something on his mind, but what? She'd have to watch her p's and q's, as her mother had always told her when she was misbehaving.

"I thought we could take a stroll. I want to show you something." He placed her hand on his arm.

"I'd love to. I've been quite bored."

"We can't have that. So I hear you've been not only bored, but sad. Things haven't turned out the way you hoped?" He opened the hotel door and led her outside.

Careful. The least indication she wasn't sincere would raise his suspicions even higher. "I really shouldn't talk about...people."

Bottoms patted her hand. "I understand. I've found it

hard to speak with others about certain people. I don't have many friends that I can trust."

Nice words, so why was she so leery? She knew the answer to that question.

"I want you to know, I hope I've shown you that I can be trusted. I want you to trust me."

She lifted her gaze then, stared straight into his eyes and allowed a bit of moisture to brighten her pupils. "Thank you. I do need a friend right now."

"Aren't you friends with Ruby?"

"Yes, but she is such a new one. You know, I haven't been in Roaring Springs enough to get to know the people all that much."

"I understand that. But surely you made friends while—out of town?"

Careful. He knew she'd spent time at Mr. Michael's ranch. Too much anger would give him a message of insincerity. "Yes and no."

He smiled down at her, allowing her to see the question in his eyes. "Hmmm. That's a leading comment. I suppose I'm to guess?"

She giggled a little. "There's nothing to guess. Maria, the cook, turned out to be a friend, caring for me when I was sick, and listening a little when I had a problem."

"A lady like you with problems? I find that extremely hard to believe."

"Not at all like the problems men face, but more personal problems."

"I see. I hope, then, I can cheer you up." Another pat on the arm.

She'd never cared for patting, not as a child and certainly not as a grown woman. But endure it she would, if that meant persuading Bottoms to trust her. "We shall see. Once trust is lost, it seldom can be regained."

"I hope you're not referring to me."

"Not at all, Bert. Not at all. But some—others—that I thought I could trust." She sighed and hoped he'd heard enough for now.

"Well, then, allow me to present to you the house I'm hoping to attain very soon. The house I want for my future wife, the house I want for my children to grow up in. It's the most respectable one in Roaring Springs, and I mean to own it."

She stared at the lovely house she'd entered earlier yesterday with Ruby who'd said nothing about Delia selling her house. She hoped the shock didn't show on her face. "It's lovely. But it looks occupied. Are the people selling?"

Mr. Bottoms pulled a long face. "Unfortunately, the owner can't keep up with her mortgage payments. I've extended her time, but she doesn't have the business to bring in enough for a payment and her monthly needs. I will, of course, make sure she isn't on the streets. She's a pretty woman, as far as that goes."

I just reckon you will. Anger, such as she'd seldom felt, swamped through her being, and the old stubbornness to insist on her wishes being fulfilled bloomed again. Biting her lip, she shook her head, trying to soothe her emotions.

"Are you all right? You look a little pale. You're not trembling, are you?" Mr. Bottoms searching gaze stroked over her.

"I'll be fine. I'm just a little lightheaded. I didn't eat breakfast. Can we stroll again?"

"Of course. Here, hold onto my arm."

Destiny did so, all the while feeling like she was clutching a snake.

~*~

Two days later, Destiny met Mr. Bottoms for yet another lunch. They'd gone for a carriage ride and eaten together, but so far, she was no closer to what she was asked to do. But then she didn't think Virge expected her to accomplish their goal in a week.

She picked up her glass and sipped at the sweet tea. "I'm considering going back east."

He laid down his fork. "What? Why would you do that?"

She shrugged and nibbled a bite of her sandwich. "I'm still bored. I have nothing to do all day. I need something productive to do."

He sat back in his chair, studying her. "How would you like to work with me?"

She glanced at him. "Are you serious? I've never worked in a bank before, although I was considered very smart in my studies at boarding school."

"My assistant is leaving at the end of this week. If you want the job, it's yours."

Do you think there's any way you could get to Bottoms' papers? His father was meticulous in keeping papers for everything—as far as his interest went—so we assume Hubert Bottoms would be similar in his work. Think you could come up with some way to do this without getting caught?

U.S. Marshal Virge's words replayed in her memory. It had sounded dangerous then, and now, with the opportunity just presented to her with the possibility of a good outcome...

Like Queen Esther, her favorite story in the Bible, she'd do her duty.

She didn't have to pretend the enthusiasm she put into her acceptance. "I do. Thank you so much. I'll do my best."

"I'm glad you've come to your senses."

"You don't know how glad I am for that too."

"You haven't forgotten I invited you to attend our early summer festival with me?"

"Not at all. I'm looking forward to it, and I've ordered a new hat to wear."

"I'm sure you will be the belle of the festival."

His supposed compliment to her seemed to indicate *he* would be the attention of the town. Since the festival was still weeks away, she fervently hoped it was so. The only difference would be the *way* he was the attention. By then, if all things went the way she hoped, and the good Lord saw fit, she'd have accomplished what Mr. Michael—er, Virge the U.S. Marshal—wanted.

Two hours later, back in her hotel room, her thoughts whirled in a dizzying circle. She hadn't given herself much time to think about Virge and what he'd asked her to do for him, the law and Mr. Michael. His emphasis on the danger part had slid over her head when he'd told her, but now...now this was real, and she'd need all her wits to pull it off. And not get caught.

Exhilarating. And dangerous.

Hubert Bottoms was not a good man, so Virge had said, and admittedly, she'd seen an angry, ugly side of him when she'd visited the town months ago. She'd seen it days ago when he and Lucy were arguing.

But anyone could get angry, right? No one knew that any better than her. What with killing her parents—no, she wouldn't think about that.

What had she gotten herself into? Had Mr. Michael really asked for her help? Was she up to this spying business? Could she accomplish what Virge asked of her? She was stubborn enough to persist at it. She was smart, or so her teachers back east claimed even while wringing their hands in frustration at her antics. She loved adventure and trying new things, and this—this being a spy was exciting. Ask any of her friends in Boston whether that was true, and there would be no one who could say otherwise.

She knew she could do what was being asked of her. She knew the exact couple to help her, and she wasn't the least afraid. Or at least, not much. But most of all, deep within her heart, she reminded herself, she wasn't doing it for Virge or the law...

Not at all. It was for Mr. Michael.

Chapter Twenty-seven

"**D**o you have time to talk?" Destiny poked her head inside Hubert Bottoms office. She'd been working as Mr. Bottoms' bank clerk for two weeks now. Plenty time for him to trust her. At least, that was her hope.

He glanced up. "Destiny, come in. What did you need? Surely not a raise already."

He was teasing, but she had a hunch he meant what he said. "I have an idea and wonder if I can run it past you and see if it's the craziest thing I've ever thought of or if it makes sense. Business sense."

Interest sparked in his eyes. "I'm intrigued. Please continue."

"You know that small piece of property between the hotel and the Blue Peacock?"

"Of course. It's pretty small."

"Yes, it is, but perfect for my plan."

A raised eyebrow was her answer.

"I have close friends who'd like to come west."

"Does this have anything to do with your plan?" He was teasing her.

"It does. I was pretty close to them back east. I've been friends with the family for years and spent many vacations with them."

"I see, but I don't see why your friends coming west has anything to do with me or a plan."

"It does very much. They want to come west and do something different. They suggested starting a business, and I've been trying to figure out what this town needs. Do you know what that is?"

"I'm sure you're going to tell me."

"I am. It's a bakery."

"Really? Do you think the town really has need of one? I mean the Blue Peacock has pretty decent desserts.

"Yes, they do, but Roaring Springs is growing. I

predict in a couple years' time, it will boom, to a certain degree. I'd like to help them get this going before someone else thinks of it."

"That doesn't mean there won't be competition."

"No, it doesn't, but they can reassess the situation then, sell if it seems the best option or grow with the competition."

"I suppose they have the money to get this up and running. There will be considerable cost in building and stocking supplies."

"I know that, and I think Mr. Mayfair will realize that since he's a decently successful businessman. They will want to purchase the land outright. But the building itself is another story. That's where I'm hoping you come in." She peered at him. The next few minutes would tell whether she'd pulled him into her scheme or not.

"I see." He sat back in his chair and stroked his chin. "The Mayfairs will run this business? You aren't planning on helping there?"

"I think they could handle the business just fine without me. Mrs. Mayfair is a delightful cook and prepared, without any help from her family's cook, many meals for us when I went to visit them. It was a special delight for her to do so, so I'm thinking she'll be fine with doing most of the baking. Then they'll probably want to have someone build an upstairs that could serve as both a small apartment for them and a storeroom."

Admiration erased the earlier doubts from Bottoms eyes. "You have given this some thought."

"I have."

"And what if this couple decides to increase their family soon after arriving?"

Destiny laughed. "They won't. Their children are grown. They are past that. In their late fifties and looking for some mild adventure. They are solid people. I've known them for years. Their granddaughter is a dear friend of mine."

"Hmmm. I see." He sat forward in his chair. "When would they arrive?"

"Then you think they can get the loan they need?"

"I don't see why not."

Destiny jumped to her feet. "Thank you. Thank you. They will be so pleased. I will wire them early in the morning. They should arrive before the festival begins."

"So soon?" His eyebrows rose.

"Well, I didn't mention they were coming west anyway for a visit and some adventure. They're bringing Gabrielle, their granddaughter. If they like the idea, then they'll have their belongings shipped later."

"No, you didn't mention that. Any other information I should know about?"

"Not right now, but I promise if I think of something, I'll let you know right away."

Was that a tongue-in-cheek comment or not? Destiny didn't hold her grin back, figuring he'd think she was teasing. But right now she didn't care. Her plan was succeeding.

"I'd better finish up my work for today."

He nodded, and she left the room.

~*~

Hubert Bottoms watched his newest clerk leave the room. She was a sight to be seen. That blond hair and blue eyes of hers gave her an angelic look, but he figured differently.

She had a spark about her, an air that was both interesting and dangerous. Not for her, probably, so much as for those on the other end of that brilliant mind's plotting.

And he was pretty sure she was plotting. Not against him, but those supposed friends of hers. No one was that thrilled over a new business that would harvest someone else a profit and nothing for themselves. No one, and that included Miss Destiny McCulloch with her brilliant mind.

Now how could he use that mind to aid him in a nice take-down of that business?

~*~

A week had passed since she'd talked with Bottoms about the Mayfairs and a loan. She re-read the telegram she'd received earlier today from them.

Arrived in Madison at noon. Stop. Will leave on stagecoach early morning tomorrow. Stop. Should reach Roaring Springs in two days. Stop. Mayfairs

Two days, then would begin the final stage, she

hoped, of this plan. Rash it might be, but she and the others had pinned their hopes on bringing down Bottoms and saving Mr. Michael from further trouble.

She'd not told them all the details, wanting to wait until they arrived. But they'd been interested and entirely willing to help.

Her only problem now was getting to sleep.

Blowing out the lamp, Destiny lay down and tried to relax, but her mind was whirling. She hadn't had much time to think about searching for her Caleb. But she'd found no one except Bottoms who claimed the name of Caleb. Right now, her interest was waning. Her intuition was telling her she'd never find such a person. Not now, after all these years. It was foolishness.

After all, with her confusion about the past, who was to say she hadn't made up the name as a child?

A creak outside her door caused her eyes to open wide. Destiny sat up in bed, her heart pounding. She had not forgotten the men who'd been in the room across from hers before. Nor their comments.

Throwing back the covers, she tiptoed across the floor and listened. Voices. And it wasn't Bottoms this time.

"Boss said to keep watching for that Lucy woman. Don't let 'er outta yer sight."

Lucy? Lucy from the stagecoach? Then that would mean they weren't watching her. Bottoms had someone keeping an eye on Lucy. Why? To kill her, that was why.

"You idiot. Whatcha think I'm doin'?"

"Boss sent me. He don't want you talkin' to her, puttin' her on the alert. He'll be madder'n a wet hen if you do."

"I ain't goin' do something stupid."

"You better not."

"Git outta here. I got work to do."

"Yeah. Yeah. You better not be sleepin'. You gotta job to do and if'n the boss shows up, yer a dead man."

"Get outa here."

"I'm goin', I'm goin'."

Destiny checked the lock. Breathing a sigh of relief, she pressed her back against the door and listened as the heavy boots walked away.

Caleb's Destiny

She wasn't at all sure she'd sleep tonight, but she had work tomorrow. She couldn't afford to be sluggish. She'd need all her brains for this portion of the plan.

She returned to her bed and pulled the covers up to her neck. She'd think pleasant thoughts and try to relax. Maybe that would help her sleep…

~*~

Destiny hurried toward the hotel two days later. It was her lunch time, and time for her friends to arrive. The stagecoach driver pulled on the reins and hollered out his commands. When the coach had finally rolled to a full stop, the man riding shotgun jumped down from his seat, opened the door, and the passengers began unloading.

A tall, partially gray-haired man stepped out then turned and offered his hand to the next passenger. The woman who appeared at the door, ready to step down from the coach, didn't look even close to her fifties, but Destiny knew she was. She ran toward them.

"Mr. Mayfair. Mrs. Mayfair."

They both swiveled toward her, the smiles on their faces conveying their pleasure in seeing her again.

"My dear, it's such a delight to see you." Mrs. Mayfair held her at arm's length after giving her a hug. "You look surprisingly healthy and just as beautiful as always."

"Destiny McCulloch, we are pleased to see you." Mr. Mayfair held her hand for a moment, his smile stretching almost from ear to ear.

"Did not Gabrielle come? I do hope she came."

"Here I am, here I am." The voice came from behind Destiny, and she whirled.

Flying up the boardwalk came a thin girl with freckles and the loveliest eyes Destiny had ever seen. She flew into Destiny's arms, and Destiny thought she'd been transported back to when they were fifteen. They'd both loved to run and had been reprimanded more times than not at the boarding school.

"She insisted on the driver letting her out early so she could surprise you." Mr. Mayfair's comment was almost drowned out by the squeals coming from his granddaughter.

When they finally released each other, Destiny gasped

238

out her happiness. "It is so wonderful to see you all. Come, and I will show you to your rooms. The owner is a friend of mine and very sweet. I hope you love it here as much as I do."

"Don't you worry your head about that. Alexander and I have been dying to see some adventure. I'm sure we will." Mrs. Mayfair gave Destiny a wink.

She led the Mayfairs to their room. Before she left the older couple, Destiny whispered at the door to their room, "We will talk later about the plans."

"Perfect. We're anxious to know how to go from here with these plans of yours." Mr. Mayfair nodded and shook her hand.

"Then we'll see you later, my dear." Mrs. Mayfair smiled.

The minute the door shut, Gabrielle tucked her arm in Destiny's and whispered, "I want to know everything you've been doing. The man you're in love with, this big exciting scheme you're involved in, and the good-looking bad man. Tell me everything."

Destiny laughed. "Do you think you can wait until we're in my room?"

Gabrielle wrinkled her nose. "I don't want to, but I think I can. Let's hurry."

~*~

Destiny didn't want to talk with the Mayfairs to fill them in on the plan just anywhere. She didn't want to talk with them at the Blue Peacock, with chances someone might overhear them. Then there was the situation with the men across the hall from her room. She hadn't seen Perez since she'd been back in town, and truth be told, she would have been terrified if he'd still been in the room across the hall.

But if Bottoms did have other men keeping an eye on her, then she'd have a definite problem getting away from them, let alone taking the Mayfairs anywhere for a private chat.

So what to do?

Gabrielle was leaning out the window taking in anything and everything that caught her attention and probably hoping a handsome cowboy would ride in and sweep her off her feet. She was a good friend, her best, and though not quite as rambunctious as Destiny was, she'd been good at sidelining obstructive teachers or covering Destiny's tracks occasionally and even, more times than not, joining in on Destiny's adventures.

"Gabrielle, I need your help."

Gabrielle withdrew her head from outside the window. "I'm ready. Tell me what to do."

"Do you think you can lead your grandparents outside of town while I, hopefully, can coax them..." She nodded in the direction of the hallway and the room across from hers. "...not to follow me?"

"I can do that. Being newcomers, we're bound to want to explore, and with all the work going on getting ready for your festival, I think we can pull it off." She clapped her hands with anticipation. "But do you think you can really lead them away? What if they guess it's just a ploy to do so?"

Destiny shrugged. "All we can do is try. If all else fails, then we will have to talk quietly in one of our rooms."

"Where shall we go then? There's some handsome men down there working on the festival doings."

"You keep your mind on what you need to do. You can dream about the men later."

"You're always so focused. Men are exciting too."

"They'll do in their place." Better to agree than argue with Gabrielle. She explained exactly where Gabrielle and her grandparents were to go. "Are you ready? Let's do this now. You go talk to your grandparents and I'll try to lead the men—or man—away. Remember, out of town, on the east side and go till you see the two big oak trees. You do know an oak tree from a cottonwood, don't you?"

Gabrielle gave her a shove and chuckled. "Silly. Of course, I do. Go."

Destiny nodded, opened the door, and shut it loudly as she departed. She made sure to clomp down the hallway. She'd barely reached the ground floor when she spotted a man sitting in a chair pretending to study a newspaper. So one of the men had decided to keep watch on where she went. Hmmm.

Probably couldn't even read, if she went by the way he kept flipping the paper from page to page.

She left the hotel and walked swiftly down the board walk. She already knew what she was going to do and kept a spring in her step as she walked. She darted around the corner of the hotel, ran to the back of the next building.

Peering around the building, she saw him exiting the hotel and looking around. Ha, he thought he'd lost her. He decided, as she'd hoped, to head in her direction, and as he passed, she shoved herself away from the building and strolled along the boardwalk behind him.

It took only seconds before he realized someone was following *him*. She could see him stiffen, then he darted into the next building—which happened to be a ladies' shop. Destiny followed him in there but ignored him as he darted quick, panicky glances at her before leaving. She picked up a couple unneeded items, paid for them and stepped outside again.

She hadn't figured on him leaving, but she had kept his attention. For sure, he'd keep her in sight now, afraid he'd lose her for good and earn the anger of his boss.

For that matter, why was his boss—assuming it was Hubert Bottoms—wanting her followed? Did he still not trust her? She giggled. If he only knew, he had little reason to trust her. But he didn't know.

Or did he?

That was crazy. How could he?

But if Bottoms was as crazy as Virge said, then he *wouldn't* be very trusting.

Good thing he'd given her today off to meet her friends. Tomorrow was Sunday, but Monday, she'd be working at the bank again when the Mayfairs would go talk with Bottoms. The day afterward, the festival would start.

Would any of Mr. Michael's people come? No doubt, Mr. Michael himself would shy away from it, despising the town as he did, but maybe he'd come to see Jake.

She couldn't, and wouldn't have if she could, stop the wish that he'd come to see *her*. No, not see her, take her home. Tears filled her eyes, and she blinked them away. Not now.

Up ahead was Jake's Emporium. The last stop before

she made her escape from her follower. Shoving open the door, the smells hit her again, as they always did, as they had the first time she'd set foot inside here.

Smells that were pleasant and reminded her of Boston, and particularly the boarding house kitchen. But farther back than that, memories from childhood stirred and demanded to be remembered.

She had no time now to reminisce about the past. Allowing the door to shut behind her, she hurried toward the counter and spoke hurriedly. "I need to escape from that man following me, Uncle Jake. He's outside across the street now, watching."

Jake cast a quick glance outside, then motioned. "You head back to my kitchen. My supper's stored in ice back there. Set it on the table, as if you've been eating, and when he comes in, if he insists on checking, you'll be long gone. Go, Destiny. I'll keep him entertained long enough you can escape."

Destiny fled, but she heard Jake's mutter as she did so.

"Might feed him a bullet while I'm at it. Probably hungering for one."

She turned around and called, "Jake, don't get hurt. Mr. Michael wouldn't forgive me."

"Get going and quit worrying about me or Mr. Michael."

She did as he ordered, and seconds later, was out the door running for her destination.

Destiny had known her Uncle Jake's place was the place to escape. It would set her straight on the path to meet with her friends and keep anyone from observing her rapid departure.

Five minutes later, she burst into the clearing. Mrs. Mayfair and Gabrielle had found a log to sit on while Mr. Mayfair took turns pacing and examining the foliage surrounding the area.

"There you are, my dear. We were beginning to wonder." Mr. Mayfair turned as she entered.

"Sorry." Gasping, she leaned against a tree. "I ran...the whole way. Took me...awhile...to get away. Whew."

"Come and sit down, Destiny. You must be worn out."

Mrs. Mayfair patted the place beside her.

Destiny drew several long breaths and took the seat beside Mrs. Mayfair. "Here's the plan..."

Chapter Twenty-eight

"**W**e're here, Destiny, early, we know, but we're so excited to get this going. Is Mr. Bottoms in yet?" Mrs. Mayfair's perpetually happy voice greeted her as they entered the bank.

Early, yes. Destiny had slept little last night and risen early, worried whether all would go as she'd planned.

Now, she shot a glance at Bottoms' office. His door was open, so surely he'd heard Mrs. Mayfair's comment.

"Yes, dear, we are early, but that's not important. Destiny, do be nice and check to see if he can see us now. We have so many things we want to do and see before the real work begins." Mr. Mayfair jerked his head in the direction of the office.

"Good morning, Mr. and Mrs. Mayfair. If you'll have a seat, I'll check to see if Mr. Bottoms can see you now." She indicated the two chairs lined up against the wall and scooted back her chair.

At Bottoms' door, she leaned in and spoke in a soft voice. "The Mayfairs are here, Mr. Bottoms. Early, and they are quite excited.

"Fine. Give me five minutes, then show them in. Oh, and I'll need you to take notes and witness the transaction."

"Notes? I didn't think—"

"I'm meticulous in keeping track of all transactions. I have my reasons. Nothing personal. And in loans, I particularly like to study the clients for their reactions. I'll need you to do the notes."

"Yes, Mr. Bottoms."

She withdrew and headed toward the elderly couple. "He'll be able to see you in a few minutes. Would you like some water?"

"No, we're fine." Mrs. Mayfair winked at her.

Destiny held back the grin she wanted to give the

woman and walked back to her desk.

It took closer to ten minutes before Mr. Bottoms called out to her. She'd had plenty of time to wait on two customers, one wanting to withdraw five dollars and the other depositing his weekly check.

Mr. Bottoms stood as the three entered his office. He motioned for them to have seats, and Destiny took the seat closest to his desk, her pencil and paper ready.

"Do you have an idea of what cash you'll need to build your bakery?"

"We do." Mr. Mayfair leaned forward and stated a sum. "With that, we ought to be able to complete the construction of the business, set up shop with supplies and equipment we'll need, and have a healthy start for the first couple of months."

"I see. Do you think a year will be sufficient to pay back what you owe?" Mr. Bottoms stroked his chin, his eyes squinting as if contemplating Mr. Mayfair's words.

"I believe so. We aim to prosper."

"Confident. I like that."

"I never enter into any business without knowing the facts. That's why I've done so well through the years, isn't that right, Orpha?"

"It is." Mrs. Mayfair beamed at her husband. "He's always been very good at business. I have perfect confidence that he will succeed in this endeavor too. You do not need to fear he will fail, Mr. Bottoms. Not in the least."

"I see." Mr. Bottoms glanced at Destiny. "Please make sure you make a note of the Mayfairs' healthy business success back east."

Destiny scribbled the note.

"Then I think there's nothing else to discuss. I have a form here for you to sign, if you will." Mr. Bottoms shoved the paper across his desk and laid a pen beside it.

"Of course. Of course." Mr. Mayfair picked up the pen and signed the document with a flourish but did not lay the pen down, his hand resting on top of the paper. "I assume I will get a copy of this contract?"

"Do you think you need one?"

"Oh, yes, like you, I'm a serious businessman."

"Then, Destiny, would you make a copy for us to sign?"

"I will. Give me a couple minutes."

It took only a few minutes for Destiny to recopy the form and present it to Bottoms and the Mayfairs.

As she led them to the door, Mrs. Mayfair leaned toward her and whispered. "How did we do?"

"Fine. You were wonderful."

Destiny stood at the door watching the couple stroll down the boardwalk, arm in arm. She seriously hoped this would work out. She did not want them to lose money on this scheme to bring Bert Bottoms down.

~*~

"Do you think you can finish those papers before closing tonight?" Hubert Bottoms leaned out his office doorway late Tuesday afternoon.

"I think so, but if I don't I'll stay over after closing to get them done." Destiny looked up from the scribbling she was doing to answer her employer.

He frowned. "Tonight's opening night of the festival. I have to be there to make the welcoming speech, and I want you by my side."

She smiled her assurance. "I'll be there and won't be late. You can count on me."

"Thank you, Destiny. It has been pleasant having you work here. You're smart and quick to learn. I've been able to trust you with the business when I had to leave."

"Thank *you*, Bert. It has been nice, hasn't it? Given me some purpose to stay." Truth be told, she'd enjoyed working at the bank and mingling with the towns people. Today had been especially busy with each store owner entering to deposit money into their savings. If only she didn't need to deal with this Hubert Bottoms problem.

But she did. She watched as he gave her another big smile and shut his office door. In a couple of minutes, she heard faint voices behind the door and stopped what she was doing. In seconds, she was at the door leaning in, trying to hear what was being said.

She knew he had his own private back door to come and go, but since she'd been working, she hadn't noticed him using it much. But that had to have been how the unknown person had gotten in.

"I want your men out of my way."

"But, for backup..."

There was a silence that somehow seemed sinister. Who was that man talking with Bottoms? "Don't want anyone getting in my way. If I sense that, I'll shoot, and it won't be your target."

"I just want to be sure."

"I want the rest of my money."

"You haven't done the job yet."

Another silence that was even worse than the last. A short laugh. Sounded like it came from Hubert Bottoms. A desk drawer slammed shut, then...

"There. Just make sure you get the job done. Or I'll be after you."

Wrong words obviously. The silence said it all.

"No, you won't. You're too afraid I'll kill you."

"You won't. I might need you again later."

"I don't reckon that's likely. I don't like you, Bottoms. Never liked you and still don't. After this job, you do your own killin' or call someone else. I've got other jobs, and who knows? One of them might have you as a target. Wouldn't that be funny?"

Footsteps tapped across a floor, the back door creaked open and shut. There was a brief pause, then another set of feet headed toward the inside door where she listened.

She whirled and ran toward her desk, plopped into her seat and picked up her pencil, striving to calm her rapid breaths.

Bottoms' office door opened.

"Destiny, I'm leaving. I have an important telegram to send. I'll see you tonight at seven sharp?"

"You will." She gave Bert Bottoms her best smile. "I'll lock up for you."

He sketched a wave good-bye and left, his face a bit pale.

She gave him five minutes, jumped up, locked the doors and pulled the shades. With a deep breath, she walked to his office and shut the door. If something happened and he returned, she just might have time to use the back door to leave before he caught her doing what she was about to do.

Hopefully.

She was a fast reader, able to discern quickly whether something was important or not. In a matter of minutes, she should be done.

Blood racing, she went straight to the closet where he kept files. Three boxes sat on the floor.

She pulled out his top box and shuffled through them. Nothing. The other two boxes were tied in elaborate knots, and she wasn't sure if she could untie and retie them before she had to leave. Or get caught.

Placing the box back into the closet, she headed to his desk. Only one drawer was locked, but she wasn't too worried. She'd picked many a lock at the boarding house. This shouldn't be any harder than those.

Thirty seconds later, she pulled the drawer out and hit pay dirt. There were two journals. In one of the journals, tied with a sturdy leather strap, was a list of transactions Bottoms's father had done.

Bottoms' father, had kept meticulous records of business he'd been involved in years ago. Notes he'd made, but too many to spend time on now. She gave it a cursory glance-through, but put it aside. Right now, she needed something on Hubert Bottoms.

The second journal was Bottoms'. A list of successful sales of different properties from various towns, a smaller list of properties marked takeovers, and a short list of properties in Roaring Spring. Two were Ruby's friend's house and the property the Mayfairs were interested in.

Destiny looked up and stared at the calendar he had pinned to a wall. Why would he have such a list? What was more important right now was the question: did *he* own those last two Roaring Spring properties?

But the last entry is what had her heart racing. Notes on how to take over the Mayfairs property once it was up and running. Notes on what to do if they caused him trouble...

Flipping through the rest of the journal, nothing caught her eye, and she closed it. Tapping the cover, she debated. If she didn't take it, and it was important, then she'd have failed. Bottoms would not be in the bank office much, if at all, the rest of the week. She should be safe, but then, if he decided to work there for a few hours tomorrow, and looked for his journal... No. She wouldn't think like that.

She'd take the chance. Should she leave the room and desk a mess to make him think someone had broken in? But then he might just point a finger at her.

No, she'd make sure everything was neat and locked up. Virge had planned on meeting her sometime during the festival so it could be, if he found the journal unimportant, she'd have it locked back up without Bottoms even knowing she'd taken it.

Locking up the drawer, and checking to make sure everything was as shipshape as before, she settled at her desk and finished the paperwork she had told Bottoms she would do. She hurriedly put everything in order, closed the bank receiving window, and headed for the door. She stepped outside, locked the door and turned.

"Destiny, hold up. I need to step inside for a minute."

Hubert Bottoms strode up the boardwalk, a determined look on that handsome face of his.

~*~

Michael had heard nothing from Virge, and it was past time. Restless and on edge, it was time to find out something on his own.

Hank was in the fields with most of the men, so he couldn't try to reason him out of going. Scribbling a note to Maria to tell Hank he'd be gone for a few days, Michael left the ranch a late afternoon, but before supper time, with Shyanne following along behind Jasper and him.

He'd ridden to the outside of Roaring Springs before his common sense revived. He should never have come. He should have left it up to Virge.

But when had he ever given over the reins of his life to another person?

Never.

Michael had never been and still wasn't happy with the plan the others had agreed upon. Putting this on Destiny was too much. Too dangerous. And he hadn't been able to rest until he checked that she was all right.

He wasn't about to contact Virge and have him chew him out. He might take the time to stop in to see Jake a moment, but he had no interest in anyone else except Destiny. If she was fine, he'd hightail it out of there. Hopefully, no one would be the wiser. And he'd be able to avoid the festival that was to start tomorrow night.

But how to make sure she was fine?

She'd be in the hotel unless she'd made friends and was with them. If she was in the Blue Peacock, he'd not be able to see her. He didn't want to risk being seen himself by standing in front of the restaurant looking in the windows. If he only knew which room she had at the hotel, he'd be able to see if she had a light on. Or sneak upstairs, but then that carried the same risk and defeat his purpose. Besides, he had no idea what room she had.

Minutes later, Michael left Jasper and Shyanne behind Jake's Emporium and moved on to the hotel.

The sound of a snap, as if a limb had been stepped on, stopped him dead in his tracks. He swept the area with his gaze as far as he could see, then turned his head from side to side.

There. Beneath the stairs leaned two people. Men, he thought, from the fire at the end of their cigarettes. He edged closer and caught their words.

"I heared he's waitin' till the festival to do it. He's figurin' on the killin' then. That man is scary."

Talking about Perez probably.

And who else was Perez planning on killing besides him?

He'd worry about Perez's moves later. Right now, all he was concerned with was Destiny's safety. He needed to get her to safety, and that wasn't happening tonight.

~*~

"Come inside with me."

Bert Bottoms' sober tone struck a blade of fear in her heart. Did he know she'd taken his journal? What was he going to do? Fire her? Or something much worse?

Kill her?

And what was she going to do with the journals hidden beneath the shawl she was carrying?

Be careful, that was what.

Destiny followed the man—her boss, the man she was trying to bring down—back into the bank and shut the door, although she would have much preferred leaving it wide open—better for a quick escape.

Bottoms went straight to his office and his desk, and she followed. After she hurriedly wrapped the shawl around the journals and placed the bundle on her desk, she followed Bottoms to his office.

Inside his room, Bottoms had opened a drawer on the left side of his desk then pulled out a small, cloth-wrapped object and stared down at it a moment. He shut the drawer and walked toward Destiny, who still stood near the doorway to his office.

"Did you need me to help with something, Bert?" Hoping he'd say no.

He didn't answer, only walked slowly toward her, still staring at the object in his hand. Then...

"I have something for you. I recently got it from a friend, well, a person, and put it back, thinking I'd sell it one day since it looks old and valuable. Here."

He handed over the material-wrapped package.

Destiny stared at him. What on earth was this? Bert was giving her a *gift*? Her conscience slapped her. Here she was trying her best to help a U.S. Marshal—and Mr. Michael—in a scheme that would prove this man's dangerous and unlawful deeds.

It took all of five seconds before her mind put up a reassuring argument. She was doing her duty, and she was doing it for Mr. Michael. A decent, responsible, true-blue, true-hearted man.

And the man she...

No, she wouldn't go there.

"I can't receive a gift from you Bert. We're friends—"

"That's exactly why you should." He reached for one of her hands. "And someday soon I hope we'll be more than that. Take it please. Wear it tonight."

"I can't."

"I insist."

Her heart would have given him the benefit of doubt except for those last two words, spoken with a tone of *I won't take no for an answer* and a *Do it now! I mean it.*

She bit her lip, began unfolding the material and thought her heart had stopped when she stared down at the object she held.

Her mother's golden locket.

~*~

Destiny chose her favorite Prussian-blue dress for the first night of the festival. The new hat, crafted by Delia here in Roaring Springs, sat on her head, accenting her blond looks. The locket, pinned to the breast of her garment, shone gold and rich, blending well with the touches of gold thread sprinkled throughout her garment.

She had to admit she looked very nice. Her mother would have been proud. And Hubert Bottoms would be pleased and think she—she enhanced his importance nicely.

So why the sad expression? *How many reasons do you need to know?* she argued with her mirror self.

I don't want to go anywhere with Bert Bottoms.

I don't want to be here in Roaring Springs.

How did Bert get my locket? He wasn't any of the men who'd robbed the stagecoach that first day—at least she didn't think so.

Had those thieves been working for him?

Had he stolen it?

A knock on her door interrupted her debate with herself. Turning, she headed for the door. It'd be Gabrielle...

When she opened the door, Gabrielle pushed her way into the room, bubbling over with enthusiasm.

"Are you ready to go? You look very fetching. How do you like my dress?"

Her chatter sent Destiny's spirits soaring. Why worry about Bottoms now? She'd enjoy the evening regardless of *him*.

"I love that claret red dress with those freckles of yours. And your hair looks very beautiful tonight." Destiny tucked her arm in Gabrielle's after locking her own door. "Let's go down."

"Don't mock my poor freckled face." Gabrielle pouted.

"I'm not. I adore those freckles. I wouldn't mind having a few, and yours are so pale they're hardly noticeable. They give your face character. Besides, your brown eyes pull everyone's focus to you."

"Thank you, I think." Gabrielle paused at the top of

the stairs. "I do hope I meet someone divinely interesting tonight. I'm getting bored."

Destiny laughed and took the first step down. "You're always bored without attentive men around you."

"Not as long as I'm around you..."

Gabrielle's chatter abruptly stopped, and Destiny looked first at her friend, then down at the bottom of the stairs.

Of a sudden, her head swirled, and, if Gabrielle hadn't still been locked arm in arm with her, she was sure she'd be falling down those stairs.

Three men stood at the bottom, dressed to a T. Three handsome men.

Hubert Bottoms.

Mr. Michael.

And Richard Burke.

Chapter Twenty-nine

It was a good thing he always kept a nice suit at Jake's place, otherwise, he'd have been up a creek without a paddle, or so his Pa used to say.

Not being able to contact Destiny had sent him straight to Jake's place right before sunrise. For one thing, Michael hadn't wanted to be seen, and another, a strange and irresponsible idea had bloomed—like that wild weed that was always growing beyond its bounds—in his head, and he'd gone straight to Jake's, hoping the man would talk him out of it.

That hadn't happened.

Jake had promptly told him that Destiny was going to the festival with Hubert Bottoms. Michael had gone from being angry with Destiny for doing such a fool thing—pacing up and down Jake's rooms till the man had had to settle him down—to being worried about the danger surrounding her.

He'd fallen asleep when Jake insisted he had to open the emporium before someone came around to see what was wrong. It was early afternoon before he'd wakened and realized what he was going to do.

Jake had vetoed the idea, arguing, reasoning and finally giving in.

"You hate this town." Jake's desperation to persuade him shone in his eyes.

"Yep." That was the truth.

"You've got a big situation here you're trying to solve."

"I know that."

"You're liable to get killed. You know Bottoms has men all over the place."

"That's true."

"Then listen to me. You need to go home."

"Can't do that."

"Why not?"

"Can't say right now."

Jake straightened. "You're the most cantankerous person I know."

Michael grinned. "Now why would you say that?"

Jake shook his head, walked over to his closet and pulled out a dark suit.

Michael was going to the festival.

~*~

"I have to go back to my room." Destiny had stopped descending the stairs and now stared at the three men at the bottom.

"Destiny. That's Richard, down there."

"Are you sure? I was thinking I was in a nightmare, and he was a figment of my dream. Pinch me please."

Gabrielle pinched her arm and grinned. "Go to your room. I'll go down and greet these three handsome men. I so seldom get that privilege."

Destiny shot her a look of irritation. "You always have three men hanging around you."

"Not like these three. Or I should say two of them. Richard doesn't count. And here in the Wild West, gunslingers, no less."

"Really, Gabrielle, Autumn Mayfair? I love you, but right now, I could shoot you myself."

"No, thanks, not interested. I'm going down. Do what you want." Gabrielle released her arm from Destiny's and took a step down.

Destiny wanted to scream in frustration. The least her best friend could have done was get her out of this mess. But she couldn't leave it to Gabrielle to steer them away. She'd have to take care of this mess herself.

If she wasn't careful, Mr. Michael and Bert Bottoms would be shooting at each other. Richard, on the other hand, would probably be off to the side, shouting platitudes of peace at the two of them which would accomplish nothing but generate more anger. If he wasn't cowering somewhere. She was pretty sure he'd never been in such a situation in his lifetime.

Where was Virge—or Hunter—when she needed him?

She descended the last two steps and took a deep breath.

"Destiny, we really should go now. The festival is due

to start any minute now." Bert's imperious voice insisted she listen to him.

He was saying more, but her attention was drawn to Richard's rather snobbish words.

"I've come all the way to this dirty place to take you home. When you didn't answer my telegrams, I was worried. And you know how busy I am. You have been rather thoughtless in..."

Destiny wanted to clap both hands over her ears. She'd forgotten how self-absorbed he could be.

Only one person stood a few feet back and didn't say a word. He didn't have to. His eyes did the talking, and Destiny's heart nearly broke at what she was getting ready to do.

She held up a hand. "Please. I want to talk with all of you, but I made a promise awhile back that I would go to the opening night of the festival with Bert. I must keep that promise."

Hubert Bottoms settled his hat on his head, but couldn't hide his satisfaction at her words.

She turned to her almost-fiancé. "Richard, please, let's talk later tonight? Or even at breakfast? I have to go."

She shot a quick glance behind the two men before Bert took her arm to guide her away.

Mr. Michael was gone.

~*~

Destiny stood at the bottom of the platform where Bert Bottoms was speaking, eloquently to be sure, but to her ears it sounded hollow. Self-serving. Boring.

Her gaze wandered, not that she cared, but wondering where Richard had gone to.

More importantly, where had Mr. Michael gotten to? He didn't like the town, didn't like the people so why was he here? Didn't he realize he might get hurt? Virge had said...

Was that...

It was. Virge stood at the far left corner of the lot, over by the livery, and that tilt of his head told her what he wanted.

She glanced at Bottoms, and he was still talking. Could she get away without him noticing?

Probably.

She went, edging away, a few steps at a time, until in the back of the gathering of people, she figured she was safe. Then turning she half-ran toward the livery and away from the prying eyes of the townspeople. She edged around the corner of the building, and a hand shot out to grasp her arm.

"Shh."

Virge.

"Are you doing all right? Let's get inside the livery before someone spots us."

"Yes. Well, mostly. I guess so." Not counting the three she'd have to console later. That is, if Mr. Michael stood around waiting to be consoled.

That was doubtful. No doubt that man was riding full tilt toward his ranch, shaking the dust of the town off his boots and the sight of her out of his mind.

"Which is it?"

"It doesn't matter. I have something for you. But I have to get it back into his desk before he finds out I've taken it, so you have to look at it now." She was babbling she knew.

"Show me."

Destiny drew the journals from the bag she carried and handed them over.

Virge headed toward the lantern inside the livery and lit it, then opened one of the journals, reading and flipping pages. It was a long five minutes later before he looked up.

"Destiny McCulloch, you've done yourself proud. Do you know what's in this?" Virge tapped a finger on the cover of the journal.

"What is it? Will it help?"

Virge grinned. "It sure will. This, my dear girl, is the thing that's going to take down the Bottoms family. Dates, lists of people he and his father swindled in deals made, with plenty of notes on how, why and what went on in each transaction. And, more important, a short list of gunslingers he called in to eliminate certain people. Including..." He glanced down at her.

"Who?"

"Mr. Michael. And Perez's name is here, with the date

he contacted him."

"Does this mean you have him?"

"Yes." He lifted the journal and shook it a bit. "This must be more of a personal journal for him, but there's enough information in here to convict him, if I'm not mistaken, and I seldom am."

"Really? Are you serious?"

"Very. You've done well."

Destiny let out a long breath of air. "Then I'm done here. I can go..."

Go where? Back to Boston with Richard?

She didn't want that.

To the ranch with Mr. Michael?

He didn't want her there.

Then what on earth was she going to do?

~*~

Michael stood at one corner of the emporium, hidden from the crowd gathered to listen to Bottoms' opening speech, but still able to keep an eye on the crowd, but more specifically, an eye open for Perez.

Destiny stood near the front of the crowd, dressed in a shimmering blue dress that accented her figure perfectly. She'd looked stunning coming down those hotel stairs with that golden locket pinned to her dress.

That locket. He'd seen it before. But he had no more time to think of it. He needed to keep his mind on Perez.

He was pretty sure the man was coming for him tonight. Bottoms would have told him he was here in town, if the gunslinger didn't already know it. He had no doubts about that, and he knew what he had to do. Enough running.

It was time to put an end to the horror from the past. He had to keep Destiny safe. He had to keep his ranch people safe. And even Jake, who at any time might become the next target of Bottoms. Too many people had had to live with tragic memories, and whatever the cost, he was going to do what he needed to do. Tonight.

His gaze moved from one building to another, then satisfied nothing was amiss—for now—moved closer to the hotel.

Just as he settled in for another study of the town, he caught the brief movement, shadow, or flicker from the building two down, but when he edged his glance that direction, he couldn't see a thing.

Nerves? He grimaced.

Time to move again. He headed toward the stable. At the corner, he searched the stable area, but saw nothing out of the way. He slipped inside and saw the shadowy form standing on the far side of the barn, and Mr. Michael ducked...right before a bullet slammed into the post beside him.

He didn't have to think, but moved again, and another bullet hit the stall wall.

Michael hesitated. This guy was good, better than him. He threw himself on the floor and peeked around the corner of the stall. Nothing. No, wait. Was that...? It was.

Two booted feet were walking slowly toward him. Cautiously, he could tell. Slipping in and out of hiding places, but ever coming nearer.

He squirmed against a side wall as tight as he could, his head as flat as he could lay it on the straw-covered floor...and waited.

He wouldn't have heard it if he'd been moving. The faint, like a gentle puff of air, movement of feet, and then he saw it. The tip of one boot then two, and Michael rolled onto his back and shot in one move.

He stared at the man trying to kill him, the man who now stared down at him, his eyes shocked as he raised his hand to his chest, glanced at the hand and then returned his gaze to Michael.

"You've done...what no one...else has ever...done." Giving the faintest of nods in recognition of the feat, Perez toppled to the floor and lay still.

Footsteps sounded in the stable and drew nearer. "This is the United States Marshal. Show yourself with your hands up."

"It's me, Virge."

Michael didn't move. He was still too stunned at what had just happened. And he knew he'd have to face what he'd done. The one thing his pa had asked him not to do.

Chapter Thirty

Michael tossed on the lumpy bed he lay in at Jake's. It was too late. He couldn't turn the clock back, couldn't take back what he'd done this evening, couldn't take back the rage that had consumed him over what the man had tried to do to Destiny.

No matter how much Virge had assured him it'd been a justifiable killing. That he'd heard Perez shoot at him twice and seen the man stalking Michael. He'd have done it himself, Virge had insisted, if Michael hadn't shot first.

It hadn't been because of himself or even his ranch that he'd shot the man. Deep inside him had bubbled a cold rage that had finally gotten the best of him. In spite of the control he'd kept through all these years since Pa's murder. In spite of pretending yesterday he was going to town to talk everyone into a peaceful solution.

He was a murderer, and as Pa had warned, he'd never be able to undo that.

Michael groaned and rolled his head from side to side, the misery demon goading him like a savage wild dog.

"God, what have I done? What have I done? Are you there, God? I've not paid much attention to you all these years since Pa died. And I guess you have a right to ignore me now. But I've got to tell you, I can't face Destiny tomorrow if you don't give me some peace."

He listened but didn't hear a word. Was God even there?

He shut his eyes and breathed in slowly. In and out...in and out...

~*~

"I want you to come with me. You've had your fun, now it's time to settle down and be a respectable woman of Boston. I intend for us to be socially busy, and you to be one, if not the top, example there, while I give myself to the ministry."

Richard's words were praise-worthy, but somehow they didn't resonate much with her. How could she ever have thought they'd have a future?

"I'm not ready to go right now to Boston, and I might never be ready." Destiny looked at him and realized she'd never been in love with him. Only the prestige of having someone so handsome and desired by the other girls had enticed her into thinking she was in love with him.

Now she knew she wasn't. And had never been. She shouldn't have encouraged him to think she was. She should have severed the relationship earlier.

But she hadn't, and now she had to deal with it.

"Richard, I don't want to go to Boston, and I don't want to marry you."

He stared at her as if she'd lost her mind.

She reached for his hand. "You are a good man. I know you'll find someone in Boston who will cherish you and be all you want in a companion. It's just not me. I'm sorry."

For the first time since she'd met him, he seemed confused. "Are you being serious? I know you have a streak of mischievousness in you now and then. How could you not want—"

Him? "I'm very serious and mean every word I said."

He pulled his hand away and turned from her. "Then I must go and pack. I want to catch the next stagecoach out of this miserable place as soon as I can. I've had my fill of this dirty town."

Without even a good-bye, Richard rose from the Blue Peacock table where they were having breakfast, and left.

So much for love.

Destiny propped her chin on her fist and stared down at her over-easy eggs that were growing increasingly colder the longer she sat there. She'd lost her appetite, but not because of Richard or his departure.

"Are you going to let those eggs go uneaten or are you contemplating whether to serve them to any hungry man who comes along?"

She blinked and looked up.

Mr. Michael stood there, but not for long. He slid into Richard's former seat and studied her. "Has your beau's departure rendered you speechless?"

"He's not my beau"

"But I was under the impression—"

"Then you were wrong."

He scratched his head. "Well, that's a first for me."

"Why do I not believe that?"

"I couldn't begin to guess."

She gave him a frown. "Why are you here in this town that you hate?"

The surprise on his face was real, and sweet and wonderful.

"Why else? I've come for you."

All this time she'd heard the saying about a cat having someone's tongue and thought it was nonsense. But now she knew. It was real. Because although she saw no cats in the Blue Peacock, one had decidedly stolen into the place and taken hers.

~*~

"Tell me the truth. Why did you come after me? You insisted I leave..." Destiny reached down and patted Shyanne's neck. "Good girl."

Mr. Michael cast a side-ways glance at her. "You really want the truth?"

"I wouldn't ask if I didn't." At least, that was what she thought she wanted. She'd been so angry at him forcing her to leave. And now, here she was, riding Shyanne back to the ranch with him.

Fortunately, he'd invited the Mayfairs to join them at the ranch in a few days, after everything in town was sorted out. With Bottoms about to be arrested, meaning no banker, it was up in the air whether there would even be a bank in Roaring Springs now.

"Since you left, Maria has spoken to me only when absolutely necessary. She was furious that I'd sent you away, and had quite a bit to say about my intelligence, manners and general upbringing. I figured if I didn't come to get you, she'd ban me from my own home, that's if she didn't shred me into strings and toss me into the wind."

Destiny burst into laughter. "You deserve it."

"Well, maybe. She's quite the monarch when she wants to be. She's taken me down a notch or two more than once."

"I'd love to have been a fly on the wall watching that."

"You do know you are quite the sassy girl?"

"I've been told that a time or two." Destiny tossed her head. "By the way, you brought Shyanne with you. What made you think I'd return to the ranch after being sent away?"

"Destiny. I only did that to try to protect you."

"I want to believe you."

"Please do."

His brown eyes implored her, and she felt herself forgetting her doubts.

And then the memory of Lucy and her fight with Hubert Bottoms hit her. "Mr. Michael, I almost forgot."

"What is it?"

"Do you remember Lucy, the woman who was in the stagecoach when I arrived?"

"I do."

"She was in the hotel while I was there."

"I don't suppose they wouldn't give her a room."

"She wasn't after a room."

"Then?"

"She was arguing with Bottoms."

"How did she even know Bottoms?"

"I took it she knew his family back east. Mostly it was about his father's taking advantage of her family in financial matters and then killing them."

"I see. And why do I need to know that?" Mr. Michael gave her an unbelieving glance. "Since when have you become a friend to her?"

"Listen to me. The way I understand it, Bottoms cast her aside after using her and promising to give her money. I don't know if he set her up in a room or what, for his doings, but he was downright cruel to her. I might not care for her personally, she wasn't very pleasant to me, but it sounds to me like she had a raw deal."

"It does, but what can I do about it?"

"She has no money and doesn't want to go back to her old way of living. If Bottoms has money, then why can't it go to her? He'll be in jail. The Bottoms' family owes her, and if and when he gets out, let him start over."

"Didn't know you could be so hardhearted."

"I'm not. I'm just thinking, what if it was me? I'd want someone to see the injustice in my life and help me."

"Destiny McCulloch, you are a good person."

She grinned. "I know."

"I don't see what I can do except maybe talk with Virge. He can put in a good word with the judge of the case. Could be it'd go in her favor."

"That's what I wanted to hear. Thank you."

When they approached the spring area, Mr. Michael offered to stop for a few minutes.

"Give us time to stretch our legs and get a drink."

"Sounds good to me."

Mr. Michael pulled off the trail beside the stream but didn't give her time to dismount on her own. He was at Shyanne's side, lifting her off as if she weighed little more than his canteen.

Again, he didn't let go. "You're not wearing that beautiful locket from night before?"

"I decided it was safer to keep it in my carpet bag."

"Smart girl."

"I wouldn't have thought you'd notice it."

"Why not? It's a lovely piece, and if I'm not mistaken fairly valuable. Has it been in your family long?" He settled her on the ground.

"I think so. My mother told me once my father gave it to her—and it'd been passed down from generation to generation—and then passed to my mother and then me as a child. I've always loved it. It is beautiful, isn't it?"

"For sure. Let's get a drink and rest—"

"Not so fast. I think I have both of you to thank for the trouble back in Roaring Springs."

Destiny felt as if she was moving in slow motion as she turned to face the man she thought she'd helped Virge bring down only a day before.

Mr. Michael slid his hand toward his holstered pistol.

"I wouldn't if I were you. I've got you covered, and though I figure you're good, I can't believe you're good enough to get me when my gun's already drawn and yours isn't." Hubert Bottoms coughed out a coarse laugh. "I've shot a man or two in my life-time. Guess I can shoot as well as the next."

"You want to prove that statement you just made?" Mr. Michael stepped forward a couple steps and didn't move his hand, but held it steady.

"Really don't want to have to shoot you until I take care of that beautiful, but deceitful lady beside you. Then, and only then, will you get what you've deserved all these years."

The anger that flooded Destiny was so sudden and fierce that she followed Mr. Michael's advancement several feet toward him before she gave it a thought. "Really, Bottoms? You sound like a petulant child that is angry at his friends because he can't have his way. Why don't you let this go and forget your imaginary injuries?"

"Shut up, Destiny." Mr. Michael's warning was soft but urgent.

"I've always known you're a smart woman, Destiny. Just not smart enough for me."

"You're disgusting."

Destiny's savage remark wiped the grin from Bottom's face. "You're mine. For how long will be up to you."

"I am not *yours*."

"We'll see about that."

He moved toward her, and she snapped at him. "Stay away from me, or I'll scratch your eyes out."

"Destiny." Mr. Michael's soft reprimand caught her attention, but did nothing to stem the flow of anger swelling inside her.

"After I make you pay for ruining my business—" He took another couple of steps toward her.

"—and you? It's what you get for holding a grudge so long." Destiny baited.

"Get over here now before I just shoot you." Bottoms snarled at her, his patience at an end.

"Coward." Destiny snapped.

Bottoms' gun raised a smidgen.

From the corner of her eye, she saw Mr. Michael's hand slide downward—slowly. Fear gripped her as the thought of him getting shot flooded her mind. "No!"

"Drop your gun, Bottoms. This is the United States Marshal."

Bottoms swiveled, gun blasting and staggered as two

bullets tore into his chest. He twisted and fell into Destiny. His last words were barely audible as he stared at her.

"I really did like you."

~*~

The sight of Bottoms' blank expression, the blood spatter on Destiny and her sudden flight toward him had Michael reaching for her. She plowed into him, and he clung to the sobbing girl, soothing her, whispering words of assurance that all would be all right.

But his gaze lifted heavenward, and his lips spoke the words even though no sound came from his throat.

"Thank you."

Maybe God had seen his despair last night after all.

Chapter Thirty-one

Destiny woke days later in her room at Mr. Michael's ranch, feeling all snuggly warm. The last few days had been cooler, especially in the mornings and late evenings. Spring was over, and—Mr. Michael had declared—summer was on them. The busiest time of the year for the ranch.

Gabrielle and her grandparents had arrived shortly after Destiny had returned, and entertaining them, and specifically Gabrielle, had kept her busy. Her friend had been so anxious to see everything, and Destiny had obliged.

Stretching, Destiny turned over, smiling at the sight of her carved kitten once again sitting on the table beside her. She was loathed to arise, but that mood didn't last long. She heard Gabrielle's laughter from somewhere outside, and that gave her the prod she needed to get up.

She dressed quickly and ran lightly down the stairs. In the kitchen, Maria was already preparing a noon meal, but she looked at Destiny. "I'm going to say this again. It's awfully good to have you home, Miss Destiny. We've missed you."

"Oh, Maria, you don't know how I hated being in town. I missed you and all the men and, and...do you have anything I can do to help you? I'd love to do something for you."

If for no other reason, then that scolding Mr. Michael said Maria had given him was worth working like a dog for Maria.

"No..."

"Please?"

Maria smiled. "Then go, child. Gather all those heavy quilts on the line. But if they're too much for you, you call Maria, do you hear?"

"Yes, ma'am. Thank you." She hurried outside. There was still a little bit of crispness to the air, but already, the sun was chasing away the nighttime coolness.

Ten beautiful quilts hung on the line. But only one caught her attention. Was it...? Surely not. Would Mr. Michael allow even Maria to take that beautiful quilt from his chest to air out? Well, since it was Maria, he probably would.

The quilt drew her like a magnet. It would, no doubt, be the only time she could look at it closely, run her fingers over the delicate stitching. She couldn't resist.

She cast a glance around, but saw no one watching. Stretching out an arm, she touched the quilt then moved closer, allowing herself to take in the colors, the needlework, and she felt herself going faint. Her memory was playing tricks on her, pulling her back to her childhood. To her mother's handmade quilt, one that looked so very similar to this one.

She gave in and examined every inch of the quilt, once even wrapping herself partially in the still hanging beauty. Until...her fingers found the tiny lettering at the edge of one corner and she pulled the quilt down, the better to study it. Sitting down, she let the quilt, the best she could, fall into her lap and leaned over to read the stitching.

SMG

Shannon McCulloch Grey.

Her mother's initials. Destiny let herself fall backward to the ground and tugged the quilt tightly around her. She studied the blue, blue May sky, the occasional fluffy cloud scooting across the heavens. She listened to the wind blowing softly, a horse now and then snorting or baying at nothing. Anything to keep from facing the truth.

She allowed her fingers to run over and over again the lettering, but refused to think what it meant.

It was only when a shadow fell across her face that she looked at Maria standing over her, arms akimbo.

"What are you doing to that quilt, Miss Destiny? It is Mr. Michael's favorite one, and he does not even like me to air it. But Maria knows when he will be gone, and I always, twice a year, sneak into his room, and bring this beautiful quilt out where it can get some sunlight love. He will not only be angry at me, but at you for allowing it to get dirty."

Her head was shaking no, this could not be happening, but Destiny shut her eyes against the sight. "No, Maria, it is not Mr. Michael's quilt. It is my quilt."

"Miss Destiny, what are you saying?"

It was true shock in the woman's voice.

Destiny sat up. "Never mind, Maria. I will explain all later. Right now, I need to go to my room."

Standing she wrapped the quilt around her, and ignoring Maria's faint protesting walked straight into the house, up the stairs to her room, and shut the door. She would not leave it till she could confront Mr. Michael.

~*~

When Michael returned home late that afternoon, he went straight to the kitchen, figuring Destiny might just be there helping, or hindering, Maria. But the woman only looked at him, a worried expression riding her features.

He stopped just inside the doorway. "What's wrong, Maria?"

She shook her head.

"Tell me."

"There's something wrong with Destiny. I think she's gone loco."

"What?" Michael laughed. "She might seem crazy with all the crazy stuff she pulls off, but, I assure you, she is not that."

Maria shrugged. "If you say so."

A trace of worry ran through his veins. Could Maria be right? He studied his cook then pulled out a chair. "All right. Tell me what's going on."

"You will be angry."

"I'll get over it. Tell me."

"I always, when I know you will be gone all day, air out a quilt or two."

"I know that. That's fine."

"But, what you don't know, is..." She drew in a deep breath. "...I also air out...that quilt...in your chest."

Her voice had sunk so low that, at first, Michael was

sure he hadn't heard her correctly. "What?"

"I told you you'd be angry." She swung away from the table.

"Maria, I am not angry. Tell me again what you said."

"I air out the quilt in your chest."

"No! I should fire you."

Her sudden shocked look tore at his heart. He shouldn't tease her so. "Maria, I've known for years, you air out that quilt in my chest. And I don't say anything because I like the smell of fresh air on it when I check it out afterwards."

"You knew?"

There went those hands on her hips. He was the one in trouble now.

"You should be ashamed for treating Maria that way. Here she is working herself to death caring for you, and you tricking her like this. She may not live to see another day. That's how shocked she is."

He loved her even more when she talked as if she was another person. Michael rose and went to her, grabbing her in a big hug, smothering any more protesting she would have done.

"There's no way you could make me get rid of you. Nothing, do you hear? You are family. I owe everything to you."

She pulled away from him, tears in her eyes, and shook a finger at him. "Then never let me hear you talk to your Maria like that again."

He raised surrendering hands, as he backed away. "I won't. I promise. I just couldn't resist…"

He left as a spoon hit his shoulder, then clattered on the floor behind him. Maria really did have the most effective way of making him listen.

Michael took the stairs two at a time. He paused a second, listening, at Destiny's door, but heard no sound. She was either gone or asleep. Or reading. He planned on having an important talk with her later tonight. Whether she liked it or not, it was happening.

After he'd changed and bathed, he scribbled a note.

Can you meet me in the library tonight around eight? I have to talk with you. Oh, yeah, wear something pink. Or blue. And would you wear your locket?

He didn't sign it, only folded it twice and slipped it under her door when he left the house again. He had one more thing to do.

~*~

Destiny read and re-read the note. It wasn't signed, but it didn't take a genius to know who it was from. And what was the *pink or blue* order about? He'd never learn she hated to be ordered.

She swiped at her cheeks. Again. How could she face Mr. Michael, knowing that he'd had her mother's quilt all these years? Where had he gotten it? She didn't want to go there tonight and spoil all the good thoughts, the good feelings she'd had about him.

Smoothing a hand over the quilt, she tugged it tighter around her and walked to the window. Mr. Michael was walking toward the barn in long-legged strides, and Destiny's heart beat a little faster. He was such a good looking man—such a good man—but what did she know?

When he disappeared inside the building, she turned away from the window.

She would meet him tonight all right and demand answers. She'd not leave until she got them. It was time to know what he knew. For better or worse.

~*~

At precisely two minutes after eight, Destiny started down the stairs. She'd purposely waited and hoped fervently he said something—anything—about her being late.

But on the first stair lay a rose petal, and Destiny stopped her descent to stare at the velvety piece of flower. She started to go on, to take another step, when she realized every step on the stairs held a red rose petal. Every. Single. One.

She could feel her cheeks heating up, her heart melting. She glanced down at the quilt wrapped around her, and her heart hardened again. He needn't think he was going to get off easy.

Taking every step carefully that she didn't trip over the cumbersome quilt, and careful she didn't step on even one of the petals, she reached the bottom of the stairs and found a white stemmed rose lying on the floor.

What on earth?

She wanted to pick it up. Wanted to very much, but she bit her lip and resisted the temptation. Not yet. Not yet.

Walking down the hallway, avoiding the stemmed roses lying every six feet, she finally reached the library and realized she didn't want to go in. She started to turn away, and the door swung opened.

Hernandez stepped back, smiling, waiting, and Destiny waited too.

"Come in, Destiny."

Mr. Michael.

Drawing in a breath, she moved inside, hesitating a second, then stepping across the floor to where Mr. Michael stood by the fireplace.

The door clicked behind her, shutting, she assumed, as Hernandez exited.

Mr. Michael's gaze skimmed over the quilt wrapped tightly around her. "You're wearing a lovely gown tonight, Destiny."

"Is that supposed to be funny?"

"Given your usual sunny disposition, I hoped you would think so."

"Well, it's not." she snapped. She blinked, holding back the tears, knowing what she was about to say.

"You're angry about something."

"I'm hurt and angry and confused. I don't understand..."

Mr. Michael stepped closer. "What don't you understand, Destiny?"

They were coming and there was absolutely nothing she could do to stop them. The tears rained down her cheeks and instead of being angry and demanding an answer, she was sobbing out a plea.

"Where did you get this? Where? Do you know where it came from?" She pulled the corners of the quilt away from her body. "Did you steal it? Buy it somewhere? *Kill my parents*?"

It was too much to bear. The memories of the past, the horror of her parent's murder that had loomed in the dim recesses of her mind, the blame to herself that she, as a child, had created, formed such an army of terror, she couldn't bear to hear that this man had caused it all.

"Destiny. Come here." Mr. Michael touched her arm, then wrapped his arms around her as she leaned backward a little to stare at him. "You want to know where I got this beautiful quilt? Then I will tell you."

She nodded but didn't speak.

"A long time ago, I found a young child hiding in some brush after...well, I wrapped that child with her tiny little white kitten in the only thing I could find nearby—this beautiful quilt, and carried her back to my home, sitting in front of me on my horse."

"You did?"

"I did. This little girl had just lost her parents, and she wouldn't talk, in the whole months' time that she lived with us, she never said a word. But my mother was sick, and Pa knew if she didn't get well, we'd never be able to care for a young girl child. We were living in a dangerous time, and if something happened to us, then she'd have nobody to care for her."

Destiny stared at Mr. Michael, registering his words, soaking them in, hoping, hoping they'd ease the hurt breaking her heart.

"About that time, Pa was finding the gold, and that gave us and Pa's partners plenty of trouble. So Pa decided the best thing for the child was to send her east. With the gold, that child was able to grow up, in the best of schools, to learn and become the most beautiful person she could be."

"Mr. Michael, you're talking about—"

He held up a hand. "Wait just a minute. You see, when that child went east she left the quilt behind. So I took it, wrapped it in some extra cloth my mother had, and hid it in my room. I saved it because I hoped someday I could give it back to that little girl, who I knew would grow up to be as beautiful in spirit as she was in looks."

Destiny looked at him then with tears in her eyes, but not angry tears. Tears of happiness. "Mr. Michael, that's a beautiful story. I wonder when you'll ever see that beautiful child grown into a woman again."

He started to speak, but Destiny placed a hand over his mouth.

"I have something I have to do. I'll be right back." She pulled from his arms and ran to her room, stopping each time she came upon another rose and even the rose petals. She flung open her door to her room, pulled off the quilt and refolded it just as she remembered it in Mr. Michael's chest, then laid it gently on her bed.

Hurrying to her closet, she opened the doors. It was time to get dressed. Again.

~*~

He'd known it would be a traumatic moment. From the minute he'd faced the fact that the little girl had come home, he'd known. He'd tried to keep it all back, but it was a hopeless endeavor. Nothing would stop this ending. Not his actions. Not his planning. Not even his knowing it might end in misery.

Destiny was upset. She might even now be packing. To go back to Boston. To that disagreeable Richard.

Michael walked to the window where he gazed at his mother's rose garden, the bustling around of some of his men getting ready for the evening, the sky and a few stars beginning to appear. He felt in his pocket for the tiny object that lay there hidden.

~*~

Destiny began her descent down the stairs again, and again she avoided disturbing the rose petals. At the bottom, she looked at Hernandez, now standing at Mr. Michael's library door, waiting to open it for her.

"Hernandez, would you please see that all these roses are placed in a vase for me?"

"I will, Miss Destiny." His dark eyes smiled his pleasure at her request.

"Oh, and don't forget the rose petals. Could you please place them in a basket? I'll sprinkle them on my bed tonight. I think they will help me sleep pleasantly, don't you agree?"

"I do think so. My Maria will have just the right basket for your petals."

"Thank you. Now I must go see Mr. Michael, don't you think, Hernandez?"

"I do indeed, Miss. You must go now."

"Yes. You're right. I will go." But she stood still for a second longer, thinking. Breathing deeply. Preparing. Then she looked at Hernandez. "I'm ready."

Hernandez opened the library door, and Destiny walked into the room.

"Caleb, it's me. I've come home."

~*~

Michael turned from the window at Destiny's words and felt his heart beating faster. She'd left the quilt behind and was dressed in the blue dress that matched her eyes, that lit a glow in her eyes.

No, that glow came from within her. A spirit so filled with life that it radiated out on those whose lives touched hers. She was like one of those sparkling stars in the sky, only a real live one. Here and now.

"Destiny." Was that his voice, almost breathless?

"Caleb."

"You know me."

"I do. How could I not? I should have known sooner. From the moment I rode behind you on Jasper after the stagecoach problem, when I first spotted your home, I felt that warming in my heart. I should have known then. No other place has ever given me that feeling."

"You should have." He smiled as he said the words.

"Did you know then?"

"No, but I should have too. Your big eyes never left my memory. I've never seen anyone with eyes like yours."

"I had other clues too."

"You did?"

She nodded. "I did. The carvings in your cabinet here in the library. They are so similar to one a little boy gave to me years and years ago. I thought it was a coincidence, but it wasn't, was it, Caleb?"

"I think you might be right on that one. And I'll confess, I saw your little kitten carving sitting on the table in your room. And I sneaked a peek at it, and knew for sure."

"Mr. Michael. You went into my room?" Her eyes laughed at him, her voice teased him.

"I did. But you weren't in there. You were out making mischief. Somewhere or other."

"I never make mischief, just fun."

"Why do I not believe that?" He reached into his pocket. "I have something for you."

"You do?"

"I do. Shut your eyes and hold out your hand."

He took her hand and gently laid the object on her palm, then closed her fingers around it. For a second he held onto her closed fist, then let go.

Her gaze dropped even as her fingers opened, and Caleb watched as the shock swept across her face. For a long moment she didn't move, then her gaze met his.

"Is this... Is this what I think it is?"

"It is. Maria and Hernandez joined us soon after Pa was murdered. Right before Hank and I tore down Pa's cabin, Maria found it that little key. I kept it, hoping someday, somewhere I could return it to you."

"And you have."

Her gaze didn't drop from his, and he saw the moisture in her eyes.

She lifted her other hand and unpinned the locket on her dress bodice. With shaking fingers, she inserted the tiny key, and the barest of clicks—so minute if one hadn't listened closely they'd have never have heard it—pinged into the room. Destiny looked at him again.

"Do you know how long I've waited to see what's inside my locket?"

"I do, Destiny."

Drawing in a deep breath, she opened the locket and stared down at the two little pictures inside.

"My mama and papa." She smoothed a finger across the picture. "I'd almost forgotten what they looked like. I look like my mama, don't I?"

Caleb moved to stand beside her. "You do. Your mother was a very pretty woman."

"And Papa. He was such gentle, strong man, or so Mama always said to me. He was my hero as a child." She sighed. "But I lost him when I was barely four years."

"But, Destiny, how could that be? There was a man with your mother—"

She didn't look up, only continued to stare at the pictures. "I know. It was my stepfather. Aaron Grey. My mother's name was Shannon. She insisted I keep my father's name after she married Aaron. My stepfather was a good man too."

Michael frowned. "Your stepfather was the fourth partner in our gold endeavor, wasn't he?"

She looked up, surprise on her face. "Do you think so?"

"I do. Pa found some pieces of paper with enough on them to identify him as the fourth owner, the man who was financing the gold search."

"But how could you know that? Why didn't you know I was the child you found when I returned? My last name—oh, I see."

"Right. Pa would have thought that Aaron Grey was your father, hence your name would have been Grey. I've only known you as McCulloch."

"And I've only known you as Mr. Michael. Why did you change your name from Caleb?"

"My name *is* Caleb *and* Michael. Caleb Michael. After Pa died, I was barely in my teenage years and went through such a bad spell, Hank suggested he and the ranch hands call me Mr. Michael. I guess he thought it would kind of wipe the past away. It didn't, but I didn't tell him that. Besides, I kind of liked it, thought it made me important to be called mister. But it stuck. Everyone began calling me Mr. Michael, and pretty soon it was as natural as breathing air. I was Mr. Michael."

"That means..."

"Yeah, it means, you are rich. I've kept your father's share—your share now—in the Mesquite Bank."

Destiny slipped him a sly smile. "Guess that means I can do a little bossing around, just like you do, instead of being bossed around all my life."

"I guess not. You have to have certain qualities."

She squinted at him. "Like what?"

"You have to be smart, good looking, and have money."

"Then I qualify." Her triumphant declaration was filled with laughter.

"I think you do. Very well."

For a moment, they stared at each other in perfect

harmony. Then...

He held out his hand. "Would you like to come outside with me?"

"Where are we going?"

"You're not much for secrets, are you?"

"Oh, I love secrets—those I solve myself. I just don't care when they involve me waiting."

"Are you going or do you want to stand here and argue with me all evening?

Destiny took his hand. "What gave you that idea? I'm going."

As they left the library, he caught a glimpse of Maria, Hernandez, Gabrielle and the Mayfairs at the end of the hallway, peeking around a doorway smiling and nodding.

"Where are we going?"

"To the rose garden."

As they stepped into the garden, Michael turned to Destiny and tugged her hand. "Come here."

Her sapphire blue-eyed gaze raised to look at him and without a word she came to him. He pulled her closer, then lifted her into his arms...

And the music started. A violin. A harmonica. A guitar.

And Michael began crooning.

"Meadow grass or forest green, rivers or garden fair, with eyes like gems, and skin of cream, my love is uncompared."

He began whirling—slowly, softly—in a circle, round and round, through the garden, up and down the paths, as the music played on and on by his most trusted ranch hands—Jackson, Hank and Hunter.

"A voice as sweet as a whippoorwill, at dusk she sings to me, she is my heart, my rose in spring, she is my destiny."

Destiny was staring at him, her eyes filled with the emotion he most wanted to see, the assurance he had to have, that she was his, and he was hers. Forever and forever.

"Open your heart, clasp tight my love, you've always belonged to me. I loved you then, I love you now, you are my Destiny."

Her lips opened and she whispered the words he most

wanted to hear. "I love you."

And Caleb quit whirling and kissed his Destiny.

~The End.~

Other Books by Carole Brown

Denton and Alex Davies Mysteries:
Hog Insane
Bat Crazy

Spies of World War II
With Music In Their Hearts
A Flute in the Willows
Sing Until You Die

The Appleton WV Mysteries
Sabotaged Christmas
Knight in Shining Apron
Undiscovered Treasures
Toby's Troubles

Troubles in the West
Caleb's Destiny

Women's Fiction:
The Redemption of Caralynne Haymen

Misc
West Virginia Scrapbook
Christmas Angels (WW II short story in the Anthology
From the Lake to the River)

Award winning author Carole Brown loves to weave suspense and tough topics into her books, along with a touch of romance and whimsy.

She is always on the lookout for outstanding titles and catchy ideas.

Carole and Dan, her pastor husband, reside in SE Ohio and have ministered and counseled across the country. Together, they enjoy their grandsons, traveling, gardening, good food, the simple life, and did she mention their grandsons?

Carole loves to connect with her readers. You can find her at her blog:

Sunnebnkwrtr.blogspot.com/

And facebook:

www.facebook.com/CaroleBrown.author

If you enjoyed reading this book, let others know... and bless Carole Brown with an honest review.

www.ingramcontent.com/pod-product-compliance
Lightning Source LLC
Chambersburg PA
CBHW020308200626
46814CB00006BA/2147